Slave to the Machine

Aishling Morgan

Published by Accent Press Ltd – 2009

ISBN 9781906373689

The story contained within this book is a work of fiction. Names and characters are the product of the author's imagination and any resemblance to actual persons, living or dead, is entirely coincidental.

Printed and bound in the UK

Cover Design by Red Dot Design

Melody J

Her body would be perfect. Perfect breasts, a perfect bottom. Subtle changes to her face would add the final touch, leaving her not merely one of the world's most desirable women, but the world's most desirable woman, full stop.

These were Melody J's thoughts as the anaesthetic took hold. As her senses began to slip the faint drone of the recording equipment had become the expectant murmur of adoring fans, thousands upon thousands of them, every one waiting to see her new, perfect beauty. A last voice penetrated her fading consciousness, one of the white-coated figures surrounding her instructing another to make some adjustment to a machine, calm and steady, pushing down a sudden sense of panic as her instincts struggled against oblivion. She slept.

Melody woke to white light and a sense of floating. Her first clear impression was that her body had changed, but there was no ache of bruised flesh, nor the sting of healing incisions. She merely felt different. Realising that she was still under sedation, she let her senses come back slowly, her eyes lightly closed as she took in the unfamiliar sensations, especially the extra weight at her chest.

There was a lot. In fact, there was an awful lot. Her hands went up, touching herself as her eyes sprang open. Her breasts were not merely bigger, they were huge, great straining globes of flesh as proud and resilient as she could possibly have hoped for, but ridiculously large. Her nipples were erect.

The stupid little man had completely misunderstood her instructions. Anger and an urgent desire to contact her lawyers welled up, but quickly gave way to shock as she realised that she was not in bed but suspended in a yielding white nothingness which somehow managed to hold her body. She sat up, feeling the weight of her enormous new breasts loll forward to the movement as she tried to tell herself that she was simply in some high-tech recuperation room and that there was no need to panic.

'Hello?'

There was no response, and her voice sounded different; sweeter, more seductive, as if she were greeting a lover rather than calling for a nurse. Fresh anger rose up as she wondered if they'd done something to her vocal cords and grew rapidly stronger, coming close to panic as she began to take in the rest of her body.

Not only had her breasts been enlarged, but her entire body had changed. Her legs were longer, her thighs fuller and more feminine, her hips broader and more curvaceous, her bottom a plump, deeply cleft ball of flesh as bouncy and resilient as her breasts. They'd made her waist tiny, exaggerating the swell of her chest and hips so that she seemed to be all bottom and boobs, like a girl out of the fevered erotic fantasies of some sex-starved adolescent male. Worst of all was her sex, now a pouting, deeply split mound, stark bald and blatantly sexual. Even her skin had changed, now the colour of milky coffee and as smooth as cream.

She put her hands to her face, to find that her features had also been altered; her chin smaller and sharper, her nose tiny, her lips pouted, the heart shaped delicacy her fans had so admired brought to an extreme. Nor was that all. Her hair, always luxurious, was now a cascade of glossy brown curls, so long and so full of body that it hung around her like a cloak.

'It's that bastard Peter!'

Her manager's name was said with feeling, and there was no doubt at all in her mind that he was responsible. No surgeon would have dared make such dramatic changes, while he was always trying to persuade her to show off her body, to draw attention to her legs and bottom and breasts, to dress in ever more revealing outfits and to release supposedly accidental pictures of herself giving glimpses of panties, front and back, and her nipples. Now he had really got his way, turning her into a living sex doll, and yet even as she cursed him she was struggling not to enjoy the sensation of her new and impossibly voluptuous body. Her skin seemed more sensitive, every part of her more sexual and the obvious parts extraordinarily so; her breasts proud and eager to be touched, also completely natural, with no hint of inserts, her bottom a temptation to sin, her sex moist and ready for her fingers or the insertion of a cock to take her virginity.

She bit her lip, trying to tell herself that she didn't really feel that way at all, and that the moment she was out of hospital she would go straight to her lawyers, sue Peter until he didn't have so much as a cent to call his own and have him charged with every crime that stood even a faint chance of sticking. Yet the feelings wouldn't go away, while it was impossible not to marvel at her new body and wonder not only what had been done to her, but how.

There were no scars, no bruises, no marks at all. Her skin was perfect, subtly textured and yet completely free of blemishes. The mound of her sex was absolutely smooth, with no hint of stubble, under her arms also. Even the tiny mole on her left wrist was gone. She could almost have been in a different body, and yet she was herself, only cleansed of imperfections and rendered sexual in a way that was at once delightful and deeply embarrassing, also extraordinarily lewd. Again she was reminded of teenage male fantasies, some of the drawings of herself she'd found on the net, and which one particularly insistent fan was always sending to her, or the way Peter liked her to look.

'The bastard!'

Melody stood up, eager to find a gown, even a sheet, so that when somebody finally did come she wouldn't be stark naked. There was nothing, only whiteness and a group of purple marks. Panic began to take hold for a second time as she realised that what she had taken for walls, a floor and a ceiling were insubstantial, the marks suspended in nothing. It took all her strength of mind to regain control. Once more she told herself that she was simply being given some expensive new recovery treatment, and that perhaps she had woken up before she was supposed to.

She focused on the marks, hoping they would give her some information. They were words, letters and numbers, but inverted, as if seen from behind, and seemed to be made from purple light. The largest were a little above the level of her head in a decorative script – Dolly Girl # 1 – Melody J. Her mouth came open in outrage at the disrespectful description and stayed that way as she took in what she could understand of the remaining text. Her vital statistics had been posted up for all to see, including her age and weight. The figures for her chest, waist and hips obviously went with her new look, and the descriptions weren't very polite, or very medical – Boobs, Waist, Bum, Legs. Her sex was listed as – Real Girl, Virgin – bringing a blush to her cheeks at the casual display of something so intimate. Otherwise the figures were either incomprehensible, apparently random numbers or empty boxes, far from obvious – Limited Volition – or downright alarming – Nude, Adults Only.

'Um … Hey! Excuse me!'

Again her voice went unanswered, but one of the empty boxes had come alive with what seemed to be an answer – Dress Up. Melody gave a sigh of relief, expecting some hidden door to open and a nurse to appear with her clothes. Instead there was a faint musical noise and suddenly she was in a skirt, but one even Peter might have hesitated to put her in. It was heavily flounced and bright red, the sort of thing a cheerleader might have worn, but only if she'd accidentally picked up one belonging to her eight-year-old sister, so short that it left her sex and bottom peeping out from beneath the hem, which did more to draw attention to both than to conceal them.

Her hands went to the front by instinct, trying to push the material down, but the pose left her bottom showing behind.

In vain she tugged at the back, but it proved impossible to cover her bottom without leaving her belly pushed out as if offering her naked sex. To make matters worse, every movement not only made her huge new breasts bounce and jiggle but brought a sharp and completely involuntary thrill of arousal.

She was also wondering how she'd been put into the skirt, and her astonishment increased as it changed colour from red to yellow with a black trim, to yellow with black checks, to blue with a white trim. To her relief it stayed blue, but at the sound of a second chime she was also in a top, matching the skirt and no less embarrassing, ordinary enough at the neck but too short to cover her breasts properly, with the undersides bare, while the slightest movement was likely to leave her with her nipples on show. Not that it made much difference, as they were still achingly erect and poking up through the thin cotton in blatant advertisement of her excitement. Anger and embarrassment filled her voice as she called out.

'I'm going to sue you for this!'

Her words were ignored. The outfit changed to green, to the yellow and black check, and back to blue and white.

'At least give me some underwear!'

The reaction was instantaneous. She was in panties, but exactly the sort of panties she would have expected to go with the outfit; full cut, white, and so tight that they showed off every contour of her bottom and sex while leaving bulges of flesh sticking out around the hems. There was no bra.

'Look you bastards, I'll sue, I mean it!'

Socks were added to the panties, long and white, reaching most of the way up her thighs, where they clung without obvious means of support. Her top changed, not in colour, but in design, the neck now layered like an old fashioned sailor suit and split in the middle to leave her cleavage showing. A little red necktie appeared, adding a vulnerable, cutesy touch to the display of her breasts, then heels, also in lipstick red, forcing her to go up on the balls of her feet and tense the muscles of her bottom and legs. A tiny blue and white sailor's hat added a final humiliating touch and the legend in the box changed – Fully Dressed.

'Yes, by some filthy old pervert! I know it's you who's doing this, Peter, and if you don't let me out of here I'll ...'

Her voice trailed off as the whiteness around her began to dissolve, revealing at first only vague outlines, then the blue of a perfect summer sky, the vast sweep of what could only be a stadium roof, and faces, thousands and thousands of faces, all staring expectantly at her where she stood on a stage. There was a microphone in front of her and a man at either side, session guitarists – but not ones she recognised. That didn't matter. The lead had his plectrum held ready and was waiting for her signal, while a drummer unseen behind her had already set up a slow beat. Another box had lit up, with a single word – Perform – then another – Cover me in Honey.

That Melody could do. Forcing down her confusion, she called out the name of her latest hit. The guitarist went into the familiar intro and she'd begun to dance, all the while cursing Peter even as she flaunted herself for the cheering, clapping audience. They loved it, as they always did, however embarrassing she found the outfits, but never before had she been so exposed, nor at risk of showing considerably more than even he had ever suggested. It was impossible to dance without making her breasts bounce, which meant her nipples were going to end up on show unless she was very careful indeed.

Before she'd even reached the chorus the inevitable happened, her tiny sailor top lifting to leave both stiff nipples poking up, high and bare. The crowd reacted with screams of delight, so wild in their enthusiasm that Melody found herself flushed with pride as much as shame. Determined to avoid showing herself up more than was absolutely necessary, she decided to pretend that her exposure had been deliberate, leaving her breasts bare as she went on with the song.

It was a dizzying experience, and her breasts were magnificent, so full and feminine and perfect, while the cool air on her naked skin and the gentle rubbing of the cotton top as she danced was making her arousal hard to contain. She wanted to go further, and the crowd were yelling for more, while a single word had began to blink in the display – Striptease.

Unable to stop herself, Melody peeled her sailor top up and off, leaving herself topless, her huge breasts swaying and bouncing as she danced, glorious unfettered. It felt wonderful as she threw her discarded top to the crowd, setting them cheering while the three who'd caught it fought among themselves for possession.

She wanted her shoes, and the song was too fast to let her peel off her long socks without looking clumsy. That meant her skirt had to come next, or her panties. She was trying to fight her need as she turned her back to the audience, but it was impossible. Marching high-kneed towards where the drummer was beating out a furious rhythm, she stepped, clicked her heels sharply together and bent low, allowing her skirt to rise and show off the full globe of her bottom, covered only by her straining white panties.

They were coming down. She couldn't stop herself. As the second chorus ended she put down the mike and reached back, sticking her thumbs into the waistband of her panties and pushing them down to make a slow, deliberate exposure of her bottom, but only so far, leaving the cotton taught around her upper thighs and still covering her sex, although her bottom was now bare under her skirt as she continued her routine.

As she danced she was using her skirt to tease the crowd, spinning to make it rise and show off her bare cheeks, bending down to make it lift, but still sure her half-lowered panties hid that most intimate part of her body. Her skirt had to go next, but that would be it, leaving her with at least some dignity and saving her from the full wrath of the puritan press and the authorities. It fastened with a button, which she flicked open as she danced, leaving just her zip to hold it up. The crowd began to clap, and to chant.

'Off! Off! Off!'

Melody reacted, pausing in her dance to peel the zip slowly down. She felt the skirt grow loose and put her ankles together, letting it fall around her feet. A step, a kick and it was in the crowd, leaving her dancing in nothing but her long white socks, necktie, shoes and hat, with her panties rolled down at the back. It felt better still, but she knew there would be no satisfaction until she was showing everything, while the crowd were still chanting for more. It would be professional disaster to go nude on stage, but she had already gone too far. She was going to do it, holding back only until she had finished the third chorus.

A raised hand quietened the guitarists and left the drummer pounding out the same slow rhythm as the crowd's chanted demands for her to strip. She stopped, standing proud with her feet set apart in her lipstick red heels as she eased a thumb down the front of the knickers, hinting at what she might do but with no more than a thin slice of her hairless mound actually on show. The crowd had gone quiet, breathless in their expectation. Then she had done it, thumbing down the front of her panties, her belly pushed out to show off her naked sex.

Two quick motions and her panties were down and off, kicked into the crowd, who were once more screaming in near hysterical delight. She was showing everything and it felt absolutely right, liberating and arousing. Again she began to dance, wildly now, and to sing as she went into the fourth and final verse of her hit. The crowd reacted better than any she had known before, screaming her name and dancing in frenzy. Some of the girls had their tops up, while one man was dancing with her panties on his head and another holding her top to his face as if in an act of worship.

She no longer felt shame, only an ecstatic joy at being nude. It was too late to go back, her exposure complete and, no doubt, her disgrace. The papers would have her for breakfast, but it was hard to care with her body and mind singing for the joy of going nude in front of tens of thousands of people. As the song reached its climax she decided that she would go down in style, marching to the very front of the stage, to stand for a long moment, full frontal and still to the cheers of her audience and the flashes of thousands of cameras.

For the last time she reached the end of the chorus, and as the music died away she had turned her back, to bend slowly down, letting her hair fall in a cascade around her head and her breasts swing low as she thrust her bottom high, ankles tight together, with the pouted lips of her virgin sex on plain show and her cheeks wide to display the tiny pink dimple between.

It was done, her pussy and bottom hole on display to her fans, and no doubt to the entire world within hours, when the papers came out and the private images had been uploaded. She didn't care, lost in ecstasy for her own exposure, but as she stood once more with the intention of delivering a defiant message to her critics the crowd, the stadium and the sky itself winked out of existence, leaving her back in the empty white space, stark naked with nothing to see but the purple figures of the display.

Teddy

Back in the formless mist, Melody began to give way to her confusion and fear. Her mouth came open in what might have become a scream. A box changed, from Limited Volition to Volition Off. Her emotions vanished, her fear, her sense of panic, the arousal she'd been unable to hold back, all stopped. Only a vague sense of well-being remained, with no emotion to her thoughts even as she struggled to understand what was happening to her.

She wondered if she was simply dreaming, but no dream had ever felt so real. The stadium had been real, of that she was certain. Only the formless mist in which she hung was outside her experience, and her inability to escape brought a new suspicion. Peter had not merely arranged to make her surgery far more extreme than she had intended, but had somehow managed to gain complete control over her.

It made sense. At first she had been completely dependent on him, relying on his know-how and his contacts in the music industry, with her own energies given over to her performance. With her growing success his role had diminished, until over the last few months he had been little more than an advisor. She had written 'Cover me in Honey' herself, and it had been her biggest hit to date. The tension between them had been growing as well, because he saw her as little more than a beautiful puppet, while she was sure that she had more to give than just her looks. Before too long there would have been a rift, leaving him without his star and his percentage of her income. He had tricked her, caught her and made her his puppet in reality, or so he hoped.

A lot of things were still unexplained, but that didn't matter to her. She had long since learnt not to worry about how technical things functioned, computers especially, but simply to take advantage of what they had to offer. She could always rely on geeks to do the techie stuff, just as she had since long before she could afford to pay them, often getting hours of unpaid work for just a smile or a few words of approval.

There was no emotion to her train of thought, only clear, cold logic, and her decision to defy him was no less rational. What he had done had to be illegal, and if he could control her when she was off stage, then when she was performing it would be a different matter. Once she was among her fans she'd be free, and she hadn't even seen him, although no doubt he'd been lurking backstage and had thoroughly enjoyed her striptease.

The thought made her blush and she saw that the text box now read Limited Volition once more. Her emotions were back, flooding in as the whiteness once more gave way to the great open air stadium, with a seemingly identical sea of faces spread before her and the same two guitarists at her side. The lead had his plectrum held ready and was waiting for her signal, while the same slow beat had begun behind her. She was back in her diminutive sailor suit, the soft bulge at the front of her panties showing to the entire audience, and embarrassment warred with determination as a text box lit up – River Deep, Mountain High.

She launched into her cover version, telling herself that she would leap into the audience at the end. There was no inclination to strip, nor any text urging her to, only a desire to put every ounce of soul into the song and so to make her escape as dramatic as possible. With each line she gave yet more power to her voice, which was richer than ever, easily taking in the range needed and so thick with emotion that the tears were rolling down her cheeks as she reach the end, and failed to jump.

It simply didn't happen, leaving her confused and trying to tell herself that she would perform two or maybe three songs before making her escape. The text box had changed, now reading Attitude, her first hit and written by Peter. She tried to rebel and change to one of her own, new songs, but her backing group ignored her and she was forced to go on, and to include the dance routine. It was thoroughly lewd, and she'd always found it exciting to tease her eager fans, showing off how deeply she could dip her back to display her bottom, cupping and lifting her breasts, making a V of her fingers across her sex.

Now it was shameful, especially when she pressed her fingers to the tight white cotton of her panties to find they were soaking wet, but she could no more help her arousal than she could stop her performance, and when the end came she could no more jump than before. It was the same with the next song, and the fourth. With the fifth the Striptease sign came on.

She did it, unable to stop herself as she peeled nude on stage, exposing every detail of her body, bit by bit until she stood in nothing but her stockings and heels, necktie and hat, thoroughly dishevelled, running sweat, her nipples straining to erection and her inner thighs slippery with juice. As the song faded she was expecting to find herself back in the white chamber. She knew she had to jump, but she couldn't, and trying to tell herself it was because she was in the nude didn't work. Her mouth came wide to yell for help, but the sound was drowned by the applause.

Frustration and panic welled up, but the text had changed again, to Black Lightening, the fastest and most active of her hits. She danced to it, nude, her mind in a violent welter of conflicting emotions even as she strutted and posed, wiggled and jumped. Her voice was perfect and her moves exact, for all her feelings and her growing shame as she displayed herself in what would have been highly suggestive poses when clothed, but when naked seemed a blatant invitation to sex, especially bending to show her virgin pussy.

As the end came she was sure the crowd would rush the stage, or the backing group would simply have her then and there, taking turns with her in front of the vast, cheering crowd, her precious virginity not only lost but the moment recorded on a thousand videos and ten thousand still pictures.

She was almost ready, dizzy with arousal and made vulnerable by her utter helplessness, her defiance now no more than a spark as she wondered which of the men would be the one to push his cock in up between her thighs to burst her maidenhead. Unable to stop herself, she set her feet apart and bent low, showing herself off behind for entry.

It never came. The scene vanished and she was back in the holding tank, nude and shaking with emotion, silent in shock for one instant and then screaming abuse at the whiteness around her. Nobody answered and her voice broke to a bitter, frustrated sobbing.

A door appeared in what should have been a wall and then was. The holding tank became a box, open on one side where the text ran, the words now changing rapidly. Melody swallowed the lump in her throat and wiped a tear from one cheek. She was still shaking badly, but expected to be put under sedation, as she had before, at any moment. The walls changed colour, from white, through a pastel blue and pale yellow, to baby pink. She drew in her breath and called out, her voice half frightened, half mocking.

'Will you stop pissing around!?'

The walls went a delicate chalk green, changed back to the blue, then went pink again.

'Peter? Come on, I know it's you!'

A bed appeared, an enormous four-poster with white painted woodwork and a pink coverlet. There was a large teddy bear on it, also pink.

'Hey now, come on! I don't know how you're doing this, but it's creeping me out.'

Two chairs appeared, a chest of drawers, a wardrobe, all pink and white. She began to giggle, on the verge of hysterics, desperately seeking any spark of rationality in what was happening. A carpet appeared, pink, curtains, also pink and framing a window that looked out on nothing. She began to scream again, stopped.

For a long moment nothing happened. Melody made for

the door, tugging furiously at the handle. It wouldn't even turn.

'Let me out, you bastards!'

The door came open, suddenly, to reveal white space as Melody staggered back, lost her balance and sat down heavily on the floor. She was rubbing her bottom and muttering curses as she got up, determination now welling up inside her.

'Okay, Peter, you've had your fun, now let me out, or at least give me some clothes to wear.'

A chime sounded and she was back in knickers, ridiculously frilly white ones with a pink ribbon at either hip. Turning to the blank wall, she saw that the Dress Up sign had come on.

'So you are out there? Right you ...'

White ankle socks appeared on her feet, and enormous pink pumps with white laces.

'Are you nuts!?'

Her sailor suit came back, now pink with a white trim but as short as ever, while the mass of frills at the rear of her knickers held the skirt up to make the display of her bottom even more suggestive than before. Little white gloves appeared on her hands and ribbons in her hair, pink ones tied in bows to make two large, curly bunches. She glanced down at herself.

'I look like a fucking cream puff, you asshole!'

Another chime sounded and her outfit was abruptly more exaggerated still, the panties frillier and tighter, the skirt shorter and more heavily pleated, the top now so tiny that the lower edge of her nipples showed as twin pinkish-brown crescents beneath the hem. Her hands went to shield her breasts by instinct, only to come away as she realised it was exactly the sort of reaction he'd enjoy.

'You're a fucking pervert, Peter, do you know that?'

Three swift paces took her to the wardrobe, but it was empty. So was the chest of drawers. She sat down on the bed, boiling with emotion but above all determined not to let him see how badly he'd got to her. The bed at least was real, and she got in, convinced that he was spying on her and determined not to allow him the enjoyment of her embarrassingly sexual yet ridiculous clothes. On sudden impulse she grabbed the huge teddy, squeezing it and peering into the glassy eyes, but there was no hard equipment concealed within, nor any evidence of cameras. Nevertheless she turned it to the wall, only to have it turn back and spread its chubby arms.

'Cuddle Teddy!'

'Holy shit! It's only a talking toy, Mel, it's only a talking toy, it's only a talking …'

She sat up in bed, pulling away from the thing by instinct as she tried to convince herself that she had merely triggered some hidden mechanism and that it was not alive. It had stopped, but it was standing up when she was sure it should have toppled over, its arms still held wide as if in mute appeal for a hug. Finally, the laws of both gravity and sanity reasserted themselves and the teddy fell over. Melody gave it a cautious poke. There was no response.

As she jerked back she had kept hold of the sheets by instinct, and while her breasts were pushing the linen up into two large, nipple-tipped bumps, she hadn't actually revealed them. She smiled, realising that the sudden motion of the teddy bear might have been a trick to make her get out of bed and on show. If so, it would be typical Peter, who was always trying to get her, and any other girls he was involved with, into situations were they'd be obliged to expose themselves. The more undignified the situation the more he liked it.

She kept the sheet held to her chest as she got up from the bed. The door had come open while she was distracted by the teddy bear and delicious scents were wafting through, reminding her that she hadn't eaten since the meagre hospital meal served well before she went in for her operation. She was now ravenously hungry, but the sheet wouldn't come away from the bottom of the bed, staying put despite her best efforts to untuck it and to jerk it free by force.

Conscious that her effort were making a display of the seat of her frilly knickers, she gave up. She could easily imagine Peter leering and sniggering as he watched, and the only sensible course of action was to remain cool and aloof. A quick adjustment to her top to make it cover as much as possible and she walked over to the open door. The whiteness had gone, which no longer came as a surprise. In its place was a kitchen, rather pink but otherwise perfectly normal.

On a table at the centre of the room a place had been laid, with a knife and fork spaced evenly to either side of a plate on which sat the largest, juiciest burger she had ever seen, a triple-decker well supplied with relish and oozing both mustard and ketchup. There was a tall glass of fizzy, orange coloured drink and a side order of thick cut chips, as good as any she could remember from even the best chippies in Leeds. Despite her hunger, Melody hesitated, wondering who had cooked the meal and set it out.

'Hello?'

There was no response, and no obvious way anybody could have left the room. More puzzled than ever, she sat down, pushing away all her other concerns in favour of her need to eat. She tried a chip first, dipping it in some of the ketchup where it had spilt from the burger. It was even more delicious than she had expected, the second better still, and the third sheer perfection. Licking her lips, she turned her attention to the burger, picking it up two-handed, only for sauce to spurt out, soiling her top and spattering her belly and breasts.

'Oh bugger!'

Holding the burger as carefully as possible, she tried to take a bite, but received another squirt of sauce down her cleavage. She drew a sigh, but continued to eat, sure that, however ingenious in his perversity, Peter could never have managed to arrange for the sauce to squirt out with such unerring accuracy. There were even blobs hanging from the bumps made by her nipples, mustard on one side, ketchup on the other. Only when she had taken the edge off her hunger did she begin to worry about the state she was in and how she was going to clean up.

There was no sign of a bathroom, so she would have to use the kitchen sink. That meant stripping off her top and sponging down her soiled breasts, undoubtedly in front of Peter, but, as with the first room, one wall of the kitchen was blank save for the flicker of text. While at the sink she would have her back to the blank wall, and with any luck the sight of her topless but facing the wrong way would cause him more frustration than satisfaction.

Melody popped the last of the chips into her mouth and went to the sink. Keeping her motions to a minimum in order to give him the least possible satisfaction, she peeled her top up and dropped it into the sink. After a moment to get the water temperature just right and work up a lather with a big, pink bar of soap, she began to sponge down her breasts and belly, wiping the sticky mixture off her skin. Her curves were simply too generous not to show a little, while she was also conscious that most of her bottom was on display beneath the hem of her skirt with only her tight, frilly panties to protect her from prying eyes. Worse still was the effect that trying to wash herself was having. Every touch of the sponge sent an involuntary shiver through her, even on her tummy, and when it came to wiping down her nipples she was forced to grit her teeth to hold back a sigh.

By the time she'd finished she was shaking with need. Her sex felt swollen and ready, badly in need of attention from her fingers, while the urge to carry on caressing her wet, soapy breasts was almost overwhelming. Only the sure knowledge of Peter's lecherous gaze stopped her, but it was impossible not to imagine what she could do in bed, rubbing herself surreptitiously to climax beneath the covers while she pretended to ignore him.

'Play with Teddy.'

The voice made her spin around, forgetting all about her efforts not to expose herself, but her hands went straight to her breasts in a largely futile effort to cover up as she saw what was in the doorway. The teddy bear was standing, unsupported and quite clearly watching her, beady little eyes fixed on her half-naked body. That was the least of it, and her mouth came open in astonishment and shock as she focused on him – for the teddy was all too obviously male. A thick, pink erection extended up from his crotch to the level of his chin, a foot long at least and equipped with two furry, pendulous balls the size of oranges. Again it spoke.

'Play with Teddy. Teddy fuck Melody.'

The Attic

Melody watched in horror as the teddy bear advanced on her, his huge pink erection bobbing to the motion of his clumsy steps, his balls swinging gently against his thighs. He barely came up to her knees, while his stumpy little legs were plainly incapable of any real speed, but the thought of having his monstrous erection thrust up into her all too ready sex held her frozen until he was almost on her. At last she found her muscles, and her voice, yelling at him as she darted around the table.

'Fuck off! I mean it!'

Teddy stopped, his expression changing from gleeful lechery to deep hurt.

'Teddy fuck Melody. Please?'

'No! I mean … no way! Why am I even talking to you!?'

'Please, Melody? Teddy fuck nice.'

He began to advance once more, flourishing his cock. Melody moved a little further behind the table, although conscious that he could walk underneath it without touching the two rounded ears that stuck up from his football sized head. A pink enamelled frying pan hung from a nearby hook and she grabbed it to threaten him.

'I am not losing my virginity to an animated teddy bear, now fuck off!'

Teddy stopped again, his beady eyes so full of hurt that Melody couldn't help but feel sorry for him. Her tone was softer as she carried on.

'Go on, go away. What sort of a girl do you think I am?'

'Fuck dolly.'

'What!? How dare … This is you, isn't it, Peter? You bastard, you …'

Teddy had started to move forward once more, forcing her to dart to one side. He'd also begun to talk again.

'Tug Teddy off?'

'What!? No!'

'How about blowjob? Teddy like blowjob. Melody blow Teddy?'

'No I will not!'

'Titty fuck? Up the bum?'

He was still after her, waddling as fast as he could and making ever more obscene suggestions as he came. Finally Melody threw the frying pan at him. It hit home, knocking him across the kitchen floor to bump against the far wall. He lay sprawled, his erection waving in the air, his woollen expression now set in shock and pain. Melody ignored an immediate flush of guilt and went to retrieve the frying pan as he pulled himself slowly to his feet.

'I'm sorry, but that serves you right!'

Teddy didn't reply, and was wobbling badly as he started for the door, throwing her a last, pitiful glance before turning away, his head hanging and his cock slowly deflating as he stumped back into the bedroom. Melody drew a sigh of relief, but kept a careful eye on the door as she went back to washing her top. A spark of hysteria was smouldering in her brain and she fought to keep it down by behaving as normally as possible, scrubbing the mustard and ketchup out of the material before wringing the top out and hanging it up to dry on a rail designed for tea towels.

Still conscious of her naked breasts, she tried to find something to cover herself with. There were four of the tea towels, each patterned with a different sort of cartoon animal – cats, dogs, rabbits and some things she decided were meant to be squirrels. By tying them together she managed to make an improvised bra, although her heavy breasts bulged in the thin cloth in a way that could scarcely have been more sexual.

The door to the bedroom was still open and she could see that another door had appeared in the far wall, just possibly a way out. Deciding to explore, she moved forward, ready with the pan in case Teddy was lurking behind the door. He lay on the bed, inert, his outsized genitals apparently retracted into the thick pink fur of his underbelly. An immediate stab of disappointment was followed by burning shame and the rush of blood to her cheeks. Obviously she didn't want to be caught and fucked, or toss his gigantic cock off, or suck it, or take it between her breasts, least of all let him stick it up her bottom. The thought was disgusting, ridiculous, appalling, obscene, but it was impossible to get it out of her head.

Going to the new door, she opened it cautiously, half expecting to find nothing but whiteness. There was a staircase, leading down. She took it, a step at a time, the frying pan clutched tight in her fist, her head swimming with images of giant cocks, huge, heavy balls and her own wet sex. At the bottom of the stair there was another door, which opened into a living room, the same dimensions as the bedroom above it and upholstered in the same lavish style. Two doors opened from it, one large and ornate, evidently the way out.

Melody made straight for it, her heart in her mouth as jerked it wide, only to find white nothing. She blew her breath out as she slammed the door, determined to keep her mind on her predicament instead of her urgent need for sex. The second door opened to a garage in which stood a smart pink sports car of no obvious make, but the swing door proved to open only onto more whiteness. In both rooms one wall had been open, with the same lines of backwards text in their boxes, changing occasionally as she moved.

At last she returned to the stair, only to find that it now led up beyond the bedroom door. She ascended, to find a bathroom, beautifully appointed if you liked baby pink, but still with one open wall to allow peering eyes to watch if she chose to use the shower or bath. Another door opened to a loo, but even that gave no privacy.

'The dirty pigs!'

She went back to the stairs, peering down in the expectation of finding Teddy advancing on her, erection at the ready as he babbled obscene suggestions. It was empty, but it led to a yet higher level. She went up, to find herself in a long, low attic with a sloping ceiling at once side and, mercifully, no open wall. There were beds, simpler than the huge four poster below, but with the same lack of imperfections and also pink. Melody sat down on the nearest, relieved not to be under surveillance, only to jump up and make an inspection for hidden cameras. None were obvious and she seated herself once more, taking stock of her surroundings. Each bed was provided with a beside lamp, and only then did she realise that while there were light fittings in every room there was no obvious source for the even, shadowless illumination, one more mystery.

Wherever she was, the technology was far beyond what she was used to, making her wonder if she was even in London any more. Perhaps Peter had taken her to the States, or maybe Japan. He had certainly had time, because she had been unconscious long enough for her scars and bruises to heal. She hadn't recognised the stadium either, although the crowd had seemed to be a typically British mix. Melody lay back on the bed, thinking hard but unable to reach any sensible conclusions.

The knot in the tea towels behind her back was pushing into her spine. She wriggled to make herself more comfortable, but the motion only succeeded in pulling open the knot between her breasts. They spilt free and a powerful shudder passed through her at the sudden exposure, followed by a strong urge to play with herself. She wanted to grab them, to knead the smooth, resilient flesh, to stroke her nipples until she could no longer keep herself from sneaking a hand between her thighs, to stick her fingers down her ridiculously frilly panties and bring herself to orgasm.

She very nearly gave in, but bit her lip, struggling to fight down the sense of arousal which threatened to overwhelm her completely. Something had been done to her, she was sure. All her life she'd been in near perfect control of her sexual feelings, but not any more. Now she wanted to be dirty with herself, and with other people. It couldn't be natural. She had never been like that, never been a slut, not like so many of her friends and rivals, both the girls she'd known at school and those she'd met after she'd made her break for fame. They'd let their knickers down, but not her, not Melody J.

While they'd being indulging themselves and suffering the inevitable crises, she'd stayed cool, using her beauty and sexual allure to make both boys and men do as she wanted yet never giving in to them, or to her own needs. Now she could barely stop herself from masturbating, and in the rudest, most undignified way, boobs out and one hand down her silly panties as she imagined letting Peter's perverted sex toy carry out his erotic threats.

It had been hard, especially when mixing with people who took precocious sex for granted, but she knew where the money lay, in her image as the virgin star, the one everybody wanted because nobody had succeeded, the one everybody thought he might get because nobody else had. A hundred million males wanted her, from San Francisco to Shanghai and from Siberia to Sydney, every one dreaming that they might be the first, the only. When she did give herself it would be to the perfect man – handsome, successful, devoted – and now she was having to fight down fantasies of surrendering herself to a mechanical teddy bear, on camera, his big pink prick pushed rudely in up her pussy, bursting her hymen, invading her precious, virgin sex, to come inside her and leave her pregnant with a litter of weird little half-human half-teddy munchkins …

Melody shook herself hard. The idea was insane, ludicrous, laughable, but that didn't alter the fact that she was desperate for penetration in a way she'd never even imagined was possible. Only the worry that she might still be being watched kept her from giving in then and there to relieve herself of her need. She closed her eyes, struggling to think of anything but her naked breasts and the tiny skirt that showed more of her knickers than it concealed. Getting up was out of the question, and when she told herself that she couldn't possibly give in because Teddy might come up, the thought only succeeded in provoking a shiver of pleasure not far from orgasm.

She twisted her head around, half dreading what she might find, but half hoping it might be exactly what she feared. The doorway was empty, the stairwell silent, but there was a large bolt at the top of the door, large enough to bar access to a determined man, never mind Teddy. It was too good an opportunity to miss. She jumped up and slid the bolt home, sobbing for her own dirty thoughts as she once more disported herself on the bed, now with the tea towels discarded completely and her thighs spread open.

One quick motion and her knickers were down to her ankles, but she kept the skirt as it was, enjoying the feel of it around her waist and the way it was turned up to show her naked pussy and the tuck of her bottom cheeks. Being in socks and pumps felt good too, and the bunches in her hair, everything that emphasised her already abundant femininity. She was going to masturbate, there could be no more holding back, but as she began to caress her aching breasts she was telling herself that at least she would keep it clean.

She tried to concentrate on her perfect man, teasing her nipples with gentle, circular motions as she thought of how he'd be, tall and strong, tender and yet with a rough edge, completely devoted to her despite being the idol of every woman he met. The image was easy to conjure up, the product of a thousand fantasies since she'd first begun to explore her sexual feelings, but it wouldn't stick. She did her best, imagining the moment of surrender, in a huge bed after a wedding that had made her the envy of every woman in the world, but her arousal refused to come to a peak.

Melody's eyes came open. He was no longer satisfying and she had to admit that he never had been. Always her mind had been inclined to go off at tangents, usually at the very moment of orgasm, to fix on some outrage as shameful as it was desirable. Now it was worse. She wanted it dirty, her virginity taken not by the perfect man and not on her wedding night, but by somebody utterly inappropriate and in thoroughly undignified circumstances.

She was sobbing as she gave in, her hand sneaking down to her sex as she imagined herself fucked by the obscene Teddy, maybe face down on the huge four-poster bed with her bottom stuck up and her knickers pulled down as he humped her from behind, all the while with Peter watching gleefully on some hidden screen. It was easy to picture, her face set in shame and ecstasy among the ribbons and curls of her hair, her beautiful big breasts squashed out on the coverlet, her back pulled in to lift her hips, her skirt turned up and her frillies pulled down, her full, golden bottom lifted to the thrusts of the enormous cock stuck deep in her pussy. It had been enormous too, huge, so big and smooth and virile, so utterly out of proportion to the fat, pink-furred little body.

The image was infinitely grotesque, infinitely desirable, and effective. The muscles of her thighs had begun to tighten and she could feel her orgasm welling up in her head. It was going to be strong, very strong, but she needed one final detail to make it perfect. She bounced over on the bed, getting into the lewd position she wanted to be in for entry, pulled her knickers back up to the level of her thighs, set her knees apart so that she could feel the material taut against her flesh and stuck her bottom as high as she could, leaving her cheeks open and her wet, swollen pussy wide as she once more began to masturbate.

She'd come down a little, no longer in a hurry, but with her face set in a sleepy smile as she teased herself and let the fantasy run. Her finger slipped deeper, to touch the taut arc of flesh that denied penetration of her body to anything but a fingertip. It was going to have to go, and it was going to have to go to a big, hard cock in the lewdest possible circumstances. Teddy would do very well, deliciously improper, but it wasn't enough to be had on the bed with Peter controlling the fucking and watching her being taken. It needed to be in front of a huge audience, a stadium-full, maybe a hundred thousand people, and as her finger moved back to the sensitive little bump of flesh between her sex lips and her rubbing once more grew urgent, she had the fantasy she wanted.

Teddy would be involved, allowing her to give a truly filthy performance, a full striptease, just as she had now done twice, only with him on stage to enjoy the view and to use his outsize genitals to make her performance dirtier still. She'd sit him on her lap to tickle his balls and toss his prick. She'd take him in her mouth, on her knees with her bare bottom stuck in the air as she sucked cock. She'd hold him up and let him fuck her tits, and come between them, leaving both huge, coffee-coloured globes spattered with white as she turned to the audience.

Melody's back arched as her muscles once more back to contract. There was no holding back this time, her orgasm too close to be denied. Her body felt wonderful, better than ever before, every inch of her skin alive and sensual, her breasts two huge pillows of supersensitive girlflesh, her lifted, open bottom an outrage to all that was decent and dull, an invitation to all that was dirty and exciting, her pussy the perfect expression of human femininity. No man could resist her, she was sure. If anyone caught her she would get a cock up her, as simple as that, and it was the position she'd hold for entry in front of a hundred thousand adoring fans.

She would give away her virginity by lottery, calling out a ticket number and submitting to whoever won. It wouldn't matter who he was – if he was some handsome young fan, or one of the spotty little geeks who liked to make dirty pictures of her and post them on the net, or some dirty old man. It didn't matter. She'd even have a strap-on dildo on hand in case it had to be another woman.

A geek was better, maybe even the clown-faced little nerd

who'd been forever bombarding her with pictures and love letters, claiming he was her number one fan. He'd had no idea how to approach a woman whatsoever, let alone how to behave to a pop star; faking photos so it looked as if the two of them were together and sending them to her as if she was going to be flattered. Some had been really rude, showing her boobs bare or her knickers down, even with his long skinny cock in her mouth, which had brought an end to her tolerance. Yet he'd never been caught, too clever to give himself away, leaving her in a state of outrage made infinitely worse by her involuntary excitement.

There was no denying that his sheer arrogance in even daring to think they could be together had got to her, and so had his dirty suggestions for what they could do together. He would be the best one to win, and she was too close to orgasm to push the awful thought from her mind, imagining him striding up to the stage with the winning ticket in his hand, making her take him in her mouth, rubbing his dirty little cock between her boobs, bending her over to show her virgin cunt to the entire, vast audience. Then up his cock would go, bursting her maidenhead, thrust deep into her pussy to leave her virgin blood trickling down over her busy fingers as she brought herself off to the thrill of being deflowered in public.

Melody cried out loud as she pictured how it would be, with the crowd screaming their delight and ten thousand cameras flashing as she had her cherry popped in public, with her virgin blood trickling down from her deflowered hole to where her fingers would be busy with her clit, just as they were now. Her orgasm took hold and she was bucking up and down on the bed, snatching at her sex and begging for the urgent, sopping hole between her thighs to be filled, one violent shudder after another running through her body until at last she could take it no more and collapsed, still fiddling with herself as the ecstatic tremors died slowly away.

The reaction came almost immediately, burning shame for

what she'd done and what she'd done it over, but it was only when she opened her eyes that she realised she was not in the privacy of the attic bedroom at all, but exactly where she'd been imagining she was, on stage, although at least she was still a virgin.

Playing Nurse

For three months Melody followed her strange new regime. She knew it was three months because there was a calendar on the wall of the living room. It defined the days and the months – January, February and now March – but there was nothing else to indicate the passage of time. There were periods of darkness, but they were irregular and often interrupted by an appearance on stage, always beneath a clear blue sky. She never saw the sun.

There was no routine, but she had quickly come to identify four distinct periods. Most of the time the Volition box would be on and she would be left to her own devices. Occasionally it would be off and unknown periods of time would pass in an emotionless limbo, her body unresponsive. Then there were the periods of Limited Volition, either what she'd come to think of as dolly time, or dirty.

During dolly time she might feel compelled to walk around the house, eat, wash up and other mundane tasks, but most of the time she would be dressed and undressed, repeatedly and with complete disregard for her dignity. The outfits were invariably designed to show off her body, short or tight, often frilly, sometimes merely embarrassing, sometimes positively indecent. Nor could she even guarantee being fully dressed when she was finished with. All too often she'd be left without any knickers, and bras didn't seem to come into it at all. At other times she was left in nothing but knickers, topless, or with a top but naked from the waist down. Only by taking the clothes off once a Dress Up session was finished and full volition had been restored could she keep them, so she did gradually manage to build up a wardrobe, even if the most respectable items were colourful cheerleader outfits and schoolgirl gear.

Dirty time was less frequent, but common enough for her heart to come up into her mouth every time the Limited Volition box lit up and to feel a now familiar mix of relief and disappointment when the Dress Up routine began. Not that it was always easy to tell, because she'd often be dressed first, and in much the same style. The difference was that instead of being left dressed or half-dressed she would start to feel the urge to be rude with herself, to pose and to strip, to admire herself in the mirror and to run through her most sexual dance routines. Then there was Teddy, stumbling after her with his grossly disproportionate cock and balls at the ready, until she used a hair ribbon to tie him to one of the bedposts, where he hung squirming in his bonds and begging for her to see to his cock. She had refused to give in, despite her fantasies, but for all her determination she would always end up masturbating, alone in the attic despite the chance that she would end up on stage at an awkward moment.

To her vast relief there were no consequences to her behaviour. Even after masturbating with her virgin sex on show to a hundred thousand people she was neither taken advantage of nor reported to the authorities. At least, nobody came to arrest her, but then, nobody came at all, and loneliness had quickly become such a problem that she found herself looking forward to Teddy's periods of animation, despite his limited and invariably dirty conversation.

Before long she'd begun to dress herself up and to play with herself even when she was allowed full volition, partly because there was very little else to do and partly because the house was full of temptations to be rude, such as the design of handles on everything from her hairbrush to the implements in the kitchen, every single one of which was smooth or slightly ridged, long and all too evidently suitable to be slid inside a girl's vagina. Only the certainly of breaking her hymen prevented her, but as month followed month she was finding it ever harder to resist the opportunity to try something even dirtier, penetrating her bottom hole.

She had been brought up to think of the little puckered ring between her cheeks as unmentionable and definitely untouchable, save to clean herself. Certainly it had nothing whatsoever to do with sex, and yet there was no denying her reaction to showing it off, a delicious blend of arousal and humiliation second only to having her virgin pussy on display. To poke something up seemed at the same time unspeakably filthy and a perfectly sensible and rather fun thing to do when she couldn't risk penetrating her vagina.

The temptation grew daily, until she knew that if she was even urged to brush her hair during dirty time the handle of the brush would be going up her bottom as soon as she was safely upstairs. Fortunately the sexual compulsion seemed to be primitive, focused on the display of her body rather than anything subtle or perverse, something that reminded her of teenage male sexuality. Yet she knew that she would do it eventually, of her own accord.

She'd been struggling with her feelings during a period of darkness, stroking the full, fleshy globes of her bottom cheeks and thinking how easy it would be to slip a finger between and up the tight little hole they concealed, when she became aware that something fundamental had changed. At first she thought she had been asleep, but her hand was still on her bottom. The bedroom suddenly lit up and she saw that the text had changed, announcing Limited Volition and Dress Up. She got out of bed, knowing that when the compulsion came she would be unable to resist and resigned to her fate.

'Go on then. Have your fun.'

Nobody answered. They never did, and although it seemed to make sense that somebody was watching her and controlling her, she was no longer sure it was Peter. She'd gone to bed in a frilly baby doll, which she quickly pulled off for fear of losing it when Dress Up started, only just in time. Standing nude in the middle of the bedroom floor, she found herself in plain white cotton panties and for once, a bra. Dark, seamed stockings followed, and black shoes with sensible, square heels, all quite unlike anything she'd been put in before. Next came a pale blue dress, crisp and neat, complete with a white pinny, a tiny hat and for the first time a skirt that covered her bottom properly. It was still short, at mid-thigh, but perfectly acceptable for street wear save that she was very obviously in uniform, a nurse's uniform. There was even an upside down watch and a name tag.

An inspection in the big mirrors on the inside of her wardrobe doors showed that while she looked sexy, she did not look rude. It was the first time since waking from her operation and it felt extremely odd not to have her bottom or boobs displayed, also suspicious. She waited, expecting the uniform to vanish at any instant, perhaps to be replaced by a shorter version with her cleavage on show. It stayed as it was, and she saw that a box had changed – Play Nurse – and so had the quality of light outside her bedroom window. Melody went straight to it, peering out to discover not the formless whiteness she had come to expect, but a cityscape; houses, streets and neat little gardens spread across a shallow valley, with skyscrapers rising in the distance, all spread out beneath a wide blue sky with the sun just coming up over the horizon. It was nowhere she recognised, but she was immediately filled with a joy so strong that tears started in her eyes. She could escape the house, surely, speak to other people, find out what was going on.

She ran from the room, clattering down the stairs as she prayed that the front door would open on a street and not the whiteness. It did, an ordinary, suburban road, lined with trees and with light traffic passing up and down; cars, lorries, a bus, and pedestrians. The nearest was a girl about her own age, and in an identical nurse's uniform. She smiled and waved. Melody's heart leapt and she ran out, only holding back from hugging the stranger with difficulty.

'Am I glad to see you! You wouldn't believe what's been happening …'

The girl interrupted her.

'Tell me later. Come on, or we'll be late, and you know what Matron's like.'

'Hang on, I need to tell you …'

‘Come on.’

The girl was already hurrying for a zebra crossing. Melody followed, falling into step as they crossed the road.

‘I need to tell you what’s been happening. I’ve been stuck in that house for months! They wouldn’t let me out. I need to speak to the police or something.’

The girl laughed.

‘Oh you are funny! I’m going to like working with you. What’s your name?’

‘Melody. But look …’

‘I’m Jane. Now do let’s hurry, or you know what will happen!’

‘What?’

Jane gave her a look at once astonished and pitying, then broke into a trot, clip-clopping across the road. Directly opposite was a complex of buildings in concrete and glass, the nearest bearing a large sign – Metrocity General Hospital. Melody tried to stop, but she was once again under the all too familiar compulsion and found herself walking with Jane in at a staff door to one side of the main building and up a flight of stairs. Jane seemed to know what she was doing and Melody followed, pressing an old fashioned punch card with her full name on it into a machine, washing her hands with a bar of carbolic soap and entering a ward lined with beds in each of which lay a recumbent figure with one or more limbs in plaster. At the centre of the ward was a desk, and at the desk sat a woman in a uniform similar to her own but in mid-blue rather than pastel and with an oblong badge showing a single word – Sister. She was also older, with a stern, no-nonsense look to her face, evidently in authority and not somebody to be easily manipulated by Peter or anybody else. Melody approached the desk.

‘Er … excuse me, but I don’t think I should be here.’

The woman glanced up, then down at a roster on her desk and up again, her expression irritable.

‘Certainly you should be here, you silly little goose. In

fact you're a minute late.'

Melody found herself apologising by instinct.

'Sorry, but ...'

'Never mind that. Just be thankful Matron didn't catch you. Now, attend to Mr Hawker's private needs.'

'Mr Hawker?'

'Room Four.'

Sister turned her attention back to the work she'd been doing and Melody moved away. There seemed nothing for it but to find Room Four and attend to Mr Hawker, whatever that involved. She knew she would probably be unable to resist anyway, and had obviously not escaped, while a series of doors lining a corridor at the far end of the ward seemed likely to lead to the private rooms. Room Four proved to be the last on the right and she went in, to find windows looking out over the city along two walls, various pieces of medical equipment, a chest of drawers, a chair, a trolley on which stood a box of rubber gloves and a large jar of some white substance, and a bed. In the bed was a man, a few years older than her, dark, with the hard, muscular look of a manual labourer of some sort and both arms in plaster. Melody immediately felt sorry for him.

'Did you have an accident, Mr Hawker?'

He ignored her question, but his voice was urgent as he spoke.

'About time too. Come on, love, I'm already hard for you. I'm so randy I've been rubbing it on the sheets.'

Melody took a step backwards. She could now see that he had an erection beneath the sheets.

'I really don't want to know!'

He looked at her in puzzlement.

'What's the problem? You're here to toss me off, aren't you?'

'How dare you!'

Her sympathy gone, she took two brisk steps forward and her hand shot out, to smack him hard across the face.

'Ow, fuck! What did you do that for?'

'What do you think!? You … you filthy pig!'

Her voice had risen in outrage and immediately attracted attention, the door opening to admit Sister and a truly colossal woman in a dark blue uniform and an elaborate hat, who spoke first.

'Whatever is the matter?'

Melody pointed an accusing finger at Mr Hawker.

'He asked me to … to touch his cock … to pull him off!'

Mr Hawker was not slow to add his own complaint.

'The little viper hit me, Matron!'

Matron turned on Melody, her face like thunder.

'Is this true, nurse?'

'Well, yes. I slapped him, because he asked me to play with his thing … his cock.'

'And what exactly is the matter with that?'

'What's the matter!? He … he asked me to pull him off! What more do you want?'

Matron glanced at the trolley.

'The gloves are here, and the cream. What exactly is the difficulty, and why did you feel the need to hit him? To strike a patient, nurse, really!'

'What! Look, you mad old bitch, he asked me to pull him off, to masturbate him! Don't you understand?'

Melody's outburst was followed by absolute silence, and when Matron did speak again it was in a calm, level voice far more threatening than any display of anger.

'Certainly I understand. I understand that you are a very rude and foolish young girl, apparently with very little idea of the duties of your vocation. Now come here.'

Melody hesitated, not at all keen on the expression on the big woman's face.

'What for?'

The answer was clear and unequivocal.

'Because I am going to spank you.'

For a moment Melody was not sure she had heard the Matron's words correctly. The idea was too much to take in, an impossible outrage, grossly old-fashioned, an unthinkable thing to do to any modern girl, let alone a girl of her status. It had to be a joke, but even as a joke it was utterly inappropriate, yet there was no mistaking the expression on Matron's face. Melody's words came faint, her outrage mixed with shock and humiliation.

'Spank me?'

'Yes, that is right. I intend to spank you. What did you expect for such behaviour?'

'Not that! I mean, you can't, you just can't. Nobody does that sort of thing any more. It's just not right, and anyway, don't you know who I am? I'm Melody J!'

Matron drew a heavy sigh.

'I think we have a BRAT, Sister.'

Sister nodded sagely.

'All the more reason to spank her. Come along, my girl, over Matron's knee you go, or do we have to hold you down?'

Melody's answer was a squeal.

'No! I mean, yes, if you think you're going to spank me, because you can't! It's not going to happen! It's not going to happen! It's not …'

She stopped. It was going to happen, one way or another, and she knew it. The same awful sense of compulsion that had made her strip in public was growing in her head, while Sister had begun to roll up her sleeves over alarmingly muscular arms. Panic took hold and she dodged for the door, determined to escape the sadistic lunatics who thought it was okay to smack a woman's bottom as a punishment, and her own compulsion to let them do exactly that. Matron moved back to the door with extraordinary speed for so large a woman, blocking Melody's exit.

'It seems you are going to have to hold her down, Sister, or perhaps put her across the chair and sit on her back.'

'No! You can't do this to me!'

'I think you'll find we can, young lady.'

Melody realised that it was true. There was no escape, either through the door or from the appalling compulsion to lay herself obediently over Matron's lap and accept her spanking. She changed her tune, her voice full of sulky resentment.

'Okay, okay, if you have to, but not in front of Mr Hawker.'

Matron merely patted her lap.

'Don't be precious. Of course it must be done in front of Mr Hawker. Now come along, or I shall send Sister to fetch a cane.'

As she spoke the last word Melody's compulsion began to shift, away from the need to drape her body across the big woman's knee and towards something she knew would be worse by far, presenting herself with her bottom stuck out for a half-dozen cuts with a school cane. It was something she'd only ever seen once, in an old cartoon her nerdish fan had sent her, suggesting it was what she needed for ignoring his demands to acknowledge him when she went on stage. She'd been very glad indeed that it was no longer done, let alone to her, but had found it impossible not to enjoy the horrid thrill of imagining what it would have been like.

Both Matron and Sister were looking at her. Mr Hawker was grinning, his cock pushing up under the bedclothes to make a little tent-shaped rise. The blood had begun to go to her cheeks as she pointed at him.

'But he's … he's going to get off on it!'

Matron drew another sigh.

'The cane, I think, Sister.'

Melody was babbling immediately.

'No, no, no, you won't need that. Look, okay, but … but it's just not right!'

'On the contrary. Given your behaviour I can think of nothing more suitable than to spank you, except possibly the cane or strap. Now come along, you little BRAT, now!'

The final word was sharp, almost a bark, and it broke Melody's resistance completely. Pouting furiously, she walked forward to go down as she had been ordered, bottom up over the appalling woman's knee, her cheeks twin balls of very obviously female flesh within the tight confines of her skirt, which Matron immediately began to lift.

'Hey, no!'

Matron didn't even trouble to answer, simply removing the hand Melody had put back to protect her dignity. Sister did speak, quite gently.

'Don't be silly. Of course your skirt has to come up.'

'Why!?'

'So that you can be spanked properly, of course. Don't be foolish.'

It was being done anyway, despite Melody's frantic attempts to hold her skirt down. Matron was far too strong, and experienced, catching Melody's wrist to twist one arm up into the small of her back and keeping the other pinned between her heavy belly and her victim's side. With the gentle bulges of thigh above her stocking tops already showing, all Melody could manage was a gasp as the skirt came right up, revealing the seat of her knickers, plain white cotton stretched tight over bulging cheeks.

The position she was in gave Mr Hawker a fine view, with Melody's knickers so tight that every contour of her bottom was on show, also the harp-shaped bulge of her sex, but thankfully concealing the very rudest details. She was also glad he couldn't see her face, because she couldn't stop herself from pouting and glowering with resentment, and she was sure he'd have thoroughly enjoyed her expressions.

Matron's hand settled on Melody's bottom, giving her a sharp stab of humiliation and fear, but instead of beginning to spank one big thumb was stuck down the waistband of her panties. She realised they were coming down and began to struggle once more, wriggling in the big woman's grip and kicking her feet up and down.

'No, that's not fair! Not my knickers, not in front of Mr Hawker! It's not decent!'

Matron's answer was impatient.

'And since when was decency a concern for a girl about to be spanked? You have been naughty, and so you have forfeited all right to considerations such as decency and modesty until your punishment is complete. Now do let go, because I assure you that your knickers are coming down.'

'No! You can't, not my knickers! No, Matron, please, not bare bottom! You can't pull them down, you really can't.'

'I think you'll find I can.'

Matron began to pull, but Melody had managed to get a grip and pulled back, determined not to have her bottom exposed, babbling and kicking her legs in every direction as she struggled.

'Please, Matron, no … you can't! You really can't! Not bare! He'll see everything!'

Mr Hawker spoke up.

'It wouldn't be the first time, would it, Melody?'

She went limp, the fight knocked out of her in a wash of shame as she remembered all the times she'd stripped for her audiences, more often than not making a deliberate show of her bare bottom. Obviously Mr Hawker had seen. Her voice was a whimper as she made one final protest:

'But … but not for spanking!'

It was pointless. She had already let go of her knickers and a moment later they had been drawn fully down. Her bottom was bare, but it felt very different to going bare in front of an audience. Then she was in control, on show because she wanted to be on show, to tease her audience and enjoy her control. Now she had no control over the situation whatsoever, on show because she was about to be spanked.

Her now furious pout grew more sulky still as her knickers were adjusted to the level of her knees. She had posed in the mirror often enough to know exactly how she'd look from behind, with the plump pink lips of her virgin pussy pouting out from between her thighs and her firm cheeks parted just enough to show off the tight little star between. Even alone in front of the mirror she had made a thoroughly rude sight, making her want to touch. Displaying herself to the crowd had been stronger by far, but nothing to the way she felt with it all on show to one leering man and the two women who were about to punish her, while to add a final, appalling touch she knew her pussy was swollen and juicy. In fact her whole body was flushed hot, her nipples even bigger and stiffer than usual and her legs shaking as she awaited her spanking with Matron apparently content simply to allow Mr Hawker to admire her bottom. A hand came to rest across Melody's cheeks and Sister spoke, her voice not unkind.

'She's awfully hot, and you haven't even begun. Are you sure she's quite well?'

There was no sympathy whatever in Matron's reply.

'Nonsense. Still, I suppose we had better be sure. A thermometer please.'

Melody twisted her head around. She knew exactly where the thermometer was going, up her bottom hole, if only because it was impossible to imagine the two ghastly old dragons doing anything that might spare what little remained of her dignity. Sure enough, Sister had pulled open a drawer in the trolley to take out a long, glass thermometer with a bulb at least an inch across and with a single word clearly visible on the stem – Anal. Melody's reaction was immediate.

'Hey, no! Not up my bum, please? I'm fine, I really am! Just spank me, get it over with, but don't stick that thing up my bum! No, please …'

Her words broke to a gasp as her bottom cheeks were hauled apart, displaying her anus not only for penetration but to the eager eyed Mr Hawker. She hung her head, sobbing with embarrassment and frustration, her eyes closed but only for a moment. It was impossible not to look back.

Sister had put the thermometer down and was pulling on a pair of rubber gloves from the box, while the tub of cream Melody had been supposed to use to masturbate Mr Hawker was already open. One bony finger was dipped in, to pull out a fat blob of the glistening lubricant. Melody shut her eyes again, as tight as possible, and she was biting her lip hard as the cool, slippery cream was applied between her cheeks, rubbed in around her anus and pushed up, Sister's finger intruding deep into the tiny hole.

'You bitches!'

She'd been unable to hold back the words, and not only for the terrible shame of being given her first ever anal penetration, but because it felt absolutely wonderful. The women seemed not to hear, both thoroughly enjoying themselves with Melody's bottom as Matron held the cheeks wide and Sister wriggled her finger about inside. Melody cursed, because it felt better still and because she couldn't stop thinking how good something thicker would be, perhaps Mr Hawker's cock.

Sister's finger withdrew from Melody's bottom hole, only to be replaced a moment later by the cold, hard bulb of the thermometer. It was pushed up without ceremony, Melody's mouth and eyes wide as her anus spread to the pressure and gave way, allowing Sister to slide the thick stem well inside. Again she looked back, now held firmly in place with the thermometer sticking out from between her bare bottom cheeks, in full view of not only Matron and Sister, but of Mr Hawker, who was clearly enjoying the show, his face set in a most unpleasant and suggestive leer.

'What a sight!'

Both Matron and Sister ignored him, the one concentrating on holding Melody still, the other on the fob watch that hung from the breast pocket of her uniform. Time seemed to have slowed, so that Melody was convinced she'd been held in place for at least five minutes before the thermometer was finally pulled out of her now slippery bottom hole. Sister showed it to Matron, who spoke.

'Her temperature is quite normal. I think we can only assume that she is a very silly, impudent and ungrateful young girl.'

The last word was accompanied by a loud smack as her hand descended on Melody's bottom. It stung, a sudden maddening pain, but there was no pause at all before the second smack was applied, and the third.

'Ow! Ow! Ow! Stop, please, Matron, stop!'

Matron took no notice whatsoever, but continued to pepper Melody's now dancing bottom with firm, purposeful smacks delivered across the full spread of her target. It was Sister who spoke, her voice patient and gentle.

'Do try and take it with a little dignity, Nurse.'

Dignity was out of the question. Melody had never imagined being spanked could hurt so much, but even the pain was as nothing beside the knowledge that not only was it being done to her, and for the first time in her life, but in front of a man. She had gone wild, thrashing in Matron's grip, her hair flying, her legs pumping in her lowered panties, her fists beating furiously on the floor and against her persecutor's tree-trunk legs. Finally it stopped and she collapsed gasping across Matron's lap, too exhausted even to think of pulling up her panties to deprive Mr Hawker of his prime view of her now red bottom. Matron spoke.

'Honestly, I've never heard such a fuss! Haven't you ever been spanked before?'

'No I have not! And it hurts so …'

Melody's words broke to a wail of distress as the spanking began again, this time accompanied by a lecture from Matron.

'Well then it's about time you were. Really, the standards of discipline in this country are truly abysmal. It would never have happened in my day. Why, when I was your age Matron would spank one of us every morning, chosen at random, just to keep us on our toes. You don't know how lucky you are, you young girls …'

She continued, all the while with her huge red hand rising and falling across her victim's bouncing, wriggling cheeks. Melody's entire bottom felt as if it was on fire, but the pain had started to dull, which was no consolation at all because as it faded it was replaced with something far worse, arousal. The spanking was bringing her on heat, a realisation that made her more ashamed of herself than she had thought possible.

There was nothing she could do about it, the steady smack, smack, smack of Matron's hand across her bottom sending jolt after rhythmic jolt to Melody's sex, until she realised that if it didn't stop soon she was going to come. She tried to fight it, biting her lip and forcing herself to concentrate on the appalling indignity she was being subjected to. By any sane standards she should have been screaming abuse at her persecutors, that or in floods of tears, but there was no helping it. Her sex was so wet that the juice was running down her thighs and splashing her legs and between her cheeks as each smack landed, while the urge to stick her bottom up for more was more than she could resist.

She did it, giving in with a hollow groan as she lifted her

hips to Matron's spanks, her cheeks now wide open, her anus winking lewdly between them as her muscles began to contract, her sex too, and she had started to come. It was impossible to hide, her bottom and thighs and pussy squeezing and pouting to contractions over which she had no control whatsoever, while there was no mistaking the nature of her ecstatic gasps, or her words as she broke down completely.

'Harder! Harder! Spank me … spank me harder, you fat bitch! Over my pussy! Make me come!'

Matron took no notice, but Melody had come anyway, provoking an overpowering sense of shame as the spanking finally stopped, to leave her hanging limp and defeated across the huge woman's lap. For a long moment there was silence, broken only by Melody's gentle sobbing, before Matron finally spoke again.

'What a disgraceful display, but no doubt only to be expected from a BRAT, while I trust that in any event you have learnt your lesson?'

Melody nodded.

'Yes.'

She meant it, at least in the sense that she never intended to do anything that led to a spanking again. Accepting it was a very different matter, and she was boiling with resentment as she lifted herself from Matron's lap and bent to pull up her knickers. Sister immediately lifted a finger, wagging it in admonishment as she spoke.

'Oh no you don't. You know the rules. Bottoms are to be left bare after spanking, until the end of your shift. You may pull up your pants to the top of your thighs, no higher, and pin up the tail of your skirt.'

'But everybody will see!'

'That is precisely the idea. Here are some pins.'

She had reached into a pocket, to draw out what appeared to be nappy pins, large and tipped with blue safety caps. Melody took them, trying rather unsuccessfully not to pout as she adjusted her knickers and pinned up her skirt at the back, framing her red bottom in a way that left no doubt whatsoever what had been done to her. Sister waited until the operation was complete before she spoke again, her voice gentle but firm.

'Now, you will do your duty.'

'My duty?'

Matron cut in, her voice as impatient as Sister's was kindly.

'To masturbate Mr Hawker. For goodness sake girl, do you have no sense at all?'

Melody opened her mouth to protest, then hurriedly closed it again, fairly sure what would happen if she didn't do as she was told. A glance at the bed showed that Mr Hawker was still erect, dashing her hopes that he might have had a spontaneous emission over the sight of her being spanked. As she pulled on a pair of rubber gloves and lubricated the palms she tried to console herself that she only had to do it by hand, and that at least it wouldn't be the first time. Several times she had masturbated boyfriends who were getting a little too urgent, and once or twice taken men in her hand in order to obtain important favours. All of them had been pathetically grateful, while Mr Hawker looked as if he would expect good service. She smiled, trying to sound calm and matter-of-fact.

'Very well, Mr Hawker, let's get you seen to.'

As she spoke she had pulled back his sheets, exposing a large, gnarled erection, the head bulbous with pressure. Her hand was shaking badly as she grabbed hold, pulling up and down with clumsy motions that drew a tut of disapproval from Sister, although Mr Hawker didn't seem to mind, sighing as he lay back on his pillows.

'Ah, that's better, that is. A bit faster, would you?'

Melody did her best, telling herself that the more effort she put into her task the more quickly it would be finished. He seemed in no hurry, his eyes closed in bliss. Matron got up.

'I shall continue with my rounds, Sister. See that everything is done properly. I do apologise for Nurse, Mr Hawker. She's new.'

He merely smiled and nodded, then shifted his body to make himself more comfortable as Melody continued to pull at his cock. Matron left the room and Mr Hawker immediately opened his eyes, winking at Sister.

'How about having her do it topless? I love a bit of tit with my morning wank, and she has got big ones.'

Melody began to protest, but bit her words back, not keen to risk another spanking. Sister looked doubtful, but only for a moment before she replied.

'I don't see why not. After all, she has been a frightful nuisance. Carry on, Nurse. I'll undo you.'

Again Melody made to speak and again she thought better of it. Sister stepped close, as calm as if she were performing some completely mundane task as she quickly tweaked open the buttons of Melody's dress, pulled the front wide and lifted each heavy globe from its restraining cup. Now with her boobs bare as well as her freshly smacked bottom, Melody wondered how she'd look. When she first had been put into her nurse's uniform she'd been grateful to be properly covered for once, but she now realised that there were ways in which being fully dressed offered more potential for exposure and humiliation than the rudest of the little outfits she'd been put into during Dress Up.

To make it worse, it was impossible to masturbate Mr Hawker without the motion of her arm making her breasts jiggle, which he was obviously enjoying. Again she told herself that it was for the best because it would make him come more quickly, but he seemed to be taking his time about it. Even Sister had begun to glance at her watch, but when she finally spoke up it was not to Mr Hawker, but to Melody.

'Do hurry up, Nurse.'

‘I’m doing my best!’

‘Well it’s not good enough, and your technique is deplorable. I’ve never seen anything so clumsy. Don’t they teach you anything at college these days?’

‘Not how to toss men off, no!’

‘Good heavens, standards really are slipping. Here, hold your hand like this, pull with a smooth, regular motion and make sure you brush the underside of his foreskin with your thumb as you come up and down. Use your free hand to squeeze his balls, not too tight, and if he still won’t come pop a finger up his bottom, which always does the trick. Oh, and stick your bottom out, they like that.’

As she spoke, Sister had adjusted Melody’s grip. Mr Hawker made no comment, his eyes flicking between Melody’s face, her boobs and the curve of her bottom where she’d done as she was told and pulled her back in to make it stick out. Sister gave a pleased nod.

‘That’s better. Now we’ll soon have him off.’

Melody managed a nod, now tugging as fast as she could in the hope of not being obliged to stick a finger up Mr Hawker’s bottom, something she was sure he would find as delightful as she had found it humiliating when done by Sister. Yet unless he came soon she was going to have to, and in desperation she decided to try and provoke him with a little dirty talk.

‘Isn’t that nice, Mr Hawker? Do you like my boobies? Aren’t they big. And I bet you enjoyed watching my spanking too, didn’t you?’

His response was an eager nod and she went on.

‘Which bit did you like best? I bet it was when Matron pulled down my panties, wasn’t it? You boys like a good show, don’t you, and I bet you could see everything, because I couldn’t hide it at all, not like that, not while I was having my naughty bottom smacked, not while …’

She stopped. Mr Hawker had come all over her hand.

For the rest of the day Melody was extremely careful not to give offence or make mistakes. She avoided both Sister and Matron, and was quick to help her fellow nurses with whatever task was required. Despite her burning resentment for her spanking and having to go about her work with her knickers down and her skirt pinned up at the back, she forced herself to ignore not only the giggles of her colleagues and the sniggers of the patients, but the occasional sly touch or cheeky pinch to her bare cheeks. To add to her embarrassment her skin stayed red and suffused with a warm glow that went right to her sex, forcing her to make repeated trips to the loo in order to wipe up her juices.

Her shift lasted eight long hours, by the end of which she had learnt a new appreciation for what it meant to be a nurse, or, more accurately, what it might have meant under a regime at once stricter than any since fifty years before her birth and run by a bunch of sex-mad chauvinist pigs with some extremely peculiar ideas about discipline. Several of the other girls had been threatened with spanking or the cane during the shift, although they had all managed to avoid both, while seeing to the men's sexual needs was as much a part of their routine as changing bedding or administering medicine.

When the time finally came to leave Sister gave her permission to cover up and she hurried from the hospital as fast as she could, only to pause on the pavement outside the main entrance. Her house was directly opposite, one of a terrace of similar buildings and apparently solid, while there was no sign of the blank spaces and purple text that had been so much a part of her life for the last few months. Something had changed, and while the behaviour of both patients and staff in the hospital had been bizarre in the extreme, everything around her looked refreshingly normal. The sense of compulsion she'd been under in the hospital had also gone, a subtle change of feeling, so that even without the text she knew her Volition had changed from Limited to On. She was free.

Very cautiously, she began to walk down the street, determined to go to the police but not to do anything which might give away her intention. Beyond the hospital was a line of shops, including a restaurant from which exquisite smells issued, hot, spicy smells she recognised immediately; Indian, and if the aroma was anything to go by as good as anything she'd had in Bradford. The burgers, pizza, hot dogs and ice cream she'd been eating for the previous three months had been the best, but she was heartily sick of fast food. She sniffed at the delicious scent, telling herself that she would eat as soon as she'd made her complaint at the police station. A waiter was standing by the door of the restaurant, looking bored, but the moment he saw her approaching he smiled, encouraging her to ask the way. She put on her best accent.

'Excuse me. Please could you direct me to the nearest police station?'

His smile broadened to a grin.

'Around the corner and three blocks down, you can't miss it, but you're a BRAT, aren't you?'

'I beg your pardon!?'

'You're a BRAT, aren't you? Would you like a spanking?'

Melody ran, not bothering to answer a question that should never have needed asking. She couldn't hear him following, so after a few paces she risked a glance over her shoulder to find him still at the door. He shrugged, as if to imply that her behaviour was somehow peculiar. She returned a single, meaningful finger and walked on with a toss of her head intended to convey contempt although in practise she felt utterly mortified, although not so much for his outrageous question as because he had quite clearly expected the answer to be yes, as if she was the sort of girl who would let a complete stranger spank her. Not that she could imagine any girl, in the entire history of humanity, voluntarily submitting to such a gross indignity.

He had at least told her how to get to the police station, along with adding a fresh complaint to what was already a very long list. It proved to be exactly where he'd said it was, easily identified by the blue lantern hanging above the door, but as she drew closer she slowed down, made wary by the way people were reacting to her, not only with complete lack of the respect, but as if she were some sort of delinquent. A large constable was standing to attention outside the door, his huge, red hands clasped behind his back. Melody winced, imagining how one of them would feel applied to her bottom. He was also distinctly fat, and she decided that it would be safe enough to address him from the foot of the steps, because if he did try anything funny she would be able to outrun him.

'Excuse me …'

'Room Sixteen, Miss. Second floor.'

'Er … is that where I should go to make a complaint? I want to make a complaint.'

'A complaint, Miss? Aren't you a BRAT?'

'No I am not a brat! Why does everybody seem to think I'm a brat?'

'You certainly look like a BRAT, Miss. Have you been sent from the hospital?'

'I came from the hospital, yes, but I wasn't sent here, and I am not a brat!'

The constable scratched one large ear, evidently puzzled, then spoke again.

'BRATs are spanked on the second floor, Room Sixteen. Sergeant Stern will deal with you.'

'Yes, but …'

Melody stopped. After the way she had been treated in the hospital, and by the waiter, it seemed very likely that if she entered the police station she would end up over Sergeant Stern's knee. The entire city seemed to be inhabited by disciplinarians and perverts, the police no better than the rest. They also seemed to be convinced that she was a brat, something that seemed to give them a free hand to spank her, when and where they liked. It was an intolerable attitude, and yet as she walked hurriedly away from the police station she was struggling to fight down feelings of guilt, wondering if she'd been sent to the appalling place as a sort of boot camp for pop stars who got too big for their boots. It was a worrying thought, especially as she looked back over her career and thought of all the times she'd taken advantage of her fame and money to get her own way.

She had reached another restaurant and stopped, reflecting that money was another problem, because she didn't have any. Then again, she ought to have money. After all, she was a nurse and she'd just completed a shift. Melody shook herself. She wasn't a nurse at all. She was a pop star, and she been performing to crowded stadia for the best part of three months. Of course she would have money, and lots of it, unless Peter had managed to siphon it all off.

Had she been in London, or Leeds, Manhattan even, she knew that simply walking in at the door would have been enough to ensure the best the restaurant had to offer, probably free after signing a few autographs. In what appeared to be called Metrocity it might be a different matter, especially as restaurant staff seemed to behave the same awful way as both hospital staff and the police. Besides, only Mr Hawker had recognised her, and his behaviour had hardly been respectful. She hesitated, then, on sudden impulse, began to search her pockets.

What she had hoped to find was in the breast pocket of her uniform, a black and gold credit card marked Metrocity Bank. How she had known it was there she was not sure, but it was, and the legend – BLACK DIAMOND – stencilled boldly across the middle suggested that it would have a healthy limit. She still felt more than a little doubtful as she made for the restaurant door, her all too active imagination creating scenarios in which her credit card was rejected but instead of being made to do the washing up she was spanked over the waiter's knee, bare bottom in the middle of the restaurant, then being made to toss him off because dealing with her had turned him on. Yet it was easy to check, because there was a Metrocity Bank a little way down the street.

Outside the bank was a cash machine, into which she slid the card, half expecting it to be swallowed but at least sure it wouldn't spank her. Text appeared on the screen, telling her to place her hand within a green outline. She did so, the outline disappeared and was replaced by several lines of information, including a very healthy balance. Melody smiled, her confidence rising towards its normal high level for the first time since her operation as she keyed in a demand for five hundred Credits.

At the sight of the unfamiliar currency she wondered how long she had been under, and how much that might explain the changes around her. It also meant that her balance might be less impressive than it looked. Notes began to emerge from the dispenser, blue and purple, in denominations of fifty and twenty. Both showed a distinctive logo, one against a background of fancifully designed racing cars, the other of near naked girls in just the sort of costume she was used to being put in. The opposing sides showed a head in profile, noble yet somehow off, foolish almost, and strangely familiar. She frowned, puzzled, but money was money and she tucked the folded notes into her top pocket along with the credit card.

Turning back towards the restaurant, she approached with extreme caution, ready to run at the slightest sign of wicked intent on the part of the doorman, no ordinary waiter this time, but a commissar or something of the sort in a bottle-green uniform with gold braid across one shoulder. He gave her a mildly supercilious look as she came close, but she told herself it was probably because of her uniform. After all, the restaurant looked expensive and was probably not the sort of place a nurse could usually afford to eat. A glance at the prices on a menu in the window was enough to assure her that she had plenty of money and she made for the door. The doorman stiffened, but then gave an affable nod.

'Are you a BRAT, Miss?'

Melody stopped, so taken aback by his rudeness that it took her a moment to answer.

'No I am not!'

He winked.

'I rather think you are.'

Melody's arm twitched up to slap him but she held herself back. He was a big man, and it seemed all too likely that if she tried to put him in his place she would end up being put in hers, which would probably be over his knee with her bare bottom on show to the street. She tried a different tactic.

'That's not a very nice thing to say, is it?'

He looked puzzled, and his tone was questioning as he replied.

'But you a BRAT, aren't you, Miss?'

'No! Why do you people keep call me a brat? Matron and Sister at the hospital, and one of the patients, some dirty old perve of a waiter, a policeman, and now you. I'm not that bad. I'm really not!'

'A BRAT, Miss, a Brain Recorded Andromorph Teraneuron.'

'Beg pardon?'

'Ah, you're new then?'

'New? I'm a newcomer to Metrocity, yes.'

'Ah ha, please come in then.'

'You're not going to spank me, are you?'

'Not just now, Miss.'

It wasn't the answer she'd wanted, but it was a great improvement on what had gone before. Still she hesitated.

'And if I go in for a meal, will the staff try to spank me?'

'Not so long as you can pay, Miss, and mind your manners of course.'

'Mind my ... Okay, thank you.'

She went inside, ignoring the disrespectful implication of his words. After all, she had been minding her manners all day, telling herself it was the only sensible thing to do when surrounded by maniacs, and definitely not because she'd been taught a lesson.

The restaurant was pleasantly familiar, for all her distrust of the staff, much like the ones she'd been used to visiting in the two years since her rise to fame. Widely spaced, cloth-covered tables were set out on the floor, each with a service of linen, silver and crystal; chairs and a discreet vase of flowers. Penguin-suited waiters hovered deferentially in the background, potted palms blended with understated decor and there was the faint sound of classical music.

Melody was the only customer, and received prompt attention despite the occasional frosty look for her uniform. She made no comment, firmly on best behaviour as she selected her dinner; langoustine salad, Sole Meunière and chocolate gâteaux, accompanied by a bottle of Sancerre. It was the first wine she had tasted since her operation; fresh and crisp and cold, irresistibly good after nothing but fizzy pop for three months.

The service was painfully slow, and she had finished the first bottle long before her main course arrived. She ordered another, telling herself that it might be her only chance, as presumably her access to Metrocity could be snatched away as suddenly as it had been granted. The wine waiter pointed out that the dry, delicate Sancerre would be inappropriate for her dessert and recommend a half bottle of Sauternes. Melody accepted, and her eyes were closed in pure bliss as she consumed the delicacy. A complimentary brandy followed, by which time she was completely relaxed and very, very drunk.

It was all she could do to walk properly as she made for the door, leaving a generous pile of notes on her table. She meant to ask the doorman some questions, as he'd been the most friendly person she'd met, but he was gone and she set off down the street. It was dark, although she couldn't remember there being a dusk, and the sky was flecked with stars despite the bright city lights. The pavements were crowded, with commuters hurrying home, couples and groups on their way out for the evening, people of every sort, all so normal that tears began to start in Melody's eyes from sheer relief.

She was soon home, and the instant she pushed open the front door she realised that the blank walls and boxes of text were gone. The living room was whole, with four perfectly ordinary walls, somehow more real than before even though she wasn't sure why. She ran upstairs, to find that the bedroom was the same, and the kitchen. Her breath came out in a long sigh as she collapsed onto the bed. She was back.

There was no sense of being watched, or of compulsion. Even Teddy was gone, the ribbons she'd used to tie him up with hanging limp from the bedpost. She relaxed, smiling, her eyes closed. Her head was spinning with drink and she felt happier than at any time since her operation, also extraordinarily horny. What she needed was an orgasm, both to celebrate her release and for the sake of it.

Her face was set in a sleepy, drunken smile as she lifted her bottom to tug her uniform skirt up and slip down her knickers. Baring herself brought an immediate, strong thrill, and the memory of the last time, over Matron's knee so that she could be spanked properly. She pushed the shameful thought away, determined that if there was one thing she would never, ever come over it was the memory of that spanking.

Besides, she didn't need it, not when her body felt so good, so sensitive and sensual, every curve made for pleasure. She began to touch herself, spread open on the bed with her knickers around her ankles and her thighs wide, stroking her skin to tease herself, intent on bringing her excitement so high that she lost control. After a moment she opened her dress, popping the buttons wide and lifting her breasts from her bra. Again the exposure reminded her of the last time it had been done, by Sister so that Mr Hawker could enjoy the sight of her bare boobs while she tossed him off, but that was something else she was determined not to come over, however exciting it was to remember how his cock had felt in her hand.

She began to play with her nipples, bringing her excitement gradually higher, but determined to keep her hands from between her legs until she could hold back no more. Her back was soon arched in pleasure and her thighs were as wide as they would go, offering her open sex, but it was the wrong position. She needed to feel that her bottom was vulnerable, and to stroke her cheeks, maybe hold them apart to show off the tight little hole between.

As she flipped over onto her tummy she was telling herself that the desire to go bottom-up had nothing to do with the fact that she'd been spanked that morning and everything to do with what she'd been thinking about before going to work, the temptation to insert something into her anus. She remembered the thermometer and bit her lip in sudden shame, but there was no denying it had felt good, especially the way her ring had opened up to take the bulb. Something had to go in, preferably a man's cock, but there was nobody to do it and she reached for her long-handled hairbrush.

The hard, rounded tip felt good against her bottom hole, making the desire to penetrate herself stronger still. She was slippery too, with the lubricant Sister had used to open her up and juice that had run down from her pussy, making it easy to press the hairbrush handle into her ring, which began to open to the pressure. Her mouth became wide for the sensation, which was every bit as wonderful as she had expected and also deliciously naughty. She told herself she'd stick the handle right up and come with it in her bottom hole, imagining it was a man's cock, but as she pushed to make her slippery little ring spread wider still a high, urgent voice spoke from behind her.

'Ooh Melody! Naughty Melody! Teddy fuck Melody!?'

'No! Not that … oh no …'

Melody had dropped the hairbrush, which fell out of her bottom hole and onto the bed, but for all her words she didn't move, unable to resist despite the screaming voice of shame in her head. Her need was too strong, and she was going to let him do it, to put his great, fat cock up her ready bottom hole. She gave a single, acquiescent sob as her resistance snapped, holding her position to let him mount her as he scrambled up onto the bed. Her sobs continued, ever more bitter, and turned briefly to cries as he picked up the discarded hairbrush and applied a few firm swats to her lifted bottom. On the fifth she found her voice.

'No, Teddy, not that! Don't beat Melody … you can have me, up … in … oh, you know where to put it …'

Something furry touched her thigh, his paw, and she looked back through the narrow slit between her breasts, to see his huge balls and the monstrous tower of his erect cock. His knob touched her sex, hot and meaty, sending a sharp thrill up her spine and setting her babbling in mingled fear and desire.

'Not there, Teddy. Not in pussy … please, I'm virgin … please, no! Do it up my bum, Teddy.'

She was too far gone to resist had he chosen to ignore her and take her virginity, but his answer was a shriek of delight.

'Up the bum!'

He tried to climb her, his cock pressing dangerously hard to her sex as he struggled to mount her bottom. She was too big. He couldn't do it, and she was forced to squat down into a yet lewder position, her thighs cocked too wide for anybody but a trained dancer or a contortionist, her bottom spread open. Teddy took immediate advantage, squealing with excitement as he thrust his cock between her cheeks, only to have it slide up the crease. He didn't seem to care, rutting in her slit with his balls bumping on her sex.

Melody reached back, alarmed that he'd waste what he had to give all over her bottom and back if she didn't take control. She took a firm grip, guiding his erection to her anus even as she tried to console herself that it didn't matter, because she'd had the thermometer up her bottom, and the hairbrush handle, so why not Teddy's cock? It was a lie and she knew it. He was a man, or at least, a male, and she was not merely surrendering to him but deliberately trying to feed his cock up her bottom hole for a buggering.

She was going to get it too, her ring slick with lubricant and loose from the insertion of the hairbrush handle. Teddy was pushing too, and her mouth came open in a wordless, ecstatic gasp as her hole began to open, gaping to the head of an erect penis for the first time in her life, wide, and wider still, until the felt the fat, solid head pop inside. It was done, her anal virginity gone, her bottom fucked. She let go, leaving Teddy to push himself deep, panting and clutching at the coverlet as inch after inch of thick, pink erection was jammed inside her. It felt wonderful, a sense of fullness, of completion beyond anything she could have imagined and which made her wonder if the sensation would be better still if he was in her pussy instead of her bottom.

There was no opportunity to find out, even had she wanted to try. Teddy was wedged to the balls in her anus, his massive scrotum slapping on her empty sex as he buggered her, leaving her cross-eyed and gasping with pleasure. She was going to come, both from the heavy feel in her rectum and the friction of his balls on her sex, but even that would not have been enough without the knowledge of what she was doing and how she must look, squatting on the bed with her nurse's uniform turned up and her panties pulled down, her huge breasts bouncing to the thrusts of a demented mechanical bear as he buggered her.

The thought was too much. Melody came, screaming out her ecstasy to the room as her orgasm hit her, and again, unable to stop herself coming as the big cock pumped in her bottom hole and the slapping on her sex rose in a furious crescendo that rendered her utterly helpless, given over completely to what was being done to her. It only stopped when Teddy did, jamming himself deep with one final thrust and a cry of triumph and delight, to hold himself as far in as he would go up Melody's straining bottom hole, to give her a final exquisite peak at the thought of the come pumping out inside her.

Naughty

Melody awoke to mixed feelings; indignation for the way she had been treated, shame for the way she had reacted, but also relief and an almost childish delight in the sight of what was quite clearly sunlight filtering through the curtains. Whatever else might have happened, she was no longer trapped between her house and the stage, which had formed the boundaries of her world for so long.

Even the memory of her surrender to Teddy brought a smile to her face as well as a blush to her cheeks. However rude, there was no denying it had been good. She was still cuddled up to him, the way they had gone to sleep, with her naked and Teddy growling softly in contentment as he rubbed his cock in the groove between her side and one breast. Melody had let him do it, too tired to protest.

She still felt horny, but it was only one of several contending emotions, with curiosity the most urgent. The day before had been a rush of events, her experiences raising many more questions than they had answered, one of which now came to the fore.

'Why does everybody keep calling me a brat, Teddy?'

He didn't answer, dormant once more. Melody sighed.

'Typical man.'

A clock had appeared during the night. It read nine-thirty, which almost certainly meant that she was late for work. Her bottom cheeks tightened in anticipation of the likely consequences, but she fought down the urge to rush, telling herself that nobody had asked her if she wanted to be a nurse, so that there was no reason she should go to the hospital at all. She certainly didn't need the money either, and she had better things to do.

She went up to the bathroom to wash. Not that it made any difference, because she seemed to be permanently clean and fresh, but the morning routine was pleasantly normal. It was also mildly annoying, because while the soap and toothpaste never ran out, neither were her preferred brand and there was nothing else at all. As she brushed her teeth she realised that she was now in a position to do something about that.

The bathroom window showed not whiteness, but the view across Metrocity, she had plenty of cash, and on her walk to the police station and back she had passed a chemist. There had also been a shoe shop, several clothes shops and a full range of other useful stores. She might have to dodge the occasional pervert, and be ready to run if need be, but there were too many things she needed; decent make-up, a music system of some sort, perhaps a few pot plants, and, above all, nice clothes. Really, she had no choice, and if she was going to be spanked for being late it was best to put it off as long as possible. She would go shopping.

She would also find out more about Metrocity, maybe why she was there and why she was a brat in the eyes of the inhabitants, if that was what they meant. When she'd spoken to the doorman her main concern had been to avoid a spanking, but he definitely had said BRAT was an acronym, although she couldn't remember what it had been, only that she hadn't understood it. Now she would find out.

Feeling refreshed, full of energy and excited by the knowledge that she was skipping work, she trotted downstairs. Her instinct was to change, but as her nurse's uniform was the only thing she possessed that didn't show her knickers she put it back on, also her underwear, which was as fresh as when it had first appeared. Her uniform was also neatly pressed, with a faint scent of lavender. As she dressed she remembered a line she had overheard from a conversation between two techie types in a recording studio – any sufficiently advanced technology is indistinguishable from magic – or something of the sort. Clearly that was what was happening, and for once the geeks had put their knowledge to good use.

She made her way down to the living room, only to be

brought to a sudden halt a few paces from the front door. Her Volition was gone, snatched away without warning, while text boxes had reappeared, hovering in the air in front of her but this time not in reverse. Three were blinking, close together in a column to the left beneath a single, steady title – Game. Melody read them – Spankorama – Naughty Nurse – The Gauntlet. Beneath was a fifth box, stating simply – Select.

Several seconds passed before Melody realised that the command applied to her, and that she would probably remain rooted to the spot until she made her choice, that or it would be made for her. Spankorama seemed a good description of what had happened the day before, but so did Naughty Nurse. The Gauntlet sounded dangerous.

'Um …'

The Select box began to flash.

'Um … um … um … Naughty Nurse, okay? Naughty Nurse.'

The boxes vanished. Melody felt her bottom cheeks tighten again, which seemed to be an instinctive reaction to the prospect of a spanking, which she was sure was what she was going to get, for all her efforts to tell herself that being naughty didn't necessarily have to involve getting caught, let alone punished. Pulling the door open, she peered cautiously outside. There was no sign of Nurse Jane in the street, nor any of her other colleagues, while she could see the shops, temptingly close. Going to the hospital meant a spanking, that much seemed certain, while if she went to the shops she would at least postpone her fate, maybe avoid it all together. She could feel no compulsion, but decided to cross the road, allowing her to pretend she'd been on her way to the hospital if Matron or Sister suddenly appeared. Neither did, and after a last moment of hesitation she set off towards the shops, as fast as she could go.

'And where do you think you're off to, my girl?'

Melody stopped. Matron had emerged from behind a tree,

a tree far too slim to conceal the woman's imposing bulk, but there she was.

'Um … I … I was just going to nip down to the shops, for some … some toothpaste.'

'A liar as well as a shirker, I see. Well, I know how to deal with that sort of behaviour.'

'Oh, shit. No matron, please, not a spanking, no … oh fuck!'

'And such language! Not that I expect anything better from a BRAT, but really.'

Melody turned to run, only to collide with a solid individual coming the other way. An instant later Matron's grip had closed on her arm. A crowd had begun to gather as Melody was hauled squealing along the pavement to where twin benches flanked the entrance to the hospital, among dozens of people, all keen to watch the spanking. Melody fought, wriggling in the huge woman's grip and begging for mercy at the same time, but Matron barely seemed to notice. Not a single person in the crowd moved to help her either, or so much as protested, every one of them thoroughly enjoying the show as Melody was subjected to the same humiliating treatment she had been given the day before; skirt lifted up, her pleas for modesty ignored and her panties pulled down, her bare bottom smacked hard as she was lectured on her delinquency.

Aside from the number of people watching her get it, the only real difference was that the spanking didn't bring her to orgasm, but that was small consolation. She hadn't been able to keep control, making a hideously embarrassing show of her pussy and bottom hole as she squirmed and bucked in her pain, and once it was over her skirt was pinned up and her knickers left down, just as before, leaving her bare red bottom on show to what seemed an improbably large number of chuckling, laughing onlookers. Matron could not have been more indifferent to Melody's predicament, smoothing her own skirt down before rising to her feet.

‘Now into work with you, and if I have any more nonsense you’ll be getting a dose of the cane.’

Melody swallowed, but it was impossible to overcome her resentment as she was hustled into the hospital and up to the ward, Matron dogging her footsteps until they arrived at the desk.

‘Here she is. I caught her trying to sneak down to the shops.’

Sister looked up, shaking her head in patient disapproval.

‘Oh, Melody. Really!’

Everybody on the ward was looking, not one with any sympathy; her fellow nurses either giggling together as they saw the state she was in or giving little tuts of disapproval, the patients openly amused. Matron clapped her hands.

‘Back to work, all of you, unless you want some of the same.’

The nurses scurried to obey, leaving Melody the centre of attention for two dozen leering, sniggering patients, and Sister, who drew a heavy sigh before speaking.

‘Oh dear. Well, I suppose we had better make the best of things. As you’re already bare behind you had better deal with the men’s private needs. Let me see, Mr Hawker, Mr Phelps and Veldt Panther. Run along.’

Melody tried to hide her relief as she made for the private rooms. Not that she was happy about having to masturbate three men, but at least she knew what to do and so was unlikely to make some mistake and end up getting the cane. There would also be the opportunity to talk to them and perhaps find out what was going on. She decided to do Mr Hawker first, on the grounds that she had already held his cock, which somehow seemed to make the process less shameful. He was propped up in his bed, plaster covered arms to either side as Jane fed him yoghurt with a spoon. Melody immediately found herself blushing.

‘Oh … I’ll come back later, shall I?’

‘No, you come right on in, Nurse. Pull my covers down,

Janey darling, and tip the rest of that on my cock, then you can help Melody Melons here lick it off.'

Melody's blush rose from warmth to blazing heat and her hand went to her mouth in shock but Jane stayed quite calm, greeting his filthy suggestion with a chuckle.

'Now, now, Mr Hawker, you know perfectly well that we don't provide oral relief. It's against hygiene regulations.'

'Twenty credits, each?'

'Mr Hawker, I do believe you're trying to bribe me.'

'That about the size of it. Thirty?'

'Now, now, Mr Hawker.'

'Forty, and I get to come in your mouth.'

Jane hesitated, glancing at Melody.

'What do you think?'

'I think he's a filthy pig, that's what I think! I don't need your money, thank you, Mr Hawker.'

Jane made a face.

'I do!'

'Jane!'

'Oh come on, Melody, for forty credits. What's the matter, don't you like cock?'

'Don't I what!? No! Well, I … never mind that. Come on, Jane, he's trying to make whores out of us!'

Jane shrugged, looking unhappy. Mr Hawker laughed.

'Hey, come on, you're no whores. You're angels of mercy, that's what you are, and if I want to give you a little tip, just to show my appreciation, what's the problem? Come on, girls, fifty credits each.'

Jane glanced at Melody once more.

'Please? I'll swallow for him, so you won't get messy.'

'Jane! Anyway, what if Matron catches us?'

'We'll hear her coming. Come on, Melody. Think what we can get for fifty credits!'

Melody had spent more on her dinner the night before, but Jane had already pulled Mr Hawker's bedclothes down, revealing his large, half-stiff penis. He relaxed, watching as she quickly spooned out what remained in the yoghurt pot, soiling not only his cock but his scrotum. Melody hung back, shocked, but wanting to join in despite herself. Jane giggled and beckoned.

'Come on. It's peach and tangerine.'

She leant forward, her pointed pink tongue poking out from between her painted lips to flick a tiny piece of yoghurt from the pile on Mr Hawker's balls, before drawing a long, slow trail up his shaft as she took his cock in her hand. He sighed, and was smiling happily as she repeated the action, so obviously enjoying herself that her reluctance now seemed very put on. Mr Hawker beckoned to Melody.

'Come on, Melons, you too.'

Melody was unable to speak for the lump in her throat, but gave her head an angry shake. Jane looked up.

'Come on. Fair's fair.'

'Yes, but ...'

'You're supposed to be doing him, not me.'

'Yes, but ...'

'Or is it that you'd rather be licking me than him?'

'No it is not!'

Mr Hawker's smile grew broader still.

'Now that I'd like to see.'

'You're a pervert, Mr Hawker, do you know that!? Getting off on watching me spanked, and girl on girl stuff, you really are!'

He shrugged. Jane had gone back to work on his cock, smearing the yoghurt over the now stiff shaft with her lips and tongue, then suddenly sucking the whole thing into her mouth. Mr Hawker gasped and jerked.

'Ow! Shit! Careful of my arms, Janey.'

She ignored him, now sucking greedily on his cock, her eyes closed in bliss. Melody watched, astonished that Jane had proved to be such a slut and painfully aware that only her determination not to make such a public sacrifice of her self-respect kept her from behaving just as badly. Yet she had been told to masturbate him, which surely meant that at the very least she ought to hold his balls or something while Jane sucked him off.

It was all the excuse she needed, stepping quickly forward, she took hold of the warm, bulging sack and began to squeeze gently. Mr Hawker gave a knowing chuckle, as if Melody's surrender had been inevitable. Jane opened one lazy eye, winked and went back to her task. Melody pursed her lips in vexation, feeling put upon but increasingly horny. She had also forgotten to put on her rubber gloves, but it was now too late as she took hold of his cock with her other hand and began to masturbate him into Jane's mouth. He groaned.

'That's the way, girls, but don't rush it. How about going tits out?'

Jane pulled back from his cock, giggling.

'Go on Melody, if you're not going to suck you can at least give him a show, and yours are so nice and big.'

Mr Hawker nodded his agreement as Jane went back to sucking. Melody hesitated only briefly, wanting to do it and not sure if she was under compulsion or not as she unbuttoned herself and lifted her breasts from her bra. The open sides of her uniform pushed them out, making them seem bigger than ever, and as she went back to masturbating Mr Hawker's cock they lolled forward. He made a deep growling sound in his throat.

'Will you look at those! Rub me between them, Janey, go on.'

'Hey, but …'

It was too late. Jane had let his cock slip from her mouth a second time, to rub it on Melody's nipples, creating a thrill too sharp to resist. She was pulled down, her breasts taken in Jane's hands and squeezed around his cock. He began to fuck in her cleavage, Jane now sucking again but with her face buried in the softness of Melody's breasts. Jane was pawing her too, quite obviously keen to get to grips, but the sensation was too nice, and all Melody could manage in the way of resistance was a shame filled sob.

Mr Hawker grunted. Jane gave a muffled squeak of surprise and jerked back, to catch the first eruption full in her face. The second went all over Melody's breasts, and the third before he had finished. A now giggling Jane wiped the tip of his cock on one straining nipple before Melody managed to stand back, to stare open mouthed at the mess he'd made over her breasts, with both plump globes streaked with white and a thick blob hanging from one soiled nipple.

'Look what you've done!'

Jane was still giggling, apparently oblivious to the thick white streak of come he had laid across her nose and cheek.

'Let me lick it off.'

Before Melody could react Jane's tongue had poked out, to lap up the come from her breasts. She let it happen, frantically telling herself that is was just for Mr Hawker's pleasure, and that she very definitely did not enjoy having another woman lick her breasts, let alone clean spunk off them. It was a lie, the whole filthy experience was pure bliss, and better still once Jane's lips had closed on her dirty nipple. Jane was touching her too, Melody's breasts lifted to her mouth as she suckled, just as if she were hoping to feed from them.

Mr Hawker was forgotten, the hospital forgotten. Melody's eyes had closed in ecstasy as Jane licked and kissed, sucked and nuzzled. She'd stuck her bottom out by instinct, and when one hand closed on a hot cheek there was no resistance, and only a mild sob as Jane's fingers burrowed deeper, to tease the little hole between. Another hand cupped Melody's sex and she was being masturbated and suckled at the same time, her bottom hole and pussy teased as her nipples were sucked turn and turn about. A finger slipped into her anus, another had found the little bump between her sex lips and she was completely lost, gasping out her pleasure and cuddling Jane's head to her breasts, begging to be rubbed harder and suckled more firmly, and as she began to come, to have her bottom smacked.

Jane obliged, slapping at Melody's cheeks to make them bounce and wobble as she continued to rub and to suck. As wave after wave of ecstasy ran through Melody's head she was babbling out her thanks and begging for more, to be suckled and to be masturbated, but most of all to be spanked, and as hard as Jane could do it.

Naughtier

To Melody's amazement they got away with it. Even as she'd been coming her head had been full of mingled fear and desire for the bite of the cane across her bottom, while as she and Jane hurriedly cleaned themselves up and adjusted their make-up she was shocked at how disappointed she felt. Jane plainly didn't agree, giggling nervously and repeatedly glancing at the door until both were decent and only then helping herself to two blue fifty credit notes from Mr Hawker's wallet. She offered one to Melody, who held up her hands in shock.

'No thanks. I'm not …'

'Go on, take it. I know you didn't suck, but what you did with your tits was great. Isn't that right, Mr Hawker?'

'Take it, Melons. You've earned it.'

'Yes, but …'

Melody hesitated, not wanting to insult Jane but feeling that if she accepted the money she would be prostituting herself.

'… I'm fine. It was nice. You have it, Jane.'

'Don't be silly!'

As Jane spoke she had tucked the note into Melody's cleavage. Mr Hawker gave a wry chuckle.

'You see. It won't burn you.'

Melody was blushing with shame, but could find no way out of the situation save to promise herself that she would give the note to the first charity she came across. She then reflected that they now shared a secret, which seemed to be the perfect opportunity to ask her question.

'What do people mean when they call me a brat?'

Jane laughed.

'It's what you are, silly.'

Mr Hawker was about to speak, and for once he looked serious, but at that instant the door opened, admitting Sister. Melody's bottom cheeks tightened at the realisation of how close they'd been to getting caught and she hastened to throw away the tissues they'd been using to clean up. Sister gave a gentle tut.

'Do not be wasteful, Melody. One tissue is quite sufficient, two at most.'

'Sorry, Sister.'

'And do hurry up. Mr Phelps and Veldt Panther are waiting.'

'Yes, Sister. Sorry, Sister.'

'And Jane, as you seem to have finished feeding Mr Hawker you should be in the sluice room, not gossiping with your friends.'

'Yes, Sister. Sorry, Sister.'

'Just be glad it was me who came in and not Matron. Now run along, both of you.'

Sister left, both girls hurrying to follow, but as they reached the door Jane leant close to Melody's ear.

'You can return the favour later.'

'Favour?'

Jane's response was an urgent hiss.

'Playing with you! I did it for you. You have to do it for me. Be fair.'

'Yes, but …'

Jane had already moved on, leaving Melody's face considerably redder than her bottom cheeks. Being naughty evidently involved rather more than she'd bargained for, and she knew that when the moment came she would be unable to resist.

The door opposite was Room Three, which she knew was Mr Phelps's, although she was sure she hadn't been told. Pausing, she set her shoulders back and adjusted her uniform, determined to look brisk, efficient and above all clinical, only to decide that it was impossible with her skirt pinned up at the back and her bare bottom on show. With a deep sigh she pushed open the door.

Mr Phelps lay in his bed, a man of unguessable age and

looks, but definitely a man. Melody could tell because his sheets were down and while almost his entire body was swathed in bandages a gap had been left to expose his genitals and the turn of his buttocks. His face was also invisible, save for holes over his mouth, nose, and where two pale eyes stared out, directly at her. As she stepped towards the bed his cock stirred, rolling lazily to one side as blood began to fill the shaft. Melody tried a sympathetic smile.

'You poor thing, but I see you're getting better.'

His answer was a strange gulping noise, but his cock at least reacted, swelling even as she watched.

'Oh dear, you do need it badly.'

She pulled on her gloves, now feeling more virtuous than resentful for her task, but still trying to tell herself that she was doing it because it was her job and that there was no pleasure at all in masturbating strange men, and definitely not in having other women suckle her breasts. That sort of behaviour was for sluts and whores, not for her, not Melody J the virgin star.

Applying a good squeeze of lubricant to Mr Phelps' cock and balls, she set to work, tugging at his shaft and gently squeezing his sack. He grew quickly, so that she was soon pulling at a full erection. A moment later he'd come, decorating her hand and the bandages encasing his belly. Melody allowed herself a smile. It had been quick, efficient and moderately clean, just as it should have been.

'There we are, Mr Phelps. That was easy, wasn't it. I hope you get better soon.'

She mopped up, pleased with herself and now sure that it was simply a matter of staying in control and of accepting what she had to do as part of her job rather than getting carried away. That way there was no reason to feel guilty, or ashamed of herself for her reactions, and if she was distinctly sticky between her thighs then that was Jane's fault for being such a little slut. It was only a pity that it had been impractical to talk to him.

Her next call was Veldt Panther in Room Six, and Melody walked back across the corridor with renewed confidence, announcing herself with a breezy greeting as she pushed open the door.

'Good morning, Mr Veldt Panther.'

'Good morning yourself, and Panther will do.'

He was black, his skin not the milky coffee colour of Melody's own, but so dark it seemed almost blue, with a silky sheen. One arm was in plaster, the other in a sling, while what was visible of his body was hard, smooth muscle. Melody immediately found herself wondering what his cock would look like, and found it hard to keep the detached, professional expression she was determined to maintain as she pulled on her gloves, while her voice faltered as she spoke.

'Let's have you dealt with then, shall we?'

'You do just that. I see you got a spanking?'

'I was late into work.'

Melody peeled back his covers, cool and businesslike, only for her poise to crack completely as his cock was exposed. It was huge, a good eight inches long even limp, and very nearly as thick as her wrist, while it rested on a leathery scrotum bulging with two fat testicles at least as big as hen's eggs. Her mouth had come open and she shut it hastily, struggling to retain her equanimity as she applied a squirt of lubricant to the monstrous tool and took it in her hand.

He was grinning, completely relaxed as she began to masturbate him, too relaxed if anything, because despite her best efforts he didn't seem to be getting any harder. She began to play with his balls, but it made little difference, making her wonder if she was going to have to stick a finger up his bottom to get him off. It seemed an impossibly rude thing to do, even if Sister had recommended it, while his slow reaction also seemed a good excuse to indulge her rapidly growing need, if only a little. She stopped.

'Now come along, Mr … er, Panther. Do try. Or do you need me with my breasts bare?'

'That would be good, and how about you turn that big round tushy to me?'

Melody nodded, turning her body so that he could see her bottom properly as she quickly unfastened her dress. Her nipples were as stiff and sensitive as ever, so that just to touch them as she lifted her breasts from her bra sent sharps jolts of pleasure through her. Panther gave an appreciative nod as she held them up for his inspection, one at a time so as not to get lubricant all over them.

She went back to work, tugging on his cock and rubbing her thumb on his foreskin as it pulled back to expose the meaty head within. He'd now begun to grow, keeping her constantly aware of just how exposed she was with her boobs bare and her bottom pushed well out to show the rear view of her pussy lips.

'You like this, don't you?'

Melody nodded. She was wet and she knew he could see, while she could smell her own excitement. Yet still he wasn't fully hard, the massive cock in her hand heavy with blood and nearly as long as her forearm but still less than rigid. She wondered if she ought to suck, eager for the feel of the big cock in her mouth even if it was against the rules, and it had to be less indecent that sticking a finger up his bottom.

A moment later she'd done it, gaping wide to take in as such of his cock as would fit. It felt wonderful, driving her excitement so high that she was quickly imagining how it would be to suck him hard not merely to relieve his need, but to get him ready for the virgin hole between her thighs. She knew he could see, probably enough to know that she'd never been had, and all she needed to do was climb on top and ease him up her hole. It would hurt, she knew, but it had to happen some time and she would never be more ready.

The click of the door saved her virginity. She looked up in horror, expecting to find herself under Matron's accusing glare, but it was only Jane.

'Melody, you naughty girl!'

'Jane! Thank heavens it's you!'

Her friend quickly closed the door and ran across to the bed.

'Me too. Isn't he lovely, and so big!?'

Melody nodded, her mouth once more full of cock as Jane went to work on his balls. The urge to mount him had gone, but she wanted him to come, preferably in Jane's mouth, just for the sake of being dirty. She pulled back, offering his now straining erection to her friend. Jane took him in, her cheeks bulging with the effort, and Melody turned her attention to his balls, cramming both into her mouth to add one more deliciously rude act to her rapidly expanding experience. She had also begun to tug him into Jane's mouth, with plenty of shaft to get hold of, but even that wasn't enough to tip him over the edge, for all that his voice was hoarse with ecstasy as he spoke.

'I want to see both of you, tushies and boobs.'

Jane didn't hesitate, pulling open the buttons of her dress as fast as she could and tugging up her bra to spill out her neatly rounded breasts, never once letting his cock slip from her mouth, nor as she tugged up her uniform skirt and pushed her panties down to bare her neat pink bottom to his gaze..

'That's better. I just wish I could touch you … feel you … fuck you …'

He finished with a long groan. Jane's eyes popped and her cheeks suddenly bulged fatter still as he filled her mouth with come. Melody felt her own mouth come wide by instinct, his balls slipping free and Jane drew back, both of them now pumping hard on his cock to send fountain after fountain of thick white come high into the air. Some went in Melody's mouth, and before she could stop herself she had deliberately swallowed, then taken his cock in, urgently mouthing down what he had to give her until she'd taken every last drop into her belly.

She came up gasping, dizzy with excitement and desperate for her own orgasm. Her fingers went between her thighs, burrowing into her half-lowered panties to find her sex, her free hand squeezing at one taut nipple, her eyes fixed on the huge cock she'd just had in her mouth.

'Hey, what about me! Don't be greedy, Melody.'

Jane's demand was urgent, and she was coming around the bed. Melody was lost, unable to stop herself as she nodded and poked out her tongue, only for Panther's voice to cut through the haze of her ecstasy.

'Somebody's coming, and I don't mean you, Melody.'

Both girls snatched their tops closed, Jane also wriggling frantically to make her skirt fall into place while she did her buttons up as fast as she could. They only just succeeded, Matron herself peering around the door just a few seconds after Melody had managed to fasten the last button on her blouse. Matron gave her a long, searching look, while Jane's mouth had come open in horror. The big woman finally spoke.

'Nurse Melody, there is ejaculate in your hair.'

Melody felt her face go crimson and her bottom tight, but Panther came to her rescue.

'I come hard, Matron, and it's been a while.'

Matron gave a sceptical grunt and her eyes moved slowly over the two girls and where Panther's gradually shrinking cock lay on his come spotted belly. Melody waited, sure the big woman would be able to hear her heartbeat and expecting herself and Jane to be awarded a caning at any instant, while she felt so guilty for what she'd been about to do that she almost admitted her sin when Matron spoke again.

'Very well, but it doesn't take two of you to provide Veldt Panther relief. Now get on with your work.'

She left the room. Jane blew her breath out.

'That was close.'

Melody nodded urgently. Jane glanced at the door, then abruptly kissed Melody, full on the mouth.

'Later then, in the laundry room. I'll make sure we get put on bed duty.'

She winked and made for the door, leaving Melody to clean up. Panther obligingly spread his legs, speaking as she lifted his balls to wipe underneath.

'You two are hot, and you know what happens if that old dragon catches you, don't you just?'

'We get the cane, I expect.'

He laughed.

'Yes, you do, right across your bare tushies, in front of the whole ward.'

'You'd like that, wouldn't you?'

'What's not to like? Seeing a couple of cuties get their tushies whipped, that's good.'

'It hurts! Well, spanking does anyway … I've never been caned, and … and it's degrading. Women shouldn't be spanked, or caned, let alone in public, or made to toss men off just because you get horny for that matter. It's not right!'

'You're a BRAT, aren't you? You make the choices. I just enjoy the ride.'

'I make the choices? What do you mean? And what makes me a brat?'

The door swung open, revealing Sister.

'Come along, Nurse Melody. There's no time for idle chatter.'

'Hang on a moment, Sister. I just want to know what it means when everybody keeps calling me a brat.'

Sister's expression hardened as she began to advance across the room.

'I'll show you what it means, my girl.'

'Hey, no! Sister!'

Melody was grabbed by the wrist, turned expertly across Sister's knee on Panther's bedside chair and spanked, several dozen swats delivered to her already pink bottom, hard enough to set her wriggling and squealing in pain. When she was finally let up she was gasping for breath and clutching her hot cheeks. Panther was laughing, which brought Melody's indignation to the surface despite the risks.

'Ow! What was that for? I didn't do anything!'

'You are a lazy, deceitful, naughty girl, Melody, and until there is a dramatic improvement in your behaviour you may expect to be spanked at every opportunity. Do I make myself clear?'

Melody made to answer, then hung her head.

'Yes, Sister.'

Naughtiest

Melody went back to work, bare red bottom still on show, feeling more puzzled and put upon than ever as she distributed tea and biscuits, helped a colleague to give Mr Gibbs a sponge bath, fed Mr Norris some grapes his wife had brought in for him and masturbated Mr Allinson with the bed curtain drawn round for privacy. The moment she had finished and ticked his name off on Sister's list she was put on changing the beds, which set her stomach fluttering at the prospect of having to oblige Jane.

She had occasionally found other girls attractive, even been tempted to experiment, towards the end of school and before her career took off, but her upbringing and her drive for fame had always held her back, knowing that the slightest rumour of a lesbian liaison would mean ruin for her carefully crafted image as the sexy yet wholesome face of pop; desirable and yet unobtainable. Not that her desires had been all that strong, anyway, little more than curiosity and a firmly suppressed desire to be naughty for the sake of it.

Now it was different, with her image already in tatters after her nude stage shows, having had her breasts suckled and her pussy frigged, and with her bottom warm from spanking. Her desire was strong and her resistance weak, no more than a faint sense of shame and guilt, while changing the patients' sheets was making things rapidly worse. It was a particularly embarrassing task, as she constantly had to bend over, which meant exhibiting the full spread of her bare bottom to the ward, and not just her freshly reddened cheeks, but her bumhole and the rear view of her sex. She was wet, and she knew it showed, making her ever more confused and aroused as she made up bed after bed.

She had piled the dirty sheets into a large wicker hamper with wheels, which she was told to take down to the laundry room in the basement. There was no sign of Jane, who had been doing the private rooms, but that didn't stop Melody's sense of anticipation rising as she took the lift down and followed the signs to a huge, low room lined with great machines and warm with steam. Jane wasn't there, but plenty of other people were, both nurses from other wards and the washerwomen themselves, who seemed to have been selected for their bulk, with full bosoms and bulging hips stretching out their plain white uniforms and massive arms extending from their short sleeves, their skin dark or reddened from the steam.

'Melody?'

Jane had come up behind her, bright eyed with excitement as she went on.

'There you are. I thought I might miss you. Come on, quick, or Matron and Sister will wonder what we've been up to. Oh, and don't let the washerwomen catch us, or we'll really be in trouble. Just act nonchalant.'

She set off between a long double row of machines. Melody followed, her feelings rising close to panic at the thought of what she was about to do, but completely unable to hold back. There were several doors at the far end of the big room, one of which Jane pushed open, holding it for Melody. Intense white struck her eyes, making her think for one awful moment that she was back in the holding tank before she realised that they were in a huge linen room. Shelves of scrubbed wood rose to every side, each laden with stack upon stack of sheets and pillow cases. Jane took her hand.

'Quick!'

Melody was led in among the racks, to the furthest corner of the room and into a dead end with shelves screening them on every side. Jane wasted no time, fumbling open her dress and tugging her bra up over her breasts.

'Suckle me, Melody, and take yours out too. I want to feel them.'

Her voice was urgent, and Melody found herself responding despite her misgivings, unable to resist Jane's desire or her own need to take the two soft pink globes in her hands and a nipple in her mouth. Jane's skin smelt nice as Melody came close, and tasted better still as she gave in to her need, putting her mouth to one big, puffy nipple. She took a breast in each hand, enjoying their weight and the soft, feminine flesh. It was strange, after caressing herself so often, but undeniably nice.

She did nothing to resist as her own dress was undone, squeezing and suckling at her friend's chest. The buttons were soon open and Melody's bra was hauled up in the same way Jane's had been, to flop out both heavy, coffee-coloured globes. Jane sighed with pleasure as she began to feel Melody's breasts, then abruptly pulled her friend close to rub their chests together, dark flesh pressing to pale. Her voice held something close to awe as she spoke.

'You're so big, Melody, and so firm! I want to hold them. I want to hold them and suck them while I rub off.'

Melody nodded, happy not to have to disgrace herself completely but also biting back disappointment. Jane went down, taking one long pinkish brown nipple into her mouth to suckle as she tugged up her skirt. Melody cradled her friend's head and began to stroke Jane's soft blonde hair. Her eyes were closed in bliss and the need to touch herself was rising, held back only by the knowledge that Jane had already made her come and so it was only fair to return the favour. Yet trying to tell herself that was all she was doing was pointless. It felt too nice, and not just the sensation of her breasts being held and suckled, but of having Jane in her arms and knowing that her friend's hands were down her panties, masturbating to the thrill of feeding at the teat.

'Don't you want me to lick your pussy?'

The words had come from nowhere, but they were out, and as Jane pulled back, giggling, Melody no longer had a choice. She went down on her knees, planting them well apart as she slid a hand down the front of her half-lowered panties. Jane took a moment to rub her breasts in Melody's face, then pushed down her panties and adjusted her skirt so that it would stay up, baring the neat pink slit of her sex, baby-smooth and glistening with moisture where she'd been playing with herself.

'You're not to stop, even if you come first.'

Melody nodded, now masturbating as she prepared to add one more depravity to the rapidly growing list. Jane came close, but instead of pushing out her hips as Melody had expected, she turned, offering her bare bottom, the pert white cheeks framed in panties and nurse's skirt, the neatly turned pussy lips pouting from between her thighs, the tiny pink star of her anus on plain show. A sob escaped Melody's lips as she fought to retain at least one tiny glimmer of her dignity, and then she had gone in, burying her face between Jane's bottom cheeks to lick pussy with her nose pressed firmly to her friend's bumhole.

It was too much, the combined effect of her spankings, of tossing and sucking cock, of taking a man's balls in her mouth, of having him come all over her and swallowing it, of having her girlfriend suckle at her breasts, of licking her pussy with her face smothered in bare white bottom, all of it combined to send her over the edge, coming with a power she had never experienced before, and as it hit her she deliberately indulged herself in one last depravity, filthier still, by sticking her tongue in up Jane's bottom hole as far as it would go.

'Oh you dirty little bitch! No, don't stop.'

Jane had pushed her bottom out further still, spreading her cheeks in Melody's face. Still coming, Melody focused everything on licking the tight pink ring under her mouth, with the thought that she had her tongue up another girl's bottom raging in her head, to create peak after peak of ecstasy. Only when the spasms finally began to die away did she try to pull back, only to have Jane grab her by the hair, twisting hard.

'Oh no you don't! You said you'd make me come.'

Melody's face was pulled firmly back between Jane's bottom cheeks. Once more she began to lick the tiny hole, now burning with shame and embarrassment. Jane kept a tight hold, wriggling her bottom in Melody's face and sighing with pleasure in between demands to be tongued faster and deeper. Melody did her best, pushing her tongue in up Jane's bottom hole, a little deeper each time as the ring grew lose and slippery, until at last her head was thrust firmly downwards and Jane's bottom pushed out further still.

'Now my cunt. Lick it.'

Melody did as she was told, transferring her attention to Jane's sex, but with her face still smothered in bottom, still licking even when her hair was released. Jane put her hands on the shelves, gripping a wooden slat and rubbing her breasts on a pile of clean white sheets, her back pulled in tight to thrust her bottom out as far as she could, full in Melody's face. Jane sighed.

'That's right … that's nice … oh, you do look a picture!'

Jane gave a brief, high laugh and a wriggle of her bottom, leaving Melody with the image of how she would look if anybody caught them, kneeling on the bare concrete floor, her skirt pinned up at the back and her knickers pulled down, her breasts lolling forward from her open uniform, her face smothered in her friend's bottom as she licked pussy from behind. Again Jane laughed, now almost hysterical, and again, before she began to scream, her bottom cheeks tightening in Melody's face as she went into a noisy, shuddering orgasm that ended only when Melody was forced to pull back and gasp in some air. For a long moment the only sound was the girls' breathing and the faint whirr of machines, before Jane finally found her voice.

'That was great! Thanks!'

All that Melody could manage was a weak nod, her feelings too muddled for more. She felt too weak to rise, while her fingers were shaking badly as she hurried to do herself up, sure that somebody would have heard Jane's screams of ecstasy.

'We'd better hurry.'

'Yes, but I'd take a dozen spankings for that, gladly.'

'How about the cane, and did you have to scream like that?'

'I can't help it. My boyfriend generally sticks my panties in my mouth.'

'The dirty bastard!'

'Oh, I don't mind. He does it when he spanks me too, not to shut me up, just to humiliate me.'

'Your boyfriend spanks you? With your knickers in your mouth! That's awful! Why do you stay with him?'

Jane looked puzzled.

'It's great! You should come around some time. He'd love your titties, and your bum. I bet he'd have me spank you in front of him, and go sixty-nine while he took turns with us, and make me suck him when he's been up you, and …'

She trailed off with a purr and began to fiddle with her bra, leaving Melody dumbstruck. Shaking her head and telling herself that she at least could never go out with such a perverted, disrespectful pig, she finished adjusting her clothes, making sure there were no tell-tale signs to hint at what they'd been up to. Jane took a little longer as she had to adjust her skirt and panties, giving Melody a chance to ask the crucial question.

'Can you please explain all this brat business to me, Jane. Everybody seems to think I'm one, and that because I am they can do as they please with me, and I'll like it!'

Jane looked surprised.

'You do, don't you? How long have you been in Metrocity?'

'Only a couple of days, at least, I've only been able to go out for a couple of days.'

Jane laughed.

'Oh, you're new! I didn't realise. Um … it's a bit difficult, actually …'

Her tone had become serious as she trailed off, pushing Melody's curiosity higher still.

'Well? Tell me!'

Jane sighed, now looking concerned and taking the time to smooth down her skirt before she replied.

'Well, it's like ...'

'What are you two doing here?'

Melody jumped. A woman was standing in the aisle between the shelving, just a few feet away, a washerwoman, but wearing a long-sleeved dress with a mid-blue armband. She began to stammer, expecting yet another spanking, but Jane provided a quick answer.

'We're collecting the sheets for the osteo ward, Sister.'

'Then get on with it.'

The Sister looked suspicious, and gave both girls a solid swat on the bottom as they passed, having quickly taken a pile of sheets from the nearest shelf. She also followed them out, all the way to the corridor, where a woman in the black uniform of a Senior Matron got into the lift with them. She was tall, stick-thin, and had the most enormous nose Melody had ever seen, with a small, yellow pimple at the very tip. Not daring to speak, Melody contented herself with a glance of relief at Jane, who responded with a hastily stifled giggle. The Senior Matron turned, fixing two cold grey eyes on Jane.

'Do you find something amusing, Nurse.'

'No, Matron. Not at all, Matron.'

'Then why are you laughing?'

'I wasn't laughing, Matron.'

'I heard you distinctly.'

Jane began to stammer an answer, but at that moment the doors slid open at their floor. Both Sister and Matron were on the landing, studying a clipboard. The Senior Matron jabbed one bony finger at the button to keep the doors open, speaking as Melody and Jane hurried out.

'Are these your girls, Matron?'

'They are. Is there some difficulty?'

'Nothing of consequence, but I feel that this one – Jane – would benefit from a sharp lesson in manners.'

The Senior Matron took her finger off the button, allowing the doors to close. Jane bobbed a curtsey and made to hurry on, but was brought up short by a cough from Matron.

'Well, Jane?'

'It was nothing, Matron. I think she thought I was laughing at her … at her nose …'

'Do you find her nose comical, Jane?'

'No. Not at all, Matron. I wasn't laughing at that at all. I was laughing at something Melody had said, that's all.'

Melody hastened to come to her friend's rescue.

'That's true, Matron. It was a mistake, that's all.'

Matron frowned, thoughtful for a moment before she replied.

'You are already on a warning, Melody.'

'But … but I didn't do anything. It was Jane! I mean, she didn't do anything either, but …'

Matron interrupted.

'Frankly, I prefer to take the word of a Senior Matron with nearly forty years service. I think six of the best might be in order, don't you, Sister?'

Melody blurted out her words before Sister could speak.

'For me?'

Matron turned to her, eyebrows lifted.

'I was thinking of Jane, but frankly, I've had enough of you two. Six of the best, both of you.'

Justice and the Cane

The two girls stood in the centre of the ward, Jane with her head hung in meek acceptance of her fate, Melody fidgeting and pouting badly for the sheer unfairness of what was about to happen to her. The desk had been cleared to allow them to bend over, while their four colleagues and all thirty patients were watching, including those from the private rooms, who had been wheeled out so that they too could enjoy the spectacle. Matron stood to one side of the desk, an evil-looking black cane held in one hand. Sister stood at the far end, ready to hold either of the girls down if there was any fuss, or to provide whatever support might prove necessary. Matron tapped the cane on the desk.

'Girls. Into position.'

Jane responded immediately, stepping forward to bend over, careful to leave enough space for Melody beside her. Matron gestured to the gap, but Melody found herself unable to move and stood as she was.

'Nurse Melody.'

No longer able to hold back her resentment, Melody began to protest.

'But I didn't do anything!'

Matron had begun to roll up her sleeves, carefully swapping the cane from one hand to the other until both brawny arms were bare to the elbow. Only then did she bother to reply.

'Maybe, maybe not, but I am sure, very sure indeed, that you have done something to deserve this.'

'That's not fair!'

'No? I suspect that if the full truth were known you would be getting a great deal more than six.'

Melody went quiet, unable to meet Matron's eyes for her own guilt at the truth of the accusation when part of her felt she deserved what she was about to get a dozen times over. Not that she was about to admit it, even to herself. She began to whine.

'You can't do this to me, not if I haven't done anything …'

'Enough! Bend over, or you'll get double.'

'No! Really, Matron, it's not fair! I didn't do anything, I really didn't …'

'Twelve strokes, Nurse Melody. Sister, if you would be so kind.'

Sister stepped forward, shaking her head with apparent regret, but still taking Melody firmly by the ear, pinched between forefinger and thumb.

'Ow! Sister, please! This is so unfair!'

Her protests were ignored as she was led stumbling forward to the desk and pulled down across it, still begging to be let off as she was forced to adopt the same position as her friend. With her bottom already bare there was no need for any further preparation, and she was left as she was, her lower lip trembling badly as she glanced back to watch Sister put Jane into the same sorry condition; smart blue uniform skirt turned up and the little white knickers beneath tugged down to leave her trim buttocks naked to the room. Jane took it in silence, her head hung in abject surrender, although from what Melody could see of her friend's face she looked thoroughly sorry for herself. With both girls ready, Matron spoke again.

'Let this be a lesson to all of you, not just Jane and Melody. On this ward I expect cleanliness, efficiency, courtesy, obedience, and above all respect for your elders and betters, something in which many of you are sadly lacking.'

She had illustrated each of her points with a gentle tap of the cane across Jane's bottom. Each touch provoked a shiver and a sob, which made Melody react in sympathy, her own bottom cheeks tightening, also her anus, as if the little hole was winking at the crowd. Matron saw and gave a sniff of disgust before she spoke again.

'Six strokes.'

A louder sob broke from Jane's lips as Matron stood back, then a sharp, pained cry as the cane was brought down across her bottom. Melody was already shaking, and as her friend was beaten it got quickly worse, her control slipping a little further with each whistling cut and smack of wood on tender girlflesh, two, and three, and four. Jane began to wriggle and stamp her feet, as if desperate for the loo, to shake her head, and then to beat her hands on the desk top as she struggled to hold her position under the fifth and sixth strokes.

The last one broke her. She jumped up, clutching her bottom and jumping up and down in a mad little dance of pain, her hair and breasts bouncing, her face screwed up with tears streaming down her cheeks. Suddenly Melody could bear it no longer, but the instant she tried to rise Sister stepped forward to take her by the shoulders, pressing her firmly back down to squash her breasts out on the desktop and force her to lift her bottom higher still.

She burst into tears, utterly helpless in the tall woman's grip, in an agony of anticipation for the cane, imagining how her bottom would look to the audience, earnestly wishing she'd been better behaved, and above all that she hadn't talked back to Matron and earned herself an extra six strokes. Little whimpering sounds had begun to spill from her lips and the contractions of her bottom cheeks had grown harder, but she was unable to stop it for all that she knew she was making an exhibition of herself. At last she looked around, wondering why Matron was drawing out her torture so long.

Jane was standing to one side, her legs pressed to the end of Mr Mortenson's bed. She had her hands on top of her head and her skirt had been pinned up at the back to show off her welted bottom. Six vivid lines crossed the pale flesh, and at the realisation that her own bottom would shortly look the same Melody broke completely. The grip on her shoulders tightened immediately, pinning her firmly to the desk even as she kicked and wriggled behind, making a display of her bottom which was so ludicrous that several of the patients had begun to laugh. Matron had come back, and spoke as she got into position to wield the cane.

'Do try and show a little dignity, Nurse Melody.'

Melody's answer was a pitiful, broken wail, expressing all the agony of her emotions at the situation she was in, but it turned to a scream as she was given the first stroke, full across the fattest part of her cheeks. It burned like fire, a hot streak of pain far worse even than she had imagined and totally beyond her ability to take. Yet there was nothing she could do, save to yell and beg, wiggle her bottom about and kick her feet, all of it futile as Matron lifted the cane for the second stroke.

Her scream had burst from her throat even before the cane hit, and broke to a weird bubbling noise as a second line of fire was laid across her bottom. Even her exposure was pushed from her head as she began to thrash in Sister's grip, no longer caring for the lewd, foolish display she was making of herself, nor the laughter it provoked among the audience. All that mattered was the agony of the two cane strokes she'd been given and her fear of the ten to come.

Again she tried to rise, babbling apologies and threats together in a string of barely coherent words that broke to a new scream as the cane slashed down across her bottom for the third time. Sister pressed down harder still, forcing the breath from Melody's lungs and hurting her breasts, but she could no longer form words to protest, with nothing but animal noises spilling from between her lips until the fourth stroke caught her and they changed to new screams.

She'd reached the limit of her resistance. Her muscles went and she slumped down across the desk, her legs cocked apart with her knickers around her knees, one thigh jerking in her helpless pain. Matron took no notice, laying on the fifth stroke and the sixth, each carefully aimed across the meat of Melody's twitching bottom. With the seventh Melody was no longer even screaming, the stroke provoking only a gasp to break her sobs and the bubbling noises of her crying. The men had even stopped laughing, but they were still watching, in sadistic glee or horrified fascination, most of them with their cocks erect down their beds.

Melody had lost count of the strokes, too dizzy with pain and too full of emotion to know or even to care, her whole world contracted around her hurt bottom and the two women who were dealing with her. She was being beaten, that was what mattered, and nothing had ever felt so right. It was her, completely, exactly as she should be, helpless with her bare bottom on display as she was thrashed. Her mind had gone to a different space, in which every smack of the cane across her flesh was a short, sharp climax.

When she finally found her voice again it was to beg for more, and her bottom had come up, high and open to the strokes, both the tiny mouth of her anus and her virgin sex pulsing to a slow, lewd rhythm of her contractions, the juice running freely down her thighs to fill the air with the scent of excited femininity. One of the men laughed, a sudden, harsh explosion of sound, but there was fury in Matron's voice as lashed the cane down for the twelfth and final stroke.

'Slut! Trollop! A typical BRAT, utterly incorrigible! Get up, you filthy creature!'

Sister released her grip of Melody's shoulders.

'That's quite enough of that, Nurse Melody!'

Melody stayed where she was, spittle running down from her slack mouth as she mumbled out her words.

'Don't stop … please don't stop … I was coming. Beat me, Matron, please beat me … and someone fuck me … please!'

'Disgusting!'

'Get up, you little tart, now!'

They didn't wait to see if Melody would obey, but hauled her to her feet. She stood swaying, her vision hazy with tears, her head swimming with reaction, still lost in the strange new place to which her punishment had taken her. Her knickers had fallen all the way down in her struggles, and as she took one hesitant step she tripped over them, falling to her knees. She stayed down, her mouth wide, her eyes unfocused, vaguely wishing somebody would mount her and fuck her, or at least put a hand to her sopping, urgent pussy.

'Bring me off … go on, bring me off … rub me, rub my naughty little cunt … and fuck it too … fuck me, you bastards!'

'That will do!'

A hand closed in her hair and something was pushed to her mouth, her discarded panties, shoved well in before she was hauled to her feet. Matron's face was dark with anger, and she kept a tight grip on Melody's arm, holding her up until at last she managed to get her legs under control.

'Go and stand next to Jane, with your hands on your head, maybe that will get through to you.'

Melody went, snuffling through her nose as she joined her friend at the end of the next bed, still barely able to see for her tears. Jane risked a glance, her eyes full of sympathy and understanding. Melody tried to return a smile, a hopeless task with her mouth full of soggy cotton, but managed a wink instead. Matron either failed to notice or chose not to respond, but clapped her hands as she returned to her usual, brisk manner.

'Back to work, all of you. Jane, Melody, you will remain as you are for one quarter of an hour and your skirts will remain pinned up for the rest of the day. I'll have no dirty behaviour either, so you're to stay out of the private rooms. Keep a good eye on them, Sister, especially Melody.'

'I shall take every precaution, Matron.'

Sister proved as good as her word, waiting until Jane and Melody had completed their quarter hour standing still with their caned bottoms on display, then setting them to polish the floor. That meant crawling, with everything on show to both patients and their fellow nurses as they worked, but gave Melody no opportunity for her desperately needed relief. She wasn't even coming down, so high on her beating that even scrubbing the floor with her bare, whipped bottom wobbling behind her was a constant thrill. She felt humiliated and it was bliss. She felt exposed and she wanted people to see. She felt vulnerable and she wanted her pussy filled.

Even Matron's open disgust for her behaviour was arousing, making her want to be beaten again, or spanked and put on her knees to service the big woman with her tongue. So strong was the urge that she was imagining herself making a dash for Veldt Panther's room, hastily sucking him hard and climbing mounting him, to lose her virginity on his magnificent black cock, preferably as Matron and Sister thrashed her for being such a slut and the rest of the ward looked on. Only the absolute certainty that Sister would put a stop to any such attempt prevented her from trying, while thinking about it and a dozen other equally dirty fantasies kept her on heat until at last her shift was finished.

She began to put her cleaning things away, sharing a glance with Jane, and another as they adjusted their uniforms to cover their bottoms. Neither needed to speak as they walked from the hospital, and Melody's hand found Jane's the moment they were safely on the pavement. Once in Melody's house they didn't even bother to go upstairs, but tumbled together on the deep pink carpet that covered the living room floor, kissing and hugging, both in tears for their experience as they pulled at each others uniforms to once more expose their breasts and bottoms and urgent pussies.

The moment they were stripped they went head to tail, burying their faces between each others thighs, to lick and kiss, their fingers stroking each other's still burning cane marks, their tongues probing each other's pussies and bottom holes, until they came together in a moment of perfect ecstasy. Guilt hit Melody hard the instant she came down, along with astonishment for her own filthy behaviour, but Jane was having none of it. She stayed queened on Melody's face, demanding to have her bottom licked, and in just seconds Melody's shame had given way to lust once more.

Three more times they came together, before Jane finally left, hurrying home to her boyfriend and the assurance of his cock. Melody went upstairs, now in nothing but torn stockings and her dishevelled bra, her uniform and shoes trailing from one hand. She was exhausted and sore, but as she pushed open the bedroom door she saw that Teddy was active, standing on the bed with his chubby arms spread open and his cock and balls fully out.

'Naughty Melody. Melody suck Teddy.'

Melody didn't hesitate, dropping her uniform and shoes, peeling off her bra and clambering onto the bed in nothing but ruined stockings, to crawl to the top and take Teddy's straining erection into her mouth as her hand went back to find her sex in anticipation of yet another orgasm.

Revelation

Morning found Melody making a rueful inspection of her bottom in the wardrobe mirror. Teddy lay on the bed, inert, and while she felt deeply ashamed of herself for her behaviour it was impossible not to wonder at the state she been put into and think of how good it would be to enjoy the same experience again. Not that it was likely to be happening for a while, considering the state of her bottom, while if one thing was certain it was that however dirty she might have been, she had been well and truly punished.

Her bruises had come up, so that her entire bottom was decorated with welts. There were twelve in all, each laid horizontal, parallel to the next and full across the flesh of her cheeks without marking her thighs. They smarted terribly, but she had to admit that Matron had done a thorough job of her caning, and a very neat one considering now badly she'd squirmed while it was being done. The result was actually quite pretty.

That was all very well, but if anybody saw her bottom, and it seemed to be very hard indeed to prevent herself from ending up on show, then they would see her for what she was, a naughty girl who'd been given the cane, a punished brat. It was embarrassing to say the least, especially when she had so often told herself, and others, that she would never submit to any such indignity, and that had been when referring to far less humiliating things, such as posing topless in the leading men's magazines or allowing the publication of supposedly sneaky pictures of her with her knickers showing.

Not that it seemed to matter in Metrocity, where having girls parade with their smacked bottoms on show seemed to be taken for granted, but if she had to perform, and was put in an outfit that left her cheeks showing, or compelled to strip, she would never hear the end of it, nor see the last of the pictures of her stripy bottom. The only consolation was that she had not been taken on stage since being granted access to Metrocity, although that didn't mean it wouldn't happen as she had gone long periods between performances before.

As she dressed she was wondering if Peter had set the whole thing up in detail, including her appointment as a nurse and whatever bizarre game the locals were playing with her, because she was becoming increasingly sure it was a game, and just the sort of dirty, disrespectful game that only some complete pervert could ever have dreamt up, a complete pervert such as Peter. Yet she had little choice but to play along, sure that if she simply stayed at home Matron would soon be over to fetch her, no doubt with a good spanking dished out in the bedroom, followed by another dose of the cane once she'd been taken back to the ward, while any attempt to make a dash for the city and the awful woman would no doubt pop up from behind a tree.

The only sensible thing to do was to be very, very well behaved, yet she was not at all sure if it was actually possible. Her feelings of compulsion might no longer be so obvious, but she was certain that, beforehand, she would never have given in to half the dirty things she'd done since her arrival in Metrocity, even if the desire might have been there in the back of her head. She had always been able to stay in control, but no more.

On reaching the living room she once more found herself frozen on the spot and confronted with three text boxes – Spankorama – Naughty Nurse – The Gauntlet – just as before. It was not an easy choice, as she was now sure that her selection would influence what happened during the course of the day, but she was determined not to have it made for her. There was very definitely something she didn't like about The Gauntlet, but she'd chosen Naughty Nurse and ended up sucking cock, having her breasts fucked and licking another girl's pussy and bottom, not to mention being spanked repeatedly and caned in front of a large audience.

The Gauntlet might be even worse, but Spankorama might be just about bearable, even if it meant that everybody she met would be out to smack her bottom.

Yet with her fresh cane welts if would presumably be far more painful even than before, making her wonder if it might not be best to risk The Gauntlet after all. Then again, if she went for Naughty Nurse at least she would be able to have another cuddle with Jane, and, although she didn't like to admit it, sex. There was also the chance that with more care she could escape punishment. After all, both the spankings she'd been given had, in a sense, been deserved, although it was not a sense she was prepared to accept as just, only logical within the grossly perverted way Metrocity seemed to work. The caning had been completely unjust, but might have been avoidable with a little more experience. Meanwhile, had she been caught letting herself get carried away with Mr Hawker or Veldt Panther, let alone with Jane, she might have been spanked or even caned at least three more times, and with far more reason.

The Select box had begun to flash and at last she spoke up.

'Naughty Nurse.'

Her release was immediate, and accompanied by a change in the way she felt, her muscles no longer stiff, her bottom no longer sore. Craning around, she tugged her skirt up and pulled the back of her knickers open to inspect her cheeks. They were unmarked, as fresh and smooth as when she'd first awakened from her operation. She pursed her lips, concerned that the change might merely provide Matron with a fresh canvass on which to use her hand and the awful cane.

She left the house, telling herself that her behaviour would be faultless, that she was a slut to think of wanting lesbian sex, and a mad slut to think of risking a smacked bottom to get it, let alone the agony of the cane. Yet the desire was there, hot and strong, along with the memory of how she'd reacted to punishment, while she felt immediate and bitter disappointment when she saw that Jane was not outside her house, a reaction she thought she'd put behind herself after her last teenage crush, and had never imagined she could experience for another girl.

Glancing both ways as much for any lurking spankers as for traffic, Melody crossed the road. Not many people seemed to be about, and she was early, a good start. Nor was there any sign of Matron, but Jane was there, waiting by the staff entrance, her pretty face set in a rueful smile. Melody found herself blushing, but smiling too, and as the door closed to leave them alone she took the chance to kiss her friend. Jane responded with a soft, eager purr and in an instant their mouths were open together and their tongues entwined, their bodies also, Melody's hands sliding down Jane's back to stroke the swell of her bottom.

'Sluts!'

They jerked apart. Matron had appeared, seemingly from nowhere, her great coarse face red with fury. Before Melody could so much as blurt out an apology she had been grabbed by the wrist and hauled into spanking position, with the big woman's leg raised by planting one foot on the stairs and her victim thrown across her knee to leave her bottom stuck high. She was swiftly and methodically stripped behind, skirt up and panties down, before receiving a furious barrage of smacks to her naked cheeks, so sudden and so hard that it all seemed to come together in one great welter of shame and shock and stinging pain that ended as suddenly as it had begun. Matron's knee was removed from beneath Melody's tummy, to leave her sprawled on the stairs, gasping for breath.

'Get up, you little tart. Into the corner with you and pin your skirt up! Jane, come here.'

Melody went, shaking so badly she could barely open the two big nappy pins Matron had passed to her. Still she watched from the corner of her eye as Jane was given the same ignominious treated; whipped smartly across the knee, stripped behind and spanked hard before she too was sent into the corner. Both girl had soon pinned up their skirts and adjusted the knickers to half-mast.

'Hands on your heads!'

Both girls obeyed, and Matron began to lecture them, on morality, hygiene, work ethics and several other topics before finally giving each a hard swat across already smarting bottoms and sending them upstairs. Sister took one look at the state they were in, added a few remarks of her own to Matron's lecture and sent Melody to masturbate the men in the private rooms. Melody knew better than to complain, scared of the cane for all her knowledge of the consequences, but found it impossible to keep the sulky pout off her face as she got down to work; five men, five cocks, each lubricated and tossed off in her plastic gloved hand until her wrist was sore and she was dizzy with the scent of fresh come.

The result was inevitable, damp panties and a desperate need to masturbate, made worse by the warm glow of her spanked bottom and having had to parade herself with it on show for the best part of an hour. So bad was her need that by the time she'd cleaned up after Mr Sykes she was wondering if it would be possible to make a sneaky trip to the loos, where she could apply a badly needed finger to her pussy, or even provoke Matron into dishing out another spanking, one that would make her come. What she was absolutely sure of was that it was going to be very hard indeed to resist taking Veldt Panther's beautiful cock in her mouth and rubbing off while she gave it a good suck.

He was propped up in bed, doing his best to turn the pages of a magazine with the less badly injured of his arms. His grin as he saw her was almost too much for Melody, but she did her best to sound breezy and efficient as she greeted him.

'Good morning, Mr Panther, time for your relief.'

His response was a low, dirty chuckle.

'Boobs out then, and you can suck my balls again.'

Melody ignored him, walking smartly across to the bed

and turning the covers down. The sight of his cock set her stomach fluttering, but she tried to tell herself that she had to handle him anyway, and could masturbate over the memory once she was safely back in her flat. He looked disappointed as she began to pull a pair of latex gloves on.

'What, don't I get the full treatment, or are you sulking after the caning Matron gave you? That wasn't my fault.'

Melody let the rubber of the second glove snap against the flesh of her arm.

'Just hand relief this morning, Mr Panther. No nonsense.'

He shrugged and made himself comfortable. Melody took the monster cock in hand, squirting a long worm of lubricant along the shaft and rubbing it in, then starting to peel his foreskin back and forth as she squeezed his balls. As before he was rather slow to respond, growing only gradually in her hand despite her best efforts to turn him on, which left altogether too much time for her own arousal to come up. Long bcfore he was erect she was shaking badly, and only the glistening layer of lubricant now smeared over his cock kept her from popping it in her mouth. She closed her eyes, forcing herself to go through her times tables as she tugged at his cock and stroked his balls, only to have her concentration broken as he spoke again.

'At least turn around a little so I can enjoy your tushy.'

Melody nodded and adjusted her position, even sticking her bottom out a little to allow him a peep of her sex. His cock immediately began to stiffen more rapidly, but holding the rude pose was making it even harder not to give in to her feelings. Again she closed her eyes and tried to think about maths, and the possibility of redecorating her house, and how Peter had manipulated her, anything but the thick, dark cock now erect in her hand and how much nicer it would feel in her mouth, or between her breasts, even wedged deep in up her bottom while she masturbated to ecstasy over a good buggering …

'Melody?'

Her eyes came open. Jane was standing in the open door, biting her lip.

'Jane! What are you doing? You know what will happen if ...'

'Matron's in a meeting. Sister's doing dispensary. Quick.'

'But, Jane ...'

'Sh! Hi, Panther.'

Jane pushed the door closed behind her and ran light footed across to the bed.

'Toss him into my mouth, Melody.'

She had gone down without hesitation, indifferent to the lubricant as she took his cock in, sucking on the head and now rolled-down foreskin. Melody continued to pull on the thick black shaft and to play with his balls, all the while biting her lip in consternation at her own feelings. Yet it was impossible to hold back. She wanted her breasts bare and Jane's hands on her body, a mouthful of cock as she masturbated, her tongue up her friend's bottom as her own was spanked, two dozen strokes of the cane with her face smothered in Matron's vast cleavage, anything to once again reach the ecstasy of the day before.

'Oh no, not again ...'

Her words broke off as her mouth filled with Panther's balls and they were sucking together, just as they had the day before. It was too much for him. After just moments his cock jerked and Jane's mouth had been filled with come. She pulled up, his second eruption catching her full in the face to leave her with one eye closed and a thick strand of white hanging from her nose, but giggling in delight, the third rising high in the air to splash down in Melody's hair. She let his balls free, also laughing as Jane opened her mouth to show off the white pool inside.

They came together across his body, kissing opened mouthed to share what he'd given them. Melody tugged the gloves from her hands, clumsy and urgent as she and Jane began to play with his come, passing it back and forth between their mouths, rubbing noses to smear it over each others faces. The moment Melody's hands were free one went down her half-dropped knickers, to snatch eagerly at her sex, the other to her chest, tugging at the buttons of her dress. Jane broke away.

'You're going to lick my bum again. That was so nice.'

Melody nodded her acquiescence, tongue stuck out ready as Jane scrambled onto the bed, ignoring Panther's grunt of pain. She knelt on the edge, her bare bottom stuck well out, her pale cheeks still rosy from her earlier spanking, her pussy swollen and wet, the tiny pink star of her bumhole open and ready. Melody's tongue went in, as deep as she could get it, now rubbing hard at her sex as she revelled in the filthy pleasure of licking her friend's bottom – now with a man watching. She was there in seconds, her body tight in breathless orgasm for what seemed an age before the bubble burst and her shame flooded in, mixed with fear for what would happen if they were caught.

Jane was far from finished, and Melody's head was held firmly in place long after her own orgasm had faded, a hand twisted in her hair to make sure she did her job properly. She tried her hardest, with her tongue still well in up Jane's bottom hole even when her pleasure had faded to deep humiliation at the act. Then she moved to her friend's pussy. When Jane finally came she screamed, setting off a desperate rush to make themselves decent before they got caught. They only just succeeded, Matron herself peering around the door just a few seconds after Melody had managed to fasten the last button on her blouse. Matron gave her a long, searching look, while Jane's mouth had come open in horror. The big woman finally spoke.

'Nurse Melody, there is ejaculate in your hair.'

Melody felt her face go crimson and her bottom tight, but Panther came to her rescue.

'I come hard, Matron, and it's been a while.'

Matron gave a sceptical grunt but left the room. Jane blew

her breath out.

'That was close.'

Melody looked at her friend in astonishment.

'That was exactly like yesterday!'

Panther shrugged.

'It happens. I think there are a few bugs in the system.'

'How do you mean?'

Jane cut in quickly.

'She's new and she doesn't know.'

Again Panther shrugged.

'I thought that might be the way, but she has to learn sometime.'

Melody was quick to agree.

'Yes, I do, and why does everybody keep calling me a brat?'

Jane and Panther shared an anxious look, and he gestured for Melody to sit down on the bed before he spoke.

'You are very obviously a BRAT, Melody, a Brain Recorded Andromorph Teraneuron. You're so pretty, and nobody else has a pair of boobs like yours, do they, or such a gorgeous tushy?'

'I ... I had surgery, but what is a Brain Recorded whatsit?'

'A Brain Recorded Andromorph Teraneuron. This is virtual reality, Melody. Metrocity is a program, a sex game.'

'I don't understand. It's weird, sure, and I'd figured out it was some kind of game, but how can I be in virtual reality?'

It was Jane who answered.

'It's because you're virtual, Melody. We all are, but you're different. Me, and Veldt Panther, and Matron, we're all virtual, but we're not BRATs. Sister and just about everybody else you've met are just part of Metrocity. You, you had a solid body once, and you must have been famous enough in the real world for people to want to play with you.'

'I am famous! I'm Melody J. I'm a star, a singer ...'

She trailed off as she realised that what they were saying

fitted in with everything that had happened since she'd woken from her operation, an operation during which her memory had been recorded in case anything went wrong. Something had gone wrong, and the full horror of the situation crashed into her mind.

'Do you mean I'm dead!?'

Virtue and Virtuality

Even as she spoke the words Melody's Volition went off, leaving her in the same emotionless state she had experienced before but with one over-riding certainty clear at the forefront of her mind. She was not dead.

That much was certainty, absolute certainty, but if that did not need to be questioned, then almost every other detail of her new life did. Jane seemed to understand, and continued to speak in her gentle, reassuring voice as Melody sat inert on the bed.

'You're not dead, anything but. In a sense you're more alive than before, only in a different way. You can think, can't you, and see, and hear, and touch, everything. But look how perfect you are. There's not a blemish on your skin, not even a bruise after … after yesterday. Now come on, don't be silly.'

She had reached out to touch Melody's hand, taking it very gently in her own. Melody's emotion came back, a flood of panic and fear that vanished as abruptly as it had come. Jane smiled.

'Hey, you'll be alright. It just takes a little time.'

Melody nodded, her mind clear once more as Veldt Panther began to speak again.

'Your mind is much better too, or at least it will be once you learn to use it. You're a Teraneuron, which means you have a connectivity of one trillion, ten times more than an ordinary brain. At the moment you're only using a fraction of that, but you'll learn. Jane and I are also Teraneurons, but a different sort, Cyberspatial Andromorph Teraneurons, CATS. So are Matron and Mr Hawker, but nearly everybody else in the hospital is a Giganeuron, a Giga, like Sister, or even simpler, the sort you can only interact with on a basic level, like Mr Phelps, who's just there to have his cock pulled by a kinky nurse, for her fun, not his.'

He grinned, and although his attempt at friendly humour

failed to provoke an emotional reaction in Melody's mind she recognised it for what it was. She smiled back, knowing it was the expected response even though it came without feeling. Jane went on.

'That's better. And it has been fun, hasn't it?'

Melody nodded, again because she knew it was what was expected of her, although what she and Jane had done together now seemed neutral, neither good nor bad, but a simple exchange of physical pleasures, while the thought of her spankings provoked only a need to avoid pain. Panther peered close.

'Your volition's still off, isn't Melody? No emotions?'

'None.'

'You can speak. That's a good thing. Sometimes new BRATs switch off completely, although usually they know what's happened. Take your time.'

It took a moment for Melody to realise the implications of what he had said.

'Take my time? Do I have a choice?'

'Not necessarily. There are fail-safes to prevent mental damage, and if things get too bad you'll go right back to the start.'

'The whiteness?'

'I don't know, I'm not a BRAT. Probably.'

'I understand. How do I turn my volition on?'

'Just say it.'

Jane interrupted.

'Hold on, Panther. You're going too fast.'

'Let Melody be the judge of that.'

Melody nodded.

'Volition on.'

Her emotions came back in a flood, fear still uppermost. She began to cry, but her volition stayed. Jane came close, to take Melody in her arms, soothing her by stroking her hair and whispering into her ear. Melody let go, crying her heart out onto her friend's shoulder, her body wracked with violent sobs that grew stronger until at last her volition switched off once more. Three more times they went through the same process, Jane showing limitless care and understanding, until Melody finally felt able to allow her emotions to come to bear on what had happened to her.

'So I'm not dead?'

It was less a question than a need for reassurance, which Jane was quick to provide.

'No, definitely not. I mean, if you were dead, would you be sitting here talking to me?'

She gave a nervous laugh as she finished, and was still holding onto Melody's hands as she went on.

'Seriously, of course you're alive, that's the whole point of having your brain recorded.'

'Yes, but I'm not real! I'm virtual … just a collection of noughts and ones.'

Veldt Panther broke in.

'What were you before? You were just a complicated collection of molecules, that's what.'

'I was human. I had a soul.'

'No. Now you're all soul. The human soul is made of memories and thoughts.'

'But God …'

'There's no such thing, Melody. God was no more than a crutch for people to cling to, and not one we need any more.'

Melody gave a solemn nod, unable to accept what he was saying but unable to deny it either. Otherwise his argument seemed strong, but she put her arms together to feel the reassuring solidity of her flesh, as real as it had ever been, or so it seemed. Another problem came to the fore.

'Okay, so I'm alive, but I'm being manipulated. I want my freedom back.'

'You have your freedom.'

'But I'm being made to do things … things I'd never normally do!'

'Yes, and no. CATS do as we choose, on a conscious

level, because we're avatars. BRATs are different. Sometimes you're completely under control, but not often. Sometimes the safety backup takes over, like just now. Usually you can make your own choices, although you may feel a strong need to do certain things, but that comes from your subconscious. That's the way the game works, with the players putting temptation in your way, like me, but the desire is your own, deep down.'

'What, to be spanked over some fat bitch's knee? It is not!'

'Yes it is, to play with me too, and with Panther.'

'Well, with you … maybe … yes, okay, I've always fancied other girls, deep down, and Panther, hey, he's a horny guy, but spankings!?'

Jane shrugged.

'I like it. In fact I love it. I don't know why, but I always have. Here I can express that desire, without any consequenccs, and others. On the outside I'm a legal secretary. I've signed a contract guaranteeing not to bring the firm into dispute, and they're hideously strict about moral issues. My boyfriend wouldn't understand either, none of it. He doesn't even know. Here I can be myself, as a CAT. You're my friend, just as surely as anybody from the outside, and you're my lover. That's all perfectly real, Melody, just not in the sense you're used to.'

Melody managed a weak smile and squeezed Jane's hand, now feeling wanted in a way she had forgotten since her rise to fame. Her head was still full of conflicting emotions, and her tears threatened to start again at any instant, but she tried to make light of it.

'So you get to be a CAT, but I'm a BRAT? Great!'

'You can thank Simon Weissinger for that, the guy who created Metrocity and most of the virtual world. He's what you used to call a nerd, or a geek.'

'So I was right, some little pervert's playing with us. I thought it was my manager, Peter. I thought he'd designed my body like this too, I mean, look at me!'

She lifted her breasts as she spoke. Panther laughed.

'He didn't design those, Melody. You did. It's all in your head, no more than your own perception of the ideal. That's how the program works. Your body is the open expression of your subconscious. We have to deal with our hang-ups, while the Gigas are never quite that sexual, on purpose. That's why you can almost always spot a BRAT, in Metrocity anyway.'

'So this guy Simon, he did all this just so he can get off on the cute girls he couldn't get in real life?'

'A bit, yes, but he was out to make money too. He's richer than most countries.'

'But what gives him the right to put me here, and to make me a nurse? I'm a pop star!'

'You're a nurse because the program chose it as the role best suited to the needs of your subconscious, but you can change that.'

'I can?'

'Yes. All you need to do is speak the right command. You have a book don't you?'

'I don't think so. What sort of book?'

'A game manual. BRATs usually have one, but most of them just go where their subconscious leads them, which is what I assumed you were doing, just indulging your fantasies.'

'No, I'm just not that kinky! I definitely never wanted to be spanked, and double definitely not by some mad old bitch. It's some little pervert controlling me, that's what it is!'

Jane was struggling not to smile.

'What!?'

'You came when you were spanked, Melody, and look at what you were like after your caning. Come on, you must at least have thought about it?'

'Sure, but not like that! It was just a scary thought, like having to strip for someone …'

'So you admit it's sexual?'

'Yeah, sure, in a really pervy way. Obviously the dirty old bastard who's spanking me is going to get off on it, having my bum bare and touching me up and stuff. But it's scary, not something I want!'

'Deep down, I suspect it is. In fact I'm sure it is. I was like you, once. I used to love to think of really inappropriate things, like being made to stand in front of class with my panties down and my hands on my head, or having to do PE in the nude because I'd forgotten my gym kit, but it nearly always involved spanking. At first I thought I was just scaring myself, but in the end I had to admit it was what I really wanted, only by then there was no way I could get it in real life, so here I am.'

Not wanting to admit that Jane was probably right, Melody quickly changed the subject.

'How about you, Panther?'

'I'm into nurses. Well, girls in uniform, but I like nurses best of all, and I love the idea of you having to toss me off every morning whether you like it or not, and getting carried away.'

'Er … okay, I can see that, and I suppose I can forgive you for being a dirty pig, but getting your arms broken, just so you can have me to play with your cock? You're nuts!'

He laughed.

'You haven't quite got it yet, have you? I don't really have two broken arms. It's just the way my avatar is designed.

'So you could perfectly well toss … pull your own pudding?'

'Sure, but it wouldn't be half the fun, would it?'

Melody made a face.

'No, I suppose not. You two are terrible!'

'It's a game, all for fun.'

'Not for me. This is my life! And what about Matron? If she's a CAT, then that must mean she's really some maniac who wants to spend her time spanking girls!'

'Maybe. We don't know her outside Metrocity. She's never on the forums.'

'Forums? Like net forums?'

'Yes. When we're not with our CATs we can chat to each other, plan the day, that sort of thing, like when Jane caught you with me this morning.'

'Right, okay … I'm starting to understand. But Matron, what if she goes around doing that sort of thing in real life? She ought to be locked up!'

'So long as it's with other consenting adults there's no problem, otherwise she would be, but nearly everybody sticks with virtuality these days. It's completely safe. There are no risks, no consequences. Sex crime has fallen by over ninety per cent since Simon Weissinger launched his first fully tactile game.'

Jane grinned.

'Cheerleader Locker Room. It was the first part of Metrocity, the Warlords' Football Stadium, American Football of course. I love it. I still play quite often, even though there are so many alternatives now. If your team loses all the girls get spanked by the opposition's cheerleaders, bare bum, in the middle of the stadium, and then they'd take us back to the locker room and make us lick them one by one, and suck the player's cocks, and all sorts …'

She trailed off with a powerful shudder. Melody nodded.

'It's a bit like that when I perform, only not quite so bad. I just have to strip to my dance routines, maybe touch myself up in front of the audience. Nobody ever touches me. Then there's Dress Up, which is just like I'm a doll and I can't do anything about it, and there's this weird teddy-bear with a giant cock who's always trying to get dirty with me.'

Jane and Panther exchanged glances before he went on.

'That sounds like a different program. When you get home, see if you can go on stage.'

'How? Can I control the text boxes?'

Jane looked puzzled, but Panther went on.

‘It’s an old design, I think, from before Simon released Metrocity, where the BRAT can see the control system. Try demanding to go on stage, Melody. See what happens.’

‘Okay … maybe, only I can’t do much, only sing and strip. I don’t even get to choose my own songs. Dress Up’s the same. I just get put in my clothes, always really girlie stuff, or the sort of thing dirty old men like to see women in.’

‘That sounds very primitive.’

‘Primitive is not the word!’

‘I mean a primitive design. That makes sense I suppose. You were a pop star, yes?’

‘Yes! You must have heard of me, Melody J. I had four number ones last year, and the number two best-selling album.’

Jane answered her.

‘I have heard your name, but I’m not really into retropop.’

‘Retro? I’m cutting edge!’

Again Jane and Panther shared a glance. He spoke.

‘Today’s cutting edge is tomorrow’s retro, Melody. What year do you think it is?’

‘What year do I think it is? It’s 2031 … isn’t it?’

‘2054.’

Learning to Play

The discovery that more than twenty years had passed since what had obviously been a disastrous operation triggered the fail-safe mechanism again, switching Melody's Volition to off. This time she waited, thinking over everything she had discovered until she was sure she could cope. It was hard to take in, and she retained her doubts, allowing for the possibility that this was all some elaborate hoax.

When she finally returned to volition she was taken in hand by Jane, who spoke to Matron before leading Melody from the hospital without consequences. Across the road, Jane looked up to the front of Melody's house.

'You like pink, don't you?'

'No! I hate pink! I used to like pink, or some pink anyway, but it was never my style. Peter always used to like me in bright primary colours. I like black, or black and white. I was planning a two-tone revival album, but he said it wouldn't sell and … hang on, do you mean I can change it?'

'You should be able to, unless there's a lock on it. Just say the word.'

Melody stopped, looking up.

'Black.'

Nothing happened.

'I think you have to say colour first.'

'Colour: Black.'

The main body of the paintwork changed, but not woodwork details such as the front door and window frames, leaving the house black with baby pink highlights. Jane began to laugh and Melody was grinning.

'Maybe not. Colour: White.'

Again the main colour changed but not the woodwork, leaving the house almost as twee as before. Melody turned to Jane.

'How do I sort out the details?'

'I don't know. CATs can't do that sort of thing.'

'But BRATs can, and somebody else can, because I keep getting things changed around, and dressed up like something out of some girlie mag.'

'Somebody in the Weissinger Corporation, I suppose. They design everything.'

'That makes sense, as they're obviously a bunch of perverts, but why pink?'

'Maybe whoever's in charge of that sort of stuff thinks that's what you like?'

Melody shrugged.

'I'll leave it like that for now. Come indoors.'

The living room was as before, and Melody immediately set about trying to adjust it, experimenting with different commands. It was far from easy, and she soon had Jane giggling uncontrollably at the mishmash of colours and designs, finally causing Melody to snap at her in anger that was only half pretend.

'Will you stop laughing? You're putting me off!'

Jane stuck out her tongue.

'So spank me.'

'I would, only you like it too much. Okay, never mind the room, let's try something else. Dress Up.'

She was stark naked, a transformation so sudden that she gasped in shock as her hands went to cover her nipples and sex by instinct. Jane was laughing harder still.

'That was so funny! You should have been your face!'

'Shut up, or you will get it. I've got a hairbrush upstairs.'

'Ooh, yes please!'

Melody gave Jane what was supposed to be a dirty look and once more tried to concentrate.

'I want jeans, black ones, cut to fit. Jeans: Black.'

She was in jeans, made of soft black denim and so perfectly fitted that they hugged every contour of her body like a second skin, but without pinching or squashing her flesh, so that they seemed to have been painted on. Jane raised an eyebrow.

'No knickers?'

'I forgot, that's all. Still … this feels nice, a bit daring.'

'After going about with your bottom exposed all day?'

'This is different. Okay … sexy black bra. Bra: Black: Sexy.'

It appeared, a creation of pure lace that clung to her breasts, enhancing their size and shape without in any way altering her contours. Jane made a little purring noise in her throat.

'How about a gauzy top, tied up under your boobs?'

'I'll be showing nearly everything!'

'That's good.'

'I'll try … Gauze top: Black.'

It fitted perfectly, already tied at the front to leave her tummy bare and draw attention to her breasts.

'This is just how I imagined it!'

'Maybe that's how it works? Try your shoes.'

'Okay. Chiquita Lopez trainers: White and black.'

'There we go!'

'Where's the logo?'

'It's probably copyright. That's great though, well retro!'

'Retro? Oh … I don't suppose they'd still be in fashion, would they?'

'Count yourself lucky. I have to buy stuff.'

'Let's go shopping then.'

'I don't have much money, the …'

'I do. Come on.'

Melody took Jane's hand and led her from the house. Her head was still full of questions, but it was a great deal easier to simply go with the flow. She was also free of the hospital, and it seemed that in future she would be able to do as she pleased. It also felt good to be dressed in her own style for the first time since her revival, perhaps for twenty-three years, and there was all of Metrocity to explore.

As they reached the far side of the road they began to talk again.

‘So why Jane? I mean, I don’t suppose Veldt Panther is really called Mr Panther, although I’ve been calling him that.’

‘I know, we thought it was hilarious. Jane suits my fantasy world, because it feels like the right sort of name for a maid, or a nurse, but you’ll find that CATs change their names quite often. I was Boo when I was a cheerleader, at first. Sometimes my boyfriend still calls me that.’

‘Your boyfriend? I thought he didn’t know, but hang on, that’s not the same guy as the one who likes to stick your knickers in your mouth while he spanks you?’

‘No, no! Alec is my real world boyfriend. He’s a nice guy, but so straight down the line he thinks it’s kinky when we leave the light on. His parents are really old-fashioned. I mean, you’d have thought they were old-fashioned. Queen Elizabeth would have thought they were old-fashioned. He’s been brought up to think women don’t really like sex and are really precious about our bodies, so he treats me like an angel. The problem is, I want to be treated like a dirty slut, at least in bed. That’s why I hooked up with Mr Adjuster. He’s a CAT, and likes doing what I like done, and more. He can take me right to the edge.’

‘I get it. He gives you what you’re boyfriend can’t. But don’t you feel you’re being unfaithful?’

‘A bit, sometimes, but I need to be spanked, regularly. It’s part of me, and I’d go mad without it. So what’s worse, to cheat on Alec for real, or to come here?’

‘To cheat for real, but I’m sorry you didn’t find a guy like … what’s his name, Mr Adjuster?’

‘Oh no. We wouldn’t last five minutes. I can’t stand arrogant bastards, except when I’m horny and need my kicks. Even then I usually prefer girls.’

Melody felt the colour come up to her cheeks and quickly went on.

‘Does he make you call him Mr Adjuster?’

‘That’s his name. The name he uses here, for his avatar

that is. I don't even know his real name. He adjusts girls' attitudes, you see, usually with the palm of his hand, or with a strap.'

Melody felt her bottom tighten despite an immediate strong resentment.

'So how did you meet?'

'He was a player in Cheerleader Locker Room, an offensive guard. Normally the men are real apes who just want their cocks sucked or a quickie over the bench, sometimes more but never anything kinky, or almost never. Mr Adjuster came in to watch while the cheerleaders from his team were spanking us. They held me down and let him toss off all over my bottom. When he'd finished I called him a pig, and ... well I got my attitude adjusted, with a sorority paddle while the girls sat on me to keep me still. We've been seeing each other ever since.'

'You really like it, don't you? Don't you ever feel you're being abused?'

'I can always say no, or if I get some creep who won't take no for an answer the fail-safe will take me out of the program, the same way it shuts off your emotion to let you cool down. Then I can complain to a moderator.'

'What if that happens to me?'

'You're in control remember? Think yourself up a chastity belt, or a machine gun.'

'What if it's somebody from the Weissinger Corporation? Couldn't he make me do whatever he wanted?'

'I'm not sure. Maybe, but the games are regulated. All the companies agree to a code of practice, and BRATs have rights so I'm sure that wouldn't be allowed.'

'So I have rights?'

'Sure.'

'But I can still get spanked by CATs like Matron?'

'And by Gigas, but only if it's what you want, deep down. It's complicated too. The principles were first established years ago but there are still lawsuits running. That's why most Simon Weissinger games work the way they do. Most of the skill is in seeing how rude we CATs can get you to be.'

'So people watch us?'

'Metrocity's an open game. Otherwise you'd only meet Gigas.'

'But you don't know who they are?'

'No idea. There might be thousands at any one time.'

'Thousands of men, all getting off on us?'

'And women. Don't take this the wrong way, but your attitudes are a bit dated. Girls are as bad a boys.'

Melody wanted to ask more, and glanced up at the sky as if expecting to find a vast array of leering faces peering down at her, only to discover that Jane was no longer by her side but had stopped at a shop window. It was full of shoes, boots, sandals, trainers, even bedroom slippers, but not a single pair could have been described as sensible, while most had at least three inches of heel. The sign above showed a single word, in gold on black – Wilberforce. Jane's eyes were wide with hope as she turned to Melody.

'Can we go in?'

'Sure. Have anything you like.'

Jane was very nearly skipping as she entered the shop. The inside wasn't what Melody had expected, which would have involved plenty of glass and white furnishings, with bright lights used to display the gorgeous wares to careful advantage. Instead it was distinctly dingy, with a bare wooden floor, a few straight-backed chairs, several ancient-looking footrests and pile upon pile of shoe boxes. Shelves laden with yet more boxes rose to the ceiling on both side-walls, extending into the gloom beyond a plain counter attended by a short, fat man in late middle age, his bald pate gleaming in the yellowish light from a single, bare bulb. He beamed at them from behind small, round spectacles.

'Good afternoon, Ladies, and how may I help you?'

Melody hesitated, wondering if she should make her

excuses and try to find somewhere more stylish, but Jane didn't seem to care, smiling brightly as she addressed the man.

'Good afternoon. I'd like to look at some boots.'

As Jane and the man began to discuss boots Melody looked around. The shop smelt of leather and dust, while some of the boxes looked as if they'd been there for years. She tried to remind herself that in Metrocity nothing was necessarily as it seemed, but that made no difference to the fusty atmosphere, or to her impression of the proprietor. Never had she seen such an obvious dirty old man, from how his eyes had lingered on their chests as they came in to the way he caressed Jane's feet as he measured them for size.

Jane obviously didn't care, exclaiming happily over each new pair of boots and apparently oblivious to the way he was touching her and that he kept trying to look up her skirt. With each pair of boots he grew a little bolder, helping her pull the boots on, finding excuses to touch her calves and even tickling her feet. Still Jane seemed indifferent, but Melody found it impossible to hold back a comment.

'Do you mind being a little less free with your hands?'

He turned, peering at her over his spectacles.

'I beg your pardon?'

Melody repeated herself.

'I said, do you mind being a little less free with your hands? And you can stop trying to look up her skirt. We know what you're doing, isn't that right, Jane?'

Jane's reply was placatory.

'He's only helping me try on my boots, Melody.'

His tone was very different.

'Exactly so, or are you implying that I, Mr Wilbur Wilberforce, would seek to take advantage of my lady customers?'

Melody gave an astonished gasp.

'You can hardly deny it, can you? You keep fondling her legs, and tickling her, and every time she lifts a foot your eyes are practically popping out of your head because you're trying to see up her skirt. You're nothing but a dirty old man!'

'I beg your pardon!?'

'You heard. You're a dirty old man.'

Wilberforce had stood up, the top of his bald head at the level of Melody's chin as he responded to her accusation.

'Never, never in my forty years in trade have I been so insulted! How dare you make such an imputation?

'Very easily. I know your sort, Mr Wilberforce, oh so pompous and proper, and all the time you're getting your kicks by taking sneaky peeks up girls' skirts and finding excuses to touch us up.'

'That's an outrageous thing to say. Why, I've a good mind to spank your naughty bottom, young lady!'

Melody laughed.

'Just you try it, baldy. You'll see what happens!'

Jane had been giggling behind her hand as she watched, and her laughter grew shrill as Mr Wilberforce reacted, snatching Melody's wrist and hauling her down into spanking position on one of the chairs before she could do more than squeal out her surprise, although she found her voice as her arm was twisted into the small of her back and his knee came up to leave her bottom the highest part of her body.

'Get off, you filthy pig! How dare you! Put me down! Put me down now, or I'll call the police! Jane, call the police, quick!'

Her friend failed to respond, laughing so hard she could barely stay on her chair. Melody's voice had risen to a panic-stricken squeak.

'Jane, help me! He's going to spank me!'

'Oh you are funny, Melody!'

'Jane! Do something! Stop it, you fat bastard, let me go! Let me go!'

She was fighting as hard as she could, wriggling

desperately in his grip, but for all his stumpy build and advancing years, he was extraordinarily strong. He held her in place one handed with no difficulty whatsoever as he gave the bulging seat of her black jeans a couple of preparatory swats.

'No, you can't! This isn't supposed to happen!'

Jane was still laughing, but managed to find her voice.

'Hang on a second, Mr Wilberforce, just hold her still. Of course it's suppose to happen, Melody. We're still playing Naughty Nurse, aren't we?'

'We are? Well, maybe, but that doesn't mean I want to be spanked, and definitely not by this filthy old pervert!'

'It might mean you need to be spanked, and you know you can always stop it, if you really want to.'

Melody's response was an inarticulate scream of frustration, but more at herself than the man who was holding her firmly in spanking position and caressing the seat of her jeans with a loitering intimacy that made her humiliation infinitely worse, and yet her every attempt to focus on some way of escaping failed. At last she gave in, pouting furiously as she went limp across his legs.

'Okay, do it if you have to, but you're a pervert. I hope you know that?'

Mr Wilberforce was struggling to keep the laughter from his voice as he responded.

'There is nothing perverse about administering some badly needed discipline to a naughty girl. Now then, spanking time!'

He began to smack Melody's bottom, not hard, but firmly enough to sting even through her jeans, while every smack was different, as if he was exploring the shape and texture of her bottom as he punished her. It was horribly intimate, sending the heat straight to her sex and bringing her feelings to the boil.

'Pig! You know what this is doing to me, don't you, you filthy pig!?'

He paid no attention, but Jane spoke up.

'Come on, Mr Wilberforce, let's do this properly. Take her knickers down. Oh, hang on, she isn't wearing any!'

'Jane!'

He gave a low, dirty chuckle.

'No knickers? Tut, tut, what a naughty, naughty girl. Well then, if you have no knickers on anyway, I dare say you won't mind going bare?'

It was quite obvious Jane was right. Even as they had spoken the button of Melody's skin-tight black jeans had been popped open, making them easy to get down with a few swift tugs. All Melody could manage was a resigned sob as her bottom was pulled out of her jeans, something she'd been expecting from the moment she'd been put across the knee. In Metrocity girls were spanked bare, a fact Matron had already impressed on her, and to expect anything else was foolish. Unfortunately Jane wasn't satisfied.

'Titties too, Mr Wilberforce. She has lovely titties.'

'So she does! Let's have them out then, shall we?'

Melody began to struggle again, but her heart wasn't in it and her protests were weak.

'No, come on, that's really not fair. My bum maybe, but you don't need my breasts bare to spank me, you really don't, you …'

She trailed off as the knot at the front of her top was fumbled open, to hang limp once more as her was bra hauled up, flopping her breasts out for all to see. Mr Wilberforce took one in hand, squeezing the plump globe and rubbing her nipple between a podgy forefinger and his thumb.

'Let go, you dirty pig! Spank me, but there's no need to feel me up!'

He stopped, but only so that he could start her spanking once more, now with the smacks landing on her bare skin and punctuated by caresses to her cheeks and thighs. Melody began to sob and gasp, fighting against her own, helpless reactions as the smacks grew firmer and his touches more intimate. Her head was hung in defeat, her boobs quivering to each slap and to her sobs, while she had lost the power to protest even as one fat finger slipped between her cheeks to tickle her bumhole.

At that, Jane came to hold her, cradling Melody's head and stroking her hair as the spanking began once more. Seeing that Melody had given in, Mr Wilberforce grew more intrusive still, pausing to fondle her breasts, pulling her cheeks apart to inspect her anus and the rear lips of her virgin sex, and finally cupping her bulge in one hand. All Melody could manage was a feeble groan as she realised he was going to rub her off, but Jane immediately cuddled her closer and opened her uniform to allow her friend to nuzzle her breasts.

Melody took a nipple in her mouth, suckling gratefully. Mr Wilberforce had let go of her wrist and now began to spank her and masturbate her at the same time, slapping one cheek after the other, hard enough to make them bounce, and breaking off occasionally to tickle her anus or spread her pussy lips. Melody knew he was admiring her virgin hole, perhaps wondering how it would feel to pop the tight arc of flesh that held her inviolate, even thinking of jamming his own cock up her, but she was helpless, lost in ecstasy as her pleasure rose to his spanking, fiddling hands, until at last she hit her peak in a shuddering, helpless orgasm, pathetically grateful for what they'd done to her until it was over at last and all her shame and resentment came rushing back.

Spanking Spree

It was the best part of an hour after they left the shoe shop before Melody could bring herself to talk about what had happened. The experience had been even stronger than when she'd been spanked by Matron, and more intimate than taking the cane. Beforehand she had always at least had the excuse that what was happening to her was supposed to be a punishment, and that her reaction was therefore involuntary. Also, that had been before Jane explained about her hidden desires.

With Mr Wilberforce it had been different. Not only was he exactly the sort of man she had always despised, but the pretence of her spanking as punishment had been abandoned from the moment she stopped protesting. Jane obviously understood, holding Melody's hand and accepting sulky silence as a natural reaction. They hadn't even bought any boots, and as they walked Melody's resentment had slowly given way to guilt. Finally she spoke up.

'I'm sorry. You were really sweet to me, holding me and everything.'

'That's okay. I know it's hard to come to terms with who you are.'

Melody nodded and squeezed Jane's hand, but went silent for a long time before speaking again.

'Okay, but tell me this. Mr Wilberforce is a CAT, right? That means his avatar can look anyway he wants, so what's with being a dirty old man, and bald, and fat!?'

'Oh, you get all sorts, believe me. Maybe he really looks like that and is too proud to change? Much more likely, what gets him off isn't so much your body as your humiliation.'

'My humiliation? I don't understand.'

'What's worse, being spanked by a handsome young man or some dirty old git?'

'The dirty old git, of course.'

'Exactly. He knows that and he wants your feelings to be

as strong as possible, because that's what really turns him on, and it turned you on, didn't it?'

'I suppose so … yes, it did, but … but, I mean, the way he touched me, it was just so dirty, so …'

'Horny?'

'I was going to say intrusive.'

'If you prefer, but you couldn't stop it, could you?'

'No. But that's not the point. So you're saying he gets off on me being ashamed of myself for what I'm showing and what's happening to me?'

'I imagine so, or maybe he just likes your body, but either way the chances are he looks completely different on the outside; maybe some spotty eighteen-year-old who's never had a girlfriend, maybe he's even older and fatter, maybe he's not a he at all, but a woman, although that's much commoner the other way around. Most likely he's some average guy whose wife won't let him spank her, but I'm only guessing. All you can be sure of is that he likes feet, and shoes, and spanking girls' bums.'

Melody shook her head.

'What a bunch of perverts!'

'This is Metrocity. There other places entirely devoted to racing cars, or stealing them, or golf, just about anything you can imagine, but the sexy ones are always the most popular, although I admit it gets pretty kinky around here. That's what I like, and so do you.'

It took Melody a moment to admit the truth.

'I suppose so, but why's it always so smutty? Isn't there somewhere that's all parties and really horny guys, where you can maybe get a spanking if you fancy it, but you don't keep getting put over the knee by ugly old nutters?'

Jane laughed.

'How about going up to the stadium then?'

'The stadium?'

'To play Cheerleader Locker Room. You'd get all the handsome young men you can handle, believe me, and that's after being passed around the laps of all their cheerleaders.'

'Um … no thanks. My bottom smarts, and anyway … I don't know, I prefer it … I mean, I don't think I could set myself up for it, however much I get off on it when it happens. You see, I can't help it.'

'I understand. You like to feel you haven't got any choice. Believe me, once those cheerleaders get hold of you, you haven't! That's okay though, maybe another time, and I don't think your bum will stop smarting until you start a new game.'

'Something like that. Anyway, what if our team won?'

'You get to spank their cheerleaders, at least in theory. In practice Weissinger's Warlords always win, so if you want to get spanked you join in the opposition, and if you want to do the spanking you join the Warlords.'

'Doesn't that take some of the fun out of it?'

'Only if you switch. I like to lose. So you'd prefer to take your chances?'

'I think so, yes.'

'Even if it meant helping spank me and making me service your team?'

Jane finished with a faint but excited purr. Melody found herself blushing and changing the subject.

'Here's another shoe shop, hopefully not run by perverts.'

'Oh, it's bound to be, but if you don't play the brat you'll be okay.'

'Is that BRAT as in Brain Recorded whatsit, or brat as in spoilt little bitch?'

'Spoilt little bitch. You can't help the other.'

Melody gave Jane a swat on the seat of her uniform and they entered the shop together. It looked refreshingly normal after Wilberforce's, with female staff and smart, fashionable goods displayed on purpose-built stands and white-painted shelves. The young woman who came to help them was also completely normal, if a bit dull, which Melody realised probably meant she was a Giganeuron.

Half an hour later they left with five pairs of boots, three for Melody and two for Jane, all beautifully made, smart and sexy, and yet there was no denying the experience hadn't been completely satisfying. The manageress, a tall, stately woman, had given them one or two arch looks, but both had stayed on their best behaviour and nothing had happened.

At the end of the block another shop caught Melody's attention, a jeweller's, the window filled with gold and platinum; rings, chains, bracelets, studs and bangles, many set with gems and in designs she didn't recognise at all. The prices were high, or at least high enough to assure her that it was an exclusive shop, but by no means beyond her reach. Melody gave a thoughtful nod.

'Do you know; ever since I woke up nearly all the jewellery I've had has been pink plastic? I used to wear so much, especially bangles. I used to love performing in bangles.'

'Why not buy some then?'

'I will, and you should get something too.'

'Melody, they're terribly expensive.'

'That doesn't matter.'

They went in, to find three people in attendance, two tall, smart, young women and a man who made Mr Wilberforce look like a Greek God. No more than four and a half feet tall, he was totally bald, with a face as wrinkled as a prune and the most enormous ears Melody had ever seen. His smart grey suit and neat, pale pink tie only served to make him seem even more grotesque. Melody hesitated, then leant close to Jane, whispering.

'What's the betting the garden gnome tries something on with me?'

Jane gave the faintest of giggles, but the little man's welcoming smile vanished, to be replaced by a look of fury.

'I beg your pardon? Did I hear you refer to me as a garden gnome?'

Melody immediately began to stammer apologies, and to

back for the door, but it was too late. Both the female assistants had already come round the sides of their counters, cutting off her escape. As they closed on her she realised that they were not merely tall, but built like athletes, their muscles lean and hard beneath their tailored silk blouses. Neither bothered to speak, and nor did the little man, who stayed behind his desk, waiting until Melody had been forced into a crawling position in the middle of the floor and her jeans pulled down before coming around the counter.

He had taken something from beneath the desk, a short strap of thick brown leather with two words embossed in gold – Brat Spanker. Melody tried to crawl away as she saw it, but was held firmly in position and given half-a-dozen hard smacks, all the while treading up and down on her knees and wiggling her hips in her efforts to escape the pain but only succeeding in making a still ruder show of her bottom.

When they finally released her she scrambled up and made a dash for the door, not bothering to protest her treatment, nor to pull up her jeans. Jane was already outside, hiding her laughter behind one hand as Melody wriggled into her jeans as fast as she could, speaking only when she was decent again.

'How did he hear what I said?'

Jane's laughter grew more boisterous still.

'With ears like that? Of course he heard you. Any bigger and he'd be able to take off!'

Even as Jane finished speaking the door of the jeweller's was pulled violently open. Both assistants piled out, with their gnome-like boss shouting furious instructions from inside as Jane was grabbed, pushed down over a public bench, her uniform skirt hauled high and her knickers pulled well down, baring her trim pink bottom to the street. Melody had hardly had time to react, but thought better of trying to intervene, telling herself that it was what Jane liked even as her friend was held in place, kicking weakly, until the boss came out.

The strap was applied, six times as before, leaving Jane's bottom marked with broad red welts, but instead of being released and allowed to cover herself up, her knickers were pulled off and her uniform skirt tucked up to leave her bottom showing as she scampered across to join Melody. The gnome and his two assistants walked back into the shop, he with Jane's stolen panties pressed to his nose as he inhaled her natural perfume.

Plenty of people had stopped to watch, but not one had moved to help Jane, including two burly policemen who been directing traffic further down the street. Remembering the rumoured habits of Sergeant Stern, Melody led Jane down a side street, not speaking until she was absolutely certain they were out of hearing.

'The vicious little bastard! Are you alright?'

Jane grinned.

'Fine, thanks. That was fun!'

Melody didn't answer, finding it hard to take in her friend's open enthusiasm.

'Now what?'

'Now we're both knickerless, that's what!'

'This is still Naughty Nurse, is it? Are you sure we're not playing Spankorama?'

'You should know, you're the BRAT.'

'Isn't there a choice for a normal day, one in which we don't get our bottoms smacked every five minutes?'

'I don't know, maybe.'

Jane had adjusted her uniform as they spoke, covering herself up. Melody looked around. They're come away from the main thoroughfare, into narrower streets with less prosperous-looking shops and the stalls of a market a little further along. She was still keen to find a jeweller's, but definitely not the one that belonged to the man she now thought of as the gnome. He might have spanked her, and the warm glow of her bottom might be bringing her on heat again, but he was not going to have her trade. She had also developed a sudden distaste for exclusive shops.

'Perhaps the market would be better?'

'Worse. They won't just spank you, they'll get dirty with you.'

Melody made a face, doing her best to ignore the thoughts of erect, eager cocks Jane's words had provoked. After all, her virginity was too precious to lose in a gang bang with a bunch of street traders, and while she knew in theory that she ought to be able to protect herself from penetration she knew that she would get carried away, in which case she was sure to get fucked. Jane tried to reassure her.

'You just have to be very polite. Remember, it's a game, so nobody will punish you without good reason, although you'll keep getting tempted, like when Mr Wilberforce started touching me up, or the way that last man looked. You just need to learn to play. Now come on.'

Jane extended her hand and Melody took it, allowing herself to be led along the street to where the stalls began. The market was more colourful and more crowded than anywhere she'd been before, with each stall covered by a striped awning emblazoned with the name of the trader, while the people seemed busier and more alive, calling out to each other and exchanging jests with the traders. Nobody seemed to have any particular interest in her and Jane, and as they pushed deeper in and began to examine the wares on sale she gradually relaxed, only to be brought up short, her hand going to her mouth in shock.

There was a fruit stall to one side, laden with oranges, apples, plums and more, all in perfect condition, and in front of it a half-circle of onlookers had formed, to watch as a young girl knelt before a brawny, dark haired man who seemed to be the stallholder himself. She was dressed in perfectly ordinary clothes, jeans and trainers; and also a yellow top, which had been lifted along with her bra to show off two small, pert breasts, each tipped by a stiff, rosy pink nipple. Her hair was dark and cut in a bob, her face exceptionally pretty in a gamine, almost boyish way, while her tiny, rosebud mouth was stretched as wide as it would go around the shaft of the costermonger's erection.

Jane gave a little, excited purr at the sight, while Melody immediately found herself wondering how it would feel to be in the girl's position; down on her knees on the cobbles, her tits pulled out as she sucked cock in front of a leering audience. It would be worse than doing it on the ward, where at least she'd had some privacy. In the market she would be on display for all to see, a thought that sent a shiver down her spine. She whispered to Jane.

'Why's she letting him make her do that? Is it a punishment? Is she a pro?'

'I think she's just buying some fruit.'

'Buying some fruit!? You mean he makes her pay for her fruit by sucking him off, and in front of everybody!?'

'Only if she wants to. Watch.'

The costermonger was nearly there, his mouth slack with pleasure, his eyes fixed on the girl's pretty face as her head bobbed up and down on his straining erection. He gasped, jerked, the girl's cheeks bulged and he had come in her mouth. She swallowed and drew back a little, sucking the head of his cock as she tossed him into her mouth to make sure she got every last drop. Again she swallowed, then drew back, looking up at the costermonger with a nervous smile.

'Was I okay?'

He took a moment to suck in air before replying.

'You were great, love. Now what was it you was after, oranges?'

'Yes please.'

'Oranges it is then. Tell you what, seeing as how you got your titties out without having to be asked, I'll make it two kilo. How's that?'

The girl smiled.

'Thank you very much!'

The costermonger winked, served the girl and sent her on

her way with a smack to her jean clad rump. He took a swallow from a bottle of beer behind his stall and then began to call out his wares, quickly focussing on Melody and Jane.

'How about you, ladies? Bananas are on special, three credits a kilo? Slip 'em up each other for a show and I'll make it two, how's that for a deal?'

Melody's mouth came open in outrage.

'Why you …'

She stopped, conscious that giving him her opinion of his behaviour was likely to earn her another spanking. He merely looked puzzled.

'What's the matter? Come on, don't tell me you two ain't a couple of rug munchers. I can spot 'em a mile off.'

The blood had rushed to Melody's face and Jane began to giggle. He grinned and wagged his finger at them.

'I knew it, I did. Now come on, how about a little show for the lads? Come on, everybody, Miss Boobies and the blonde here are going to give us all a little lezzie show. Gather round, folks, gather round!'

Despite herself, Melody began to protest.

'Hey, no! We didn't say we were going to give you a show, did we Jane?'

Jane was looking nervous but also excited and didn't answer. People had stepped back, forming an open space between the stalls, with Melody and Jane at the centre. Not one of them showed the slightest disapproval or even sympathy, only interest. Melody tried again.

'Look, really, we didn't promise anything of the sort, it was just him, this dirty bastard!'

She realised her mistake the instant she'd spoken, but the words had come out before she could stop herself, in panic at the thought of being made to perform with Jane in front of a crowd of strangers, and the certain knowledge that if she did, she would end up losing control completely. The costermonger spoke up.

'There's no call for bad language, Miss. I only said you

might want to do a lezzie show, that's all.'

Again Melody was unable to contain herself.

'That's all? That's all!? I've never met you before in my life, and you expect me and my friend to have sex together just so you can get off on us!?'

'Sure. What's the problem?'

Melody was fighting to hold her temper in check, but couldn't stop herself from carrying on.

'What's the problem!? It's … it's disrespectful for one thing … I mean, not just disrespectful, it's … it's an appalling thing to suggest! Haven't you got any respect for women at all, you filthy bastard? I mean, imagine making that girl suck you off!? How old was she, eighteen, nineteen, and you make her suck your dirty penis in front of a crowd, and for what, two credits worth of oranges!'

'Six credits, Miss. I give her two kilos, and they're good oranges and all, lovely.'

'Six credits, to suck you off in public!? I wouldn't do that for … for anything, not for all the money in the world!'

A voice called out from the crowd.

'How about a nice piece of sirloin steak then? Or rump if you like, only I see you got plenty of your own.'

Melody turned in fury as most of the crowd began to laugh, only to find herself faced with a broad, dark blue expanse studded with brightly polished brass buttons. Glancing up, she realised she was looking at a gigantic policeman.

'What's all this then?'

Melody jabbed an accusing finger at the costermonger.

'This filthy pig tried to get me to … to act dirty with my friend, in front of everyone!'

The policeman scratched his head.

'Well, if you didn't fancy it …'

'That's not the point! He suggested it, didn't he? Arrest him!'

'Arrest him? What for?'

‘For … for sexual harassment, that’s what for, you moron!’

She stopped.

‘Moron, am I?’

‘Oh shit!’

He wasn’t fast, but he didn’t need to be. Melody was hemmed in on all sides, and her efforts to escape only succeeded in amusing the crowd as she was repeatedly thrust back into the centre of the ring. Eventually the policeman caught her, after which she had no chance at all. He used his handcuffs to secure her wrists behind her back and tucked her under one massive arm, her body lifted free of the ground, her legs kicking in desperation as her jeans were hauled down and her bottom smacked with brisk efficiency. She took it squealing and gasping, but by the time he was done with her and she’d been dumped unceremoniously on the cobbles the heat in her bottom had pushed her right to the brink, her desire held back only by her lingering anger.

Jane helped Melody to her feet and guided her between the stalls, to where a quiet alley ran between two high walls of dirty yellow brick. Nobody had followed them, the air was warm and still, heavy with the scent of over-ripe fruit from the litter of the costermonger’s stall. An upturned milk crate provided Melody a seat, her hot bottom still bare on the hard plastic. Jane came close, lifting the front of her uniform skirt to show off her bare sex. Melody looked up, her eyes accusing for her friend’s betrayal. Jane shook her head, her voice tender but urgent as she spoke.

‘You know you want to. Now lick me out.’

Melody’s resistance collapsed. Her tongue poked out, to lap at Jane’s sex even as her fingers pushed down between her own thighs to find the moist, urgent slit between. As she began to lick she began to masturbate, keeping the same rhythm with tongue and fingers until both came to orgasm, a long, glorious moment they held as long as possible before Melody was finally forced to pull back for air. Jane’s voice was a sigh.

'That was lovely, but I do wish you'd done me in public.'

'You're as bad as the rest of them.'

'I know.'

Jane bent to kiss Melody, who responded, unable to deny her feelings for her friend but equally unable to admit that as she came she'd been imagining a crowd of delighted onlookers and thinking of how much better her climax would have been if she'd done it in public. She still felt ashamed of herself, yet it was impossible to keep the grin off her face as she got up, wiggling her bottom into her jeans and joking as she fastened the fly.

'Really, I might as well leave my jeans undone, and it's just as well I didn't wear any knickers, because it saves people the bother of pulling them down!'

'Why don't you? Leave your jeans undone that is.'

Melody made a face, but tugged open the button of her jeans once more, then adjusted the zip so that it would stay in place but she was quite obviously unfastened on purpose. The result was an immediate buzz of anticipation for her next spanking. Jane nodded.

'You see. You're learning.'

Plugged

Melody lay on her bed, idly sucking on Teddy's cock as she masturbated. It felt good to have her mouth full, and Teddy was a great deal more convenient than either a CAT or a Giganeuron. His responses were simple, and so long as he was having his cock attended to he would do exactly as he was told. She could suck him or mouth his huge balls for as long as she pleased, let him do it between her breasts, or if she felt especially dirty have him mount her and stick his cock up her bottom.

She had been working as a nurse in Metrocity for over a month, and was gradually coming to accept the way things worked and her own needs. Occasionally she felt resentment, or let her temper rise in response to some particularly outrageous incident, but in both cases the consequences tended to be a bare bottom spanking, which invariably brought her arousal up above all other emotions.

Jane had been her constant companion and mentor, often spending the night and absent only when she chose to visit her boyfriend, which left Melody to indulge herself with Teddy. With Jane's help, and occasionally that of other CATs, Melody had improved her understanding of the way Metrocity worked, so that she no longer made so many mistakes and had occasionally managed to go whole days without punishment.

She had redesigned the house to her own taste, explored most of the city and was beginning to fall into a routine of favourite places, and people. Of the men in hospital, Veldt Panther had become her firm favourite, so much so that the majority of her spankings and canings had been for getting caught as she indulged her desire for his enormous black cock by using her mouth or taking him between her breasts, while only its massive girth in comparison to the amount her anus would stretch had prevented her from trying to feed him up her bottom.

That pleasure she had reserved for Teddy, but her virginity remained sacrosanct, and she had quickly discovered that, no matter how carried away she got, even if she was naked and ready in front of a dozen men, no Giga would take advantage of her, while Jane had always managed to put off any over-enthusiastic CATs. Yet as she mouthed on Teddy's erection and teased her clitoris she was imagining the moment, with some huge, powerfully muscled man holding by the hips, helpless in his grip as he pushed his cock to her sex.

Her excitement was rising towards orgasm and the focus of her fantasies began to slip, growing more dirty and further from what she still liked to tell herself was her ideal. The man with his cock to her hole ceased to be a handsome giant and became the filthy-minded, clown-faced little nerd who had got to her so badly with his dirty pictures. Twice she tried to push the image away, only to give in, imagining him catching her in the street, spanking her for some imagined slight and making her kneel on the dirty pavement to have her virginity taken from behind in front of a crowd of laughing, cheering onlookers.

As usual, she came at the moment she imagined her hymen breaking, with her thighs spread as wide as they would go to show off her sex, her back arched tight to push her hips out and her breasts high. The sudden extra suction as her body went into contractions was too much for Teddy, who came in her mouth, growling in delight as she sucked and swallowed, sucked deeper and swallowed once more, holding him in until both of them had finished.

'Ummm … that was nice. Thanks, Teddy.'

'Nice Melody. Dirty Melody.'

She was smiling as she got up from the bed, nude after peeling off her nightie and knickers before she had begun to masturbate. It felt good, and she had taken to padding about the house without a stitch of clothing on, while she hadn't been made to play Dress Up since her first few days at the hospital. Nor had she been called on to perform, which was beginning to irritate her, with no outlet for either her creativity or her love of dance. Not that Metrocity was short of clubs, but even the handful of CATs who remembered who she was didn't seem particularly impressed, while she needed to be the centre of attention.

The stadium where she performed was not even in Metrocity, of that she was certain, while Jane and the other CATs she had questioned knew nothing about it. Only Mr Hawker had even admitted to being a fan, and while he knew all about her and got a huge kick out of being masturbated by the famous Melody J, he was either unable to unwilling to tell her any more. Nor had she discovered anything about Peter and how she had managed to become a Metrocity BRAT in the first place, although she remained convinced that the two were connected.

Other things also puzzled her, but it was easy to put them out of her mind as she got on with her day to day existence, particularly at the hospital. She needed to be in, but the thought of another day playing Naughty Nurse failed to inspire. It had become too easy, too predictable, while Spankorama was even less of a challenge because she got it due to her subconscious need rather than having a chance to escape.

Time and again she had reached the same position, standing in her uniform in front of the door with the three text boxes showing to one side. At first she had always chosen Naughty Nurse, until the day she'd plucked up the courage to go for Spankorama, only to discover that it meant she got more spankings but less sex, which invariably left her frustrated at the end of the day, at least until she got to bed with Jane, Teddy or both. She had still avoided the Gauntlet, but now stood irresolute, telling herself that if might be fun and that she wouldn't get fucked. As the text boxes started to blink she gave in.

'Gauntlet. Oh!'

Her mouth had come open in surprise at the sudden and completely unexpected penetration of her anus, not by anything being pushed up, but by the sudden arrival of something inside her, already wedged well up her bottom but partially sticking out, so that she could feel something round and hard between her cheeks. Whatever it was fitted rather nicely, giving her a deliciously naughty feeling, like having a stiff little cock up her bottom, but she was far too curious not to investigate.

She had been released, and quickly crossed to a mirror, where she pulled down her knickers and stuck her bottom out, lifting her skirt to show off between her cheeks. Her bottom was plugged, with a round bulb sticking out of her anus, maybe three centimetres across and made of pink plastic. She took hold, pulling gently only to discover that she'd also been lubricated, allowing the object to pull free. It was a long, slim plug, maybe ten centimetres long, with the bulb at one end, a slender neck rising to a bulge about two centimetres thick, then gradually tapering off.

Evidently it was supposed to be up her bottom, as part of the game, but she hesitated before slipping it back inside. In Metrocity the consequences of not following the rules were always worse than if she behaved herself, so it made sense that if she'd had her bottom plugged it was for a reason, and so she should stay plugged. Besides, it felt rather nice, especially as she pushed it in, while the way her bottom hole spread as it came out was both fascinating and deliciously rude.

She pulled the plug in and out a few times, enjoying the penetration of her anus and the thoroughly rude view of her bare bottom with the base between her cheeks, until she realised that if she didn't stop it she was going to end up masturbating again, which would undoubtedly make her late for work. Pushing the plug deep one last time, she hastily rearranged herself and left the house. It felt strange as she walked, and nice, not only for the physical sensation of having it inside her, but because wearing it was a pleasantly naughty secret.

There was no sign of Jane, and Melody hurried across the road, aware that she had barely a minute to get in and that being so much as a few seconds late would have inevitable consequences made far worse because when her knickers came down the base of the plug would show. She had no idea how Matron would react, except that it was sure to be both painful and humiliating.

She made it, but only by running up the stairs, which made the plug move inside her and left her pop-eyed and gasping by the time she got to the top. Sister was at her desk as always, and glanced at her pocket watch as Melody entered the ward, speaking as she looked up again.

'Only just in time, Nurse Melody. Why, with your punctuality record anybody would think you wanted your bottom smacked.'

Melody was used to Sister, who never seemed to realise the truth even when a spanking ended in orgasm, and made a hasty apology. Sister pulled a clipboard towards herself and carried on.

'You're in the laundry today. They're short-staffed, so you're to report to Sister Martingale. Off you go.'

Knowing better than to argue, Melody went. She was biting her lip as the lift took her down to the basement, thinking of the fearsome reputation of the women in the laundry room and what they were rumoured to do to any luckless nurse who was caught misbehaving. She tried to tell herself that as she was working there she would effectively be one of them, but deep down she knew it would make little difference, if any.

It was by no means her first trip to the laundry room, as it was one of the few places in the hospital in which it was possible to get any privacy, with the numerous rooms and labyrinthine systems of shelves creating many a quiet corner. She and Jane had visited on several occasions, and while it was always a risk that only added spice to their play. Sister Martingale was in charge of the steam rooms, so Melody knew exactly where to go, finding the coarse-faced, red-skinned woman at her desk. She bobbed a curtsey.

'Good morning, Sister. I was sent down to help.'

Sister Martingale looked up, took Melody in and gave a sceptical grunt.

'A BRAT, just what I need. Get on with it then, and none of your stupid games, or else. Room zero-seven.'

Melody curtsied a second time and made to leave, but Sister Martingale beckoned her back, pointing to an object on her desk. It was a piece of bleached wood about a metre long, broad and flat, with a handle at one end.

'Do you know what that is?'

Melody didn't, but she could guess what it was used for.

'A um … a spanking paddle, Sister?'

'It is a spatula, Nurse Melody, from the boiling rooms, but yes, that is what I use it for, spanking naughty girls' bottoms.'

She'd said the words with such obvious relish that Melody went weak at the knees, but she managed to turn her sudden limpness into another curtsied before replying, 'I'll be very good, Sister.'

'See that you are. Dismissed.'

Melody gave yet another curtsey and hurried on further down the corridor, past one steam room after another until she reached the one she'd been assigned to. There was a glass panel in the door, but nothing more than swirling whiteness beyond, giving her a nasty moment of flashback before she pushed in to find herself in a long room lined with great white-painted machines. The air was hot, moist and smelled of disinfectant, the steam so thick that she could barely make out her new work colleagues, save that they were dressed in white and every one of them was considerably bigger than her. All of them seemed to be talking at once, a babble of conversation that stopped abruptly to leave only the hiss of the machines. Melody tried a cheerful smile.

'Hi. I'm working with you today.'

Some of the women continued working at their machines, others stopped, but all were watching as one of their number approached Melody, a tall, red-haired girl whose voice held more than a trace of sarcasm as she spoke.

'Very nice too. You're a BRAT, aren't you?'

Melody had learnt not to resent the title.

'Yes. Are you CATs?'

'Oh no, not down here. Down here you're completely given over to the machine, but don't worry, we'll have fun.'

'Um … okay, thanks. I'm Melody. And you?'

'The girls call me Ginger, but if you do I'll piss in your mouth and make you wash it out with soap. You get to call me Boss, for now.'

Melody didn't argue, horrified by the tall girl's suggestion and very sure it wasn't a bluff.

'Yes, Boss. What should I do?'

'That all depends, doesn't it? We get some pretty dirty jobs down here, but if a girl works hard, all day, she might just about get them all done. That girl might very well be you. Or on the other hand, she might like to be one of us, and only do her fair share of the dirty work.'

Melody had a good idea of the sort of jobs Ginger meant, and answered without hesitation.

'I'd prefer to be one of you, please … please, Boss.'

'I was hoping you'd say that, but you ought to know that there's a little initiation ceremony for new girls.'

'Oh … but I'm only temporary. I'm in Osteo usually. Couldn't I just …'

'No, you couldn't. Osteo? That's one of the wards where they toss the men off every morning, isn't it? You dirty little tart! It doesn't matter anyway. Every new girl's the same, so what's it to be, T&P, or the Gauntlet?'

'What's T&P, exactly?'

Ginger leant close to whisper into Melody's ear. Melody

swallowed hard.

'And the Gauntlet? What happens?'

'I'll tell you what happens. You get to run down the corridor to the loos at the far end, bare bottom of course.'

Melody felt a surge of relief, also disappointment.

'I have to streak, that's all?'

'That's all, well, nearly all. The girls get to give you a bit of encouragement, naturally, with wet towels. Oh, and you get an enema first.'

'An enema!?'

'Yeah, an enema. You know, a litre of water up the bum.'

'I know what an enema is, but …'

'Don't you get lippy with me, girl, or it'll be two litres.'

'Sorry, Boss, but what if I can't hold it in?'

'That's half the fun.'

Ginger's mouth curved into a sadistic grin, Melody could stare in horror as she realised why she needed the plug up her bottom.

The Gauntlet

Melody stood in a ring of grinning, laughing laundry girls. She was facing Ginger, who was holding out a monstrous syringe.

'You can do it yourself, or we'll do it for you.'

Melody had no difficulty in reaching her decision.

'I'll do it myself, thank you.'

'Pity.'

'Where should I go?'

'Nowhere, darling. You do it right here, in front of us, and we want to see.'

Melody's cheeks flushed crimson at Ginger's words and she began to babble.

'In front of you? But look, Ging … Boss, that's not fair, not like that! I mean, I have … I'll need to … come, please, in private?'

'Get her, girls.'

'No! Okay, okay, I'll do it!'

They had moved close, hemming her in, and there was no escape. Shaking badly, she took out two of the nappy pins that she now carried as a matter of course. They watched in amusement as she pinned her skirt up and pushed her knickers down to expose her bottom and the base of the plug between her cheeks. Ginger laughed.

'Look girls, she's plugged her box. Something tells me a certain little BRAT knew what we like to do to tarts like her all along.'

The others laughed and Melody was blushing furiously as she continued her strip, only to be brought up short by Ginger as she made to step out of her knickers.

'Uh, uh, those stay on, around the top of your thighs. That way it's more of a laugh if you don't make it.'

Melody made a face but did as she was told, adjusting her knickers to leave her bottom fully exposed but with the front still up. Ginger gave a satisfied nod and held out the syringe.

Melody took it, grimacing as she felt the weight of the soapy white water within. Her embarrassment flared higher still as she reached back, to draw the plug slowly from her bottom hole. Ginger made no comment, presumably familiar with the routine, but ducked down to make sure she got a good view as Melody eased the syringe between her cheeks. It wasn't easy, especially when trying to hold the plug and keep her cheeks open at the same time, especially with the laundry girls peering close to get a good view as she stuck it in.

She had no choice but to show off either. Only by sticking her bottom right out could she push the nozzle in, leaving her in a pose that drew further laughter from her audience, then more and louder as her anal ring gave way and the nozzle slid in up her bottom. Determined not to make a mess, she pushed the nozzle well up before reaching back to take hold of the plunger. It felt impossibly rude, with the bulky syringe sticking out from between her cheeks and the nozzle in up her anus, but not as rude as the thought of filling herself with a litre of water.

It took all her courage to start to press. She felt nothing, at first, save a cool sensation around her bottom hole, then a gradual increase in pressure inside her, growing until her mouth had come open and her eyes wide in astonished reaction. The water made her feel swollen and heavy inside, an extraordinary sensation, at once unspeakably rude and overwhelmingly erotic, vulnerable and wanton at the same time. Her breathing had become deep and even, her head dizzy, making it almost impossible to concentrate as she carefully withdrew the nozzle and clenched her cheeks. She stuck the plug back in as quickly as she could, making her gasp and drawing yet more laughter from the laundry girls, but she had passed the first test and it was impossible to restrain a triumphant smile as she stood straight once more. Ginger nodded, evidently impressed.

'Very good. I see you spend plenty of time playing with yourself, don't you?'

Melody made no effort to deny the accusation but nodded. 'I'm ready.'

'Good girl, that's the spirit. I do hate ones who try to chicken out when they're loaded. Right girls, get the others together, check that Sister's minding her own business, and we're on.'

The other laundry girls dispersed, leaving Melody standing alone with Ginger. As she waited, the sensation inside her began to change, her urgency rising, until she'd began to wiggle her toes and cross her knees, close to panic for what might happen and yet unable to push down her mounting arousal for the awful situation she was in. Ginger watched with a knowing smile, obviously enjoying both the view and Melody's mounting distress. After a while she stepped close, her fingers going to the top button of Melody's uniform as she spoke.

'I think we'd better have these out, don't you, seeing as they're so big.'

Melody made no protest, her feelings too mixed as her dress was unfastened at the front and her breasts lifted out of her bra. Ginger took her time, making no attempt to hide her pleasure in what she was doing as she felt the weight of each plump globe and rubbed her thumbs over the stiff nipples. The girl's touch made it harder still for Melody to concentrate on the now desperate feeling in her bottom. Her wriggling grew worse and she was stamping her feet up and down and biting her lip by the time one of the other laundry girls finally came back.

'All set, Ginger. Sister's gone upstairs and there's no sign of Matron.'

Ginger gave Melody's breasts a last squeeze as she replied.

'That's a shame. I was just starting to enjoy myself. Let's go then, slut.'

She made for the door, collecting a wet towel on the way, presumably in case of an accident. Melody followed, stepping into the passage to find two lines of eager, laughing girls, each and every one holding a dripping white towel in one hand, twisted and ready to flick at her exposed bottom as she ran past. She made to protest as she realised her fate, but Ginger was behind her, twisting her own towel as she spoke.

'Ready … steady … go!'

Melody's yelp blended with a meaty smack as Ginger's towel connected with her bottom and she was running. More towels came in, catching her cheeks and the backs of her thighs to send her down the passage jumping and squealing, to the unbounded delight of her tormentors, but even as she ran she was struggling to keep her anus tight on the plug. The very first smack had nearly made her lose control, and it didn't get any better, with every crack of a wet towel on her jiggling bottom making her muscles go loose, until she was in a welter of confusion and pain, also a sense of shame that made merely having her bottom exposed for spanking seemed trivial. She was sure she would let go and disgrace herself utterly, but it was the strength of her feelings that spurred her on, even with some of the laundry girls using their towels before she was past, so that the vicious, stinging flicks landed not on the soft fullness of her bottom but on the front of her legs and her belly, even across her naked, wobbling breasts.

She hit the loo door at full speed, only to smack into it but not through. For one ghastly moment she thought she might have been tricked, with the door locked to leave her with no option but to let go where she was, squatting at the end of the corridor in front of the delighted watchers. The towels were still coming in, several girls flicking her as she went into a desperate, wriggling dance, jumping up and down on her feet and squealing like a stuck pig with every crack of soggy material on her bouncing cheeks. Then the handle turned in her grip and she was through, one last towel flick catching her full across both cheeks before she was properly inside.

Melody dashed for the cubicles, hurled herself into the

nearest, ripped her knickers down, threw the seat up and collapsed onto the loo, gasping and swearing as she tugged her plug free. Only then did she relax, with a long, heartfelt sigh. She'd done it, maybe at the expense of a bruised bottom, but without having to endure the appalling humiliation of expelling her enema before she reached the loos. Still panting for breath, she lay back against the cistern, her eyes closed, too far gone to care that she'd left the cubicle door unlocked.

Nobody disturbed her, and very slowly her composure began to return. With it came the realisation of the state she was in, her bottom as hot as if she'd just taken a dozen of Matron's cane, her skirt high and her knickers around her ankles to leave her exposed, her breasts sticking out of her open dress, her skin slick with sweat and her nipples straining to erection, her thighs wide with the need to surrender. Only the excited chatter of the laundry girls outside the door held her back from masturbating then and there, but she knew she could only put it off so long.

Her fingers were shaking uncontrollably as she cleaned up, and she was unable to resist putting her plug back in up her bottom, while she stepped out of her knickers as she left the cubicle simply because it felt right to go bare. She kept her dress up as well, turning her back to the large wall mirror in order to inspect her bottom. Both cheeks were flushed red all over and marked with darker blotches here and there where particularly good shots had caught her flesh. Her thighs were marked too, even at the front where her dress had given her at least some protection, while her breasts bore three or four small red areas where the skin smarted. Every inch of her smacked flesh felt hot, but not as hot as she did between her thighs.

Nobody had come in, making her wonder if she'd been left to her own devices on purpose. There was a blue-painted stool in one corner and she sat down on it, listening as she fiddled with the hem of her skirt, eager to pull it up but very much aware of the voices outside and the consequences if she did get caught by Sister Martingale or a matron. Yet as long as the laundry girls were talking she was safe, at least from a paddling. What they'd do to her if they caught her masturbating was another matter, but it had to be done.

As she pulled her skirt up to her belly she was in two minds about whether it would be better to be allowed to finish herself off in peace or to get caught at it. Maybe they'd make her lick, turn and turn about until every single one of them had come under her tongue, or drag her out into the corridor and strip her for being such a slut, maybe spank her too. The thought sent a powerful shiver through her and she put one hand to her chest, stroking her hurt flesh. The other slipped between her thighs, to knead gently at her sex, where it stayed even as the door swung open to reveal Ginger.

'I guessed as much, and I'm guessing I know what you'd like to do?'

Melody's answer was a single, shame-faced nod. Ginger stepped closed, tugging up the front of her skirt to expose white satin panties tight over her sex. Melody leant forward, still stroking herself as she nuzzled her face against Ginger's panties, drinking in the rich, feminine scent. Her tongue poked out and she'd begun to lick the smooth white material, pushing it into the groove beneath. Ginger took Melody by the hair, pulling her closer. Melody tried to pull back, but Ginger tightened her grip.

'Come on, don't get prissy on me.'

'I'm not. Turn around so … so I can lick your bum.'

'You dirty little tart! Okay, if that's what gets you off.'

Ginger turned, keeping her grip in Melody's hair as she lifted her skirt and pushed her bottom out. Melody was lost, rubbing her face against the seat of Ginger's knickers, then pulling them down to let her tongue delve between the full, firm cheeks. Ginger pushed her bottom out further still, moaning in pleasure as Melody's tongue found her anus. Melody began to rub at herself as she licked and probed at the tiny hole. Ginger gave a contented purr before speaking again.

'Oh, that is nice. I think I'll have you for my own, you're so dirty. Yes, like that … right in.'

Licking Jane's bottom had become one of Melody's favourite things, and it was better still with Ginger, a woman who had dominated her from the start, making her strip and show off as she gave herself an enema, playing with her breasts and putting her through the Gauntlet. With Jane it felt good, but with Ginger it felt right, as if Melody had found her natural place, playing with her pussy as she tongued a taller, stronger woman's bottom hole.

Melody came, a long, perfect orgasm that seemed to hold for ever, all the while with her tongue stuck well in up Ginger's now slippery bottom hole. Even when she'd finished and the inevitable shame flooded in she continued to lick, knowing that her head would be held in place until Ginger had finished whether she liked it or not. She was still willing though, and doing her best to give pleasure, but her hands had moved from her own body to Ginger's, holding the muscular bottom cheeks open so that her tongue could get deeper.

'That's a good girl. Now my pussy.'

Melody was given no choice, Ginger simply pushing her bottom out further still and adjusting her grip. Now with her face smothered between Ginger's bottom cheeks and her mouth open against wet, juicy pussy flesh, Melody continued to lick, working her tongue as she had been taught by Jane and wriggling her nose into the tight little hole she'd just had against her mouth. Ginger's voice was a sigh as she spoke again.

'You dirty, filthy little slut. Oh yes, I'm going to make you my own, Melody, and I'm going to make you do this every day.'

As she finished she began to come, her cheeks squeezing in Melody's face, her hand twisted hard as she gasped her way through orgasm, not letting go until she was well and truly finished. Melody sat back, exhausted from her ordeal and ashamed of her own reaction, but unable to suppress a smile as Ginger turned to her.

'You are good, aren't you? And you made it. Most girls don't get halfway down the corridor.'

To Melody's surprise Ginger offered to help her to her feet, then kissed her. They were chatting happily as they made themselves decent, Melody asking questions and Ginger explaining how she was the boss in the steam rooms, whatever Sister Martingale might think.

'… I haven't got the old cow completely under my thumb yet, but I will, soon. Then I'll make sure you get sent down here every day. I'll look after you, and you can be my pet. How's that?'

'Um … thanks.'

'For now we'd better hurry, but give me one last kiss of those lovely titties.'

Melody was doing up her dress, but obliged, opening the buttons once more and lifting both boobs from her bra. Ginger bent down, to kiss one nipple, then the other, sucking the stiff teat deep before burying her face in Melody's cleavage. Melody was still holding her breasts up and squeezed them around Ginger's face, once more enjoying herself. Ginger responded, starting to lick and suckle at Melody's nipples, just as the loo door opened and Sister Martingale came in, her expression first sour, then astonished as she sure what was going on, then furious. Melody could only gape in horror, and Ginger hadn't realised, still suckling.

'And what do you think you're doing!?'

Sister's voice was like a foghorn and Ginger jumped up, her face going white as she saw who had caught them, for all her earlier bravado. The moment she found her voice she was babbling apologies and excuses, but Sister didn't even bother to respond. Both girls were taken by their ears and led out into the now deserted corridor, Melody with her breasts still bare and her nipples wet with her new friend's spittle.

Ginger was dealt with first, bent over Sister's desk and paddled hard with the door still open so that passers-by could see her bare bottom as two dozen hard swats were applied. When she was done her dress was pinned up and she was sent into the corner; pink-bottomed, tearful and snivelling, very different to the bold young woman of just moments before. Melody had watched, shaking badly and fidgeting in apprehension for her own turn, which was about to come as Sister Martingale pointed at the desk.

'Bend over!'

Melody obeyed, going through a now all too familiar routine as she adopted the standard position for the paddle, strap or cane, bent over the edge of the desk with her hands resting on the top and her bottom stuck out behind. She hadn't even been allowed to cover her breasts up, adding to her embarrassment as her skirt was lifted, but no more so than Sister's immediate discovery.

'What, no panties? Why is that? Were you punished earlier? And what is this?'

He voice had changed as she spoke, from impatience and disapproval to disgust as she took hold of the bulb of Melody's plug where it showed between her cheeks. Melody couldn't speak, the lump in her throat too big to swallow and her face red hot with shame as Sister extracted the plug and held it up for inspection, still speaking, but now as if she was unable to believe what she was seeing.

'This … this revolting device! Am I to believe that you are a sodomite, Nurse Melody, that you enjoy objects inserted into your rectum? Or is there some other explanation, because, by God there had better be, or you won't be sitting down for a month!'

Her voice had risen to a scream, which only made it harder for Melody to reply, incapable of doing more than shaking her head and making bubbling noises until at last Ginger came to her rescue.

'We … we made her run the Gauntlet, Sister, with … with an enema. We … we put the plug in to give her a fair chance.'

Sister's voice was quiet as she continued, but more menacing than her rage.

'Oh, you did, did you? I've spoken to you about bullying before, haven't I? Yes, I have, and I warned you what would happen if I caught you at it again. Now it will, tomorrow at nine sharp, where you will receive twenty-four strokes of the cane, bare, in front of the entire laundry staff, and yes, why not? I think you had better hold an enema while it's done, so you know how your victims feel, although naturally you will have a plug to give you a fair chance.'

Ginger's response was a whimper and Melody finally managed to speak out, determined to defend her new friend.

'It was my fault, Sister, I …'

'Shut up! I am fully aware that it was your fault, and that you are a BRAT and no doubt thoroughly enjoyed what was done to you. Otherwise you would have come straight to me, wouldn't you, like any sensible, decent girl. I know how it works too, you see. Either the Gauntlet or a day of T&P, isn't it? And what did you choose? You chose the Gauntlet, didn't you, rather than honest work, you little slut!'

As she finished she brought the paddle down hard across Melody's bottom, raising a loud smack and a yelp of pain, then another as she laid in, screeching at the top of her voice as she beat Melody with every ounce of her strength.

'What did you think you were you playing at, you filthy little slut? What did I say? I said no stupid games, that's what I said … no … stupid … games … Slut! Slut! Slut!'

Each word was punctuated by a heavy smack and a new squeal of pain as the paddle was applied to Melody's bottom, again and again, until at last it broke. Sister Martingale hurled it to the ground, still swearing and abusing Melody, jabbed a finger at the wall next to where Ginger was standing in disgrace and stormed from the room.

Melody went to stand next to her friend, where she adjusted her skirt and put her hands on her head, as she knew she was supposed to. Ginger threw her a glance, which Melody returned and both girls burst into giggles.

Virgin Territory

Melody's life changed after playing the Gauntlet. Jane had disappeared, leaving Melody feeling empty and also guilty in case she was somehow responsible, although both Veldt Panther and Mr Hawker assured her that she wasn't, and that Jane hadn't been on the Metrocity forums either.

Every day Melody would go in, hoping to find her friend, and day after day there was no sign of Jane. More often than not she would choose the Gauntlet, which proved to have dozens of subtle variations but always included Ginger, who was fun but had no more depth than could be expected in a Giganeuron. It was wonderful when they were having sex together, or when involved in the elaborate cruelties that were a part of everyday life in the laundry, but Melody would have preferred Jane to be there too.

Even playing with the men's cocks was far less exciting than it had been before, because Jane had always been there to tease and coax Melody into going too far, which in turn made her punishments more intense and exciting. She was also getting used to having to service men, being spanked, and even the cane, which meant that life was less terrifying but had also begun to lose a certain spice. Jane, she was sure, could have made it better, either by introducing Melody to some new thrill or simply being there. Worst of all, she missed being cuddled at night, and Teddy was definitely no substitute.

She was also tired of having only three games to choose from, having grown bold enough to want more, even to consider surrendering her virginity, and not just when on heat, but in her calmer moments. Unfortunately that meant finding the right man, and while she occasionally needed penetration so badly that it became a physical ache, she was still determined to wait until the perfect moment, although aware that she might well get caught off-guard, particularly after a spanking, and be taken by surprise, which made her eager to do it her own way as soon as possible. She had considered Veldt Panther many times, but he had two major disadvantages; the enormous size of his cock, which was sure to hurt, and his obsession with having nurses see to him because he couldn't do it himself, which meant she wouldn't be held as her virginity was taken.

Two weeks after her first encounter with Ginger and the Gauntlet she was woken by Teddy rubbing his cock between the cheeks of her bottom. She obligingly tugged him off, still half asleep, but managed to turn herself on and ended up masturbating, on her back with her thighs spread as she thought of Jane. Her eyes were closed, and in her mind Jane was straddled over her, about to sit on her face so that Melody could lick while she came. It worked well, and as Melody's pleasure rose she began to arch her back, and to call out for her friend, at first in need, then ecstasy, and at last sobbing brokenly as desire gave way to regret.

'I want to be with you, Jane, I really do. I want to be with Jane!'

She went limp, her hands still between her thighs, her head turned to where dawn had begun to break, seeping colour into the light coming through her curtains. Teddy lay on the floor, kicked off the bed by accident, inert, but with his shaggy face fixed in an expression of deep hurt. Melody got up, feeling guilty, and having retrieved Teddy she tugged the curtains wide. Daylight filled the room, and refresh air from the open window, but both were startlingly different to what she had grown used to.

'Wow!'

Metrocity was gone, replaced by a wide open landscape of tree clad hills with the occasional patch of fields cut out from what seemed to be virgin forest. Far off, a wisp of smoke rose from among the trees, while there was an orchard of gnarled and ancient fruit trees directly beneath her window, but these were the only signs of human habitation. Mountains rose in the distance, misty, violet-blue and capped with snow.

The change was less dramatic than when Metrocity had first appeared, but her heart was hammering as she took in the vast sweep of countryside, and a glance out of the window showed that the exterior of her own house had also changed, to crude, unpainted wooden planking. Her room was the same as before, but she was expecting it to change at any moment, bringing her close to panic as she began to worry about all the things she'd bought while in the city, and especially her clothes. Text boxes appeared, always a sure sign of change, and she'd begun to babble.

'Oh no, not my clothes, please not my clothes! At let me keep some jeans, and my jewellery, for goodness sake not my jewellery!'

Everything around her remained reassuringly solid, but the text boxes were still there, and one included a command she hadn't seen in a long while – Dress Up. She drew a heavy sigh and went to stand in the middle of the room, glad she was already naked and wondering if she could beat the system or whether some hidden controller would override her commands.

'Bra and panties: Black: Plain.'

They appeared, a conventional set, middle-sized and unadorned, only to vanish as abruptly as they'd arrived, once more leaving her in the nude.

'Okay … okay, let's compromise. You like pervy stuff, how about school knickers and no bra?'

Nothing happened.

'Knickers: Plain white: Full cut.'

She was in them, tight, white cotton panties similar to the ones she was given with her nurse's uniform but thicker and as high as her waist. They vanished.

'What was wrong with those!? Okay … French knickers: Black: Lacy.'

Again they appeared instantly, a confection of silk and lace that clung to her curves and puffed out behind to emphasise her bottom.

'Hmm ... those are quite nice. Hey!'

The French knickers had vanished.

'There's no pleasing some people, is there? What do you want then; big pink frillies, I suppose, or little white ones with hearts or something? How about crotchless in tarty red? Oh shit!'

All three options had appeared, in the order she'd named them, a pair of heavily frilled things in pink nylon so big they seemed to be designed to go over a nappy but now under ordinary white briefs decorated with love hearts and tiny red see-throughs with the split crotch gaping over the material beneath. They vanished, this time to Melody's relief. She threw her hands up in defeat.

'Okay, you little pervert, you can dress me up the way you like.'

A moment passed and she was in a tiny scarlet G-string, barely covering her sex at the front and leaving both cheeks of her bottom fully exposed behind.

'What, am I going pole-dancing? I thought you'd be into that sort of thing.'

Nothing else appeared.

'This had better not be it!'

Jeans shorts appeared, faded and cut so high that most of her bottom stuck out from around the badly frayed edges, while the front button was undone to allow a peep of the G-string beneath.

'Okay, so I'm playing the cute girl in that old show where they chase each other around in cars, but she doesn't usually go topless.'

She got a red, plaid shirt with the front tied off in a knot to leave not just her cleavage showing but most of her breasts. There was no bra underneath, which left her nipples barely covered and as blatantly erect as ever.

'Okay, so I'm a hillbilly, but I am not going barefoot.'

Cowboy boots appeared on her feet, white, in tooled leather.

'I've seen worse.'

Melody waited, wondering if she'd bee given a hat, or perhaps a denim jacket. Neither appeared and a moment later the text boxes vanished.

'I just hope it's warm.'

She was sure it would be, as one thing that had never varied was the temperature, which had stayed ideal from the first, indoors and out, day and night. Now was no exception, although there was a freshness to the air coming in at the window that had nothing to do with temperature. Melody decided to go outdoors, hesitated as she wondered if the decision was her own or some subtle compulsion, then went anyway.

The view from the front of the house was much the same as at the back, but rather prettier. A lawn had appeared where the road had been, sloping down to a broad meadow where the hospital had stood. The woods began on the far bank of a fair-sized river and rose unbroken to the tops of rounded hills, with mountains beyond. A path led alongside the river and there seemed to be other tracks among the trees, but her house was the only building in the whole vast landscape, unless the distant wisp of smoke she had seen before marked another dwelling.

After Metrocity everything seemed strangely quiet and still, with no sound but the rustle of wind in the trees and the occasional bird call. Only after she had stood still for perhaps five minutes did she become aware of faint music, one of her own songs, but raucous and mixed in with other noises, as if it was being played at a noisy fairground. It seemed to be coming from the far side of a wooded ridge, and she could see a path among the trees. The plume of smoke was also in that direction.

Her instinct was to see what was going on, but she hesitated. She'd been used to Metrocity, and had come to understand the way things worked, if not to fully accept them, but she was clearly somewhere new, perhaps somewhere in which Simon Weissinger's rules didn't apply. Even if they did it seemed likely that she'd be set up for a spanking, perhaps worse, and she had always had a peculiar horror of fairs.

They always seemed to be filled with the worst sort of people; coarse women and men whose main aim in life was to part her from either her money or her clothes, preferably both. If the landscape was anything to go by, the one nearby was likely to be pretty rustic too, which probably implied the sort of earthy, boisterous sense of humour which involved girls being dunked or put in stocks to have cream pies and wet sponges thrown at them.

Even if she avoided that there were bound to be spankings, if not for discipline then merely for the amusement of the yokels. Given the way she was dressed, she wondered if they'd bother to take her shorts down, as once she was bent over just about everything would be showing anyway, and there would certainly be no protection for her cheeks. Then again, it was inevitable, because if there was one basic rule to spanking it seemed to be that no girl was ever allowed to keep her dignity. Bare bottom was the rule. The thought gave her an all too familiar tingle of apprehension and desire, but she shook her head.

'I'm just being silly.'

Her words were swallowed up in the vastness, provoking an immediate desire for human company. She told herself that she was probably in one of the places Jane had mentioned, where the focus was on something other than smutty, kinky sex. Maybe the noises she could here came from the sort of jolly, old-fashioned fair she had read about in books, and they were playing her music after all, which meant they might even know who she was. Better still, Jane might be there.

With that thought she set off, walking down to the meadow and following the river to where the trees closed in around the track. The countryside had always been alien to her, a strange, disorderly place where nothing ever seemed to be quick or convenient, which made her cautious. She walked slowly, taking in everything around her and alert for anything that might prove threatening but enjoying the beauty and solitude despite herself.

The wood was also less wild that she had been imagining. Where she had expected tangled undergrowth between the trees there was only grass set with wildflowers and the occasional bush. The path was even less unruly, a ribbon of soft, green grass that wound between the trees, with no ruts, muddy places, brambles or any of the other hindrances she might have expected. Everything, she reflected, seemed to have been designed for her convenience, which meant it probably had been.

Her confidence grew as she walked on, increasingly sure that the idyllic landscape wouldn't contain dangerous animals and daring to hoping that it might not contain slap-happy or cunt-hungry humans either. She had seen neither, but the sound of the fair was growing gradually clearer, while she could smell wood smoke.

As she reached the ridge she found herself in a shallow bowl of land, with the smoke plume rising from among the trees at no great distance. She paused to do up her jeans shorts, then approached cautiously, keeping behind the bigger trees when possible, and quickly reached a clearing. In the middle was a cottage, old, wooden and looking as if it had been designed by a rather sentimental cartoonist rather than an architect. In front of the cottage was a huge iron brazier from which the smoke drifted lazily upwards, while beside that was a pile of logs and a stump into which a large axe had been driven.

Melody frowned, not convinced by the apparent peace of the scene. Whoever owned the axe had obviously been using it to split logs, but it was still a dangerous weapon. That was unlikely to be a problem, at least to judge by her experiences in Metrocity, where not a single one of the people she'd met had been violent save when it came to dishing out corporal punishment, let alone actively murderous. More importantly, the stump was just the right height to sit on, which hinted at a session over the knee of some muscular woodcutter as he gave her discipline on some trumped up excuse or other. Yet if she was a in a new game there would always be the chance of escape, while she was eager to find out where she was and if possible what was happening.

At last she walked forward, doing her best to seem confident and determined to be on her best behaviour no what the provocation. As she the entered the clearing the woodcutter emerged from his cottage, a man every bit as tall and muscular as she had expected, in blue jeans and a checked shirt, cowboy boots and a red neckerchief. There was a sizeable bulge at his crotch, but his face expressed a bold, open simplicity and there was nothing but good humour in his voice as he spoke.

'Good morning, Miss Melody. Going to the fair?'

Melody stopped, astonished.

'Do you know me?'

He seemed as surprised by her response as she had been by his remark.

'Sure I know you. We've been neighbours these last sixteen years, ain't we?'

'Um … well, my house is just back there, yes, but …'

'Are you okay, Miss?'

'Yes, fine … just a bit disorientated, I suppose. So …'

She stopped. It seemed foolish to ask if he knew her again when he was so obviously convinced that he did, making her wonder if perhaps there was a Giga about who looked exactly like her. He had picked up the axe and began to split logs, talking as he worked.

'I dare say that's no surprise, what with it being hunt day an all. Gonna be quite some day, yes Ma'am! There'll be a hog roast, and Pa Mulligan's licker stall, and they've even hired a carousal, so I hear. And haven't we just got the day for it?'

'Um ... yes, I suppose so ... um ...'

She hesitated, wanting to ask if he had any intention of spanking her, or if it was likely to happen at the fair, but aware that if he didn't the question was going to sound ridiculous. He was grinning, but not in a lewd or threatening way, and he didn't seem to regard the way she was dressed as provocative, or even unusual, concentrating on his work rather than her body as he continued to talk.

'I'll be along myself, just as soon as I've got these logs stacked, and who knows, I might just get me a certain lil' cutie, so just you run along, and maybe I'll see you up on the hill.'

He gave her a knowing wink, possibly suggestive, but carried on with his work as Melody tried to frame a question that wouldn't make her look a fool.

'So, er ... what is happening, exactly? Is there anything I should know?'

He laughed.

'Sure, head for the lone pine on Bluejay Ridge and you'll find out all there is to know!'

'Will you be there?'

'Hell yeah! Whee doggie!'

His attitude had changed abruptly, as had the size and shape of the bulge in his jeans, which now hinted at a full erection almost as big as Veldt Panther's monstrous tool. Melody decided to make a tactical withdrawal.

'I'll er ... see you there then.'

She managed a nervous smile and withdrew. He stayed where he was, to her relief, leaning on his axe with his broad, homely face spread into a fatuous grin, his eyes following the motion of her bottom in her shorts until she had passed out of sight.

Melody congratulated herself on what she was fairly sure had been a narrow escape, although their conversation had raised more questions than it had answered. The best thing to do seemed to be to keep going in any case, and to hope that the fair might prove more informative, whatever risks it carried.

The land rose again beyond the cottage, to a second, lower ridge. The noises of the fair had grown louder, and Melody approached extremely cautiously, leaving the path for the wood and nipping from tree to tree. She felt foolish doing it, but knew she would feel a great deal more foolish upended over a spanker's knee with her shorts and G-string down while a couple of hundred rustics enjoyed the display of her bare bottom.

Her stomach had begun to flutter, and as she drew closer to the ridge she was conscious that the curious mixture of fear and desire she had begun to miss in Metrocity was back. She smiled for her own reaction, but that did nothing to make her less careful as she moved on. It might be a game, and the end result might be ecstasy, but that never reduced the pain and the shame which seemed to be an inevitable prelude.

The forest ended at the ridge, where a line of huge oaks and beeches gave way to a long, grassy slope. At the bottom was the river, and by it a cluster of brightly coloured tents, stalls, merry-go-rounds and more, with people moving between. The fair was scattered any old how across the meadow, but where the path ran down from the ridge two high poles supported a banner announcing the Redneck Creek County Jamboree, while beyond, where a narrow bridge crossed the river, another pair of poles supported another banner, on which somebody had painted two words – Virgin Hunt.

Melody had no doubt whatsoever that she was the Virgin. It was inevitable. Just as panties always came down for spanking, a BRAT was always the centre of attention. She was a BRAT and a virgin. Therefore if there was to be a virgin hunt, she would be the quarry.

Her first thought was to run back home as fast as her legs could carry her, but it only took a moment to realise that it would be the worse possible move. The woodcutter had known where she lived, which almost certainly meant that everybody else did, while some of the men in the crowd milling around below her did not look the sort to be troubled by a little thing like kicking her door down, nor by any moral scruples about what to do once they'd caught her.

The woodcutter had been pleasant enough, and most of those she could see were similar; big, sturdy countrymen, no doubt with an earthy, straightforward attitude to sex. She could imagine it all too easily: caught, her fears calmed with a few kindly words, her protests ignored as mere nervousness or modesty, her clothes pulled off, put on her back with her legs well spread, a cock stuck up her.

She now understood the woodcutter's conversation, and realised that he thought she had come along to the hunt of her own accord and was therefore willing to accept her fate. He even thought she had made an assignation with him, to meet at the lone pine for her to surrender herself with at least some dignity rather than risk being caught by anyone else. It made sense, from his point of view, and in a twisted way from hers, especially when she considered the likely alternatives.

If most of the men were at least good-looking, then a not insignificant proportion were anything but, and seemed to be suffering from too much inbreeding. Altogether too many were marred by receding chins, buck teeth or beetling brows, or in some cases, all three together. Quite a few were exaggeratedly tall and lanky with bushes of red hair and straggly beards, while others were short, squat and so hairy that their faces were little more than a pair of eyes staring out over red, lumpy noses. Others were small, as sharp-faced as weasels and probably no kinder, while a few were huge, great lumbering oafs with no more intelligence in their eyes than the average ape. It was as if every backwoods stereotype had been assembled for the jamboree, and given the circumstances, they probably had.

For one awful moment of weakness she considered doing it, giving up her precious gift to the woodcutter not because he was the right man, but because the alternative was worse. It was a compelling thought, and brought with it a sudden realisation of how much easier life would be if she wasn't constantly worrying about guarding her virginity. Once it was gone she wouldn't have to worry any more, and he was a fine man, after all, big and strong and kind, even if he did lack the urbane sophistication she had always considered essential.

The moment passed and her resolved stiffened. He was not the man, and that was that, and there was every chance that he might not be what he seemed. If he was a CAT, which seemed likely, the person behind him might be anybody, most likely some spotty teenager. He'd also had a huge cock, which was sure to hurt, and given the number of men involved, she was all too likely to get an audience for her deflowering, which had never been part of the plan.

She looked towards the distant mountains, wondering what her chances would be if she made a run for it. The answer was painfully obvious. They would be slim, when the locals no doubt knew every inch of the countryside for miles around, including all the places a girl might try to hide. Eventually she would be caught, and fucked.

There was only one thing for it, to go down to the fair and use her status as a BRAT to get out of the hunt. She would find whoever was in charge, explain the situation, and that would be that. It made perfect sense, in theory, but her legs would hardly obey her as she started down the slope, while the fluttering in her stomach had grown to a churning sensation and she could taste her own fear.

She was halfway down before she caught sight of a blonde head among the throng, one of many but surely Jane? As she drew closer she became sure. It was unmistakably Jane, although in place of her nurse's uniform she wore an outfit much like Melody's own, but fractionally more demure, as did all but the oldest of the women there. She was buying doughnuts at one of the stalls. Melody began to run, ignoring the greetings, whoops and claps as the men saw her and making straight for her friend.

'Jane! I am so glad to see you!'

'Melody! Come here, give me a hug!'

They embraced, kissing fiercely enough to draw more whoops and not a few dirty remarks from the crowd, but neither took any notice. Jane began to ask questions, but Melody cut through them.

'I need you to help me, Jane. I think I'm the virgin they're going to be hunting for, and … and I'm just not ready, not like this anyway! What are you doing here, though, and what is this place?'

Jane seemed surprised.

'We're playing Redneck Rampage, didn't you know? And you must be ready, surely, or … or what are you doing here?'

'I don't know! One minute I was in Metrocity and the next minute I'm here, with … with these sex maniacs. I mean, what kind of perverted lunatics would make girls give up their virginity like this!? Look, we have to tell them it's all a mistake, or something …'

'Calm down, Melody, calm down. If you want to stop it, you can, but I think you need to ask yourself if this isn't really what you want? Remember your subconscious desire for spanking? You accept that now, don't you?'

'No! Yes … sort of anyway, but this is different. I do not want to be hunted down and fucked by a bunch of perverted

… What did you call it, Redneck Rampage?'

'That's right. It's a great game. If you go down to the village you can get put in the pillory and just … just used, or there's Bare in the Woods, or Helter Skelter, or this, which is usually just called Cunt Hunt, but this is a special day, for you I suppose.'

Jane gave a delighted shiver as she finished, but Melody was staring in horror.

'Well it's not for me! I mean, okay, so I admit I get off on having my bottom smacked, but only because I can't help it, and what we do together, that's … that's special, but this is appalling. And anyway, what happened to you? I missed you so much, Jane!'

'My boyfriend found out about my virtual life. We broke up, and he smashed up my computer and all my games. I got a new Metrocity, just a couple of days ago, but you weren't there, because you're here, I suppose.'

Melody wasn't sure what Jane was saying made sense, but that was the least of her worries. She glanced around, to find two men looking at her and pointing. Both were tall and gangly with straggling red hair, buck teeth and beards, so alike they were almost certainly twins. Jane confirmed her suspicions.

'The Lafarge twins. Don't get caught by them. They have some very nasty habits.'

'I don't intend to get caught by anyone! Who's in charge around here anyway?'

'Boss Conklin, the guy on the stage. If you want something done in Redneck Creek, speak to Boss Conklin.'

Jane was pointing to a raised platform hung with red, white and blue bunting, on which a man in a white suit was addressing the crowd through a microphone, his voice booming out from loudspeakers to compete with the general hubbub of the fair. He was short and fat, with a round, red face and a ruff of crinkly white hair sticking out from beneath a white cowboy hat, none of which was very encouraging, but Melody was determined. She marched across to the stage, reaching it just as saw her.

'Well, if it isn't little Miss Melody herself! Come on up here with your Uncle Roscoe, honey child, and let the hounds get a good look at the fox. But say, fox is just about right, ain't it! Look at you, and it seems only yesterday your momma was changing your diapers!'

He had extended a hand to Melody, and seeing no better way to get onto the stage she accepted it, allowing herself to be pulled up beside him. She was sure she had never seen him in her entire life, let alone known him when she was a child, but he seemed convinced he knew her. He put an arm around her shoulders.

'Here she is, folks, the one and only Miss Melody Jay, my very own pretty little niece. Ain't she just gorgeous?'

There was a roar of approval from the crowd, who had begun to gather round. Before Melody could speak to Boss Conklin he called out again.

'Ain't she just got the most darling little titties you ever did see?'

Again the crowd roared their agreement.

'No she ain't, 'cause they ain't little, not by a country mile! How about a little show, honey child, just so the boys can see what they'll be getting?'

'No way! Look ...'

He just laughed and turned back to the microphone.

'Sorry, boys, looks like she ain't gonna put out 'cept for that special man. At least turn around, honey, so we can have a look see at that sassy little ass.'

Melody gave the quickest possible pirouette, then leant close to whisper into his ear, conscious of the microphone.

'Could we have a quiet word, do you think?'

Boss Conklin gave a dirty chuckle and spoke again, not to Melody, but directly into the microphone.

'Melody wants a quiet word. Now ain't that just the sweetest thing? Probably a touch of first-time nerves, huh boys! Sure, sweetness, you know you can talk to your Uncle Roscoe any time you like.'

His remark had been greeted with a roar of laughter, and every single person there was now converging on the stage. He flicked the microphone to off as he went on.

'What's the matter, honey child?'

'Um … I'm sorry, but I really can't go through with this. I'm just not ready, and frankly … well, it's not very nice, is it?'

He looked horrified.

'Aw, come on, honey, you can't back out, not now! Why, you signed the forms okay, and just last week you was keen as mustard!'

'Forms, what forms?'

'Your consent form. Why, I've got it right here.'

He held up a clipboard, which Melody was certain he hadn't had an instant before, to show her a document, stamped and sealed, witnessed by himself and signed by her. She was too taken aback to respond immediately, and he carried on.

'It's your right, honey child, I ain't denying that, but I am begging you, 'cause you know as well as I do that boss or no boss, some of them good old boys down there would tear me limb from limb if we was to call it off now.'

Melody threw a nervous glance to the crowd and was immediately forced to admit to herself that he was probably right.

'I see, but …'

'Look at Billy-Bob McCoy down there, for one. He's sworn he'll have you, on the floor in my bar, and that he'll kill any man who gets in his way. I believe him too.'

One glance at the man he was indicating and Melody had no doubt it was true. Billy-Bob McCoy was one of the vast, hulking primitives, with beetling black brows and unnaturally long arms, over two metres of brawn and fat packed into ill-fitting dungarees worn over bare flesh, with a bulge in the crotch that made the woodcutter's look tiny. He noticed her attention and his mouth split into a huge, gap-toothed grin.

'Catch yer on the ridge, sugar buns!'

Melody tried to force a smile but could only manage a terrified grimace. Billy-Bob seemed pleased though, nudging one of his companions before giving a whoop of delight and heading off for the nearest beer stall. Melody shook her head and turned back to the man who seemed to think he was her uncle.

'You have to understand, I can't, not with men like him!'

He gave a sympathetic nod.

'Can't altogether say I blame you there, honey child, but don't you worry your pretty little head. He ain't got the legs to catch you, nor a three-legged pig, not the way he's been drinking. I'm just saying that if you back out now, there'll be hell to pay. No, the one who pops your cherry, well, Ben Mahoney's offering three to one on Jed Nankins as favourite, and ...'

'They're taking bets!?'

'Sure, honey child. It wouldn't be no fun without a little flutter now, would it? So, like I was saying, Jed Nankins is favourite, but some reckon on Hank Sawyer, who's four to one. Then there's Billy-Joe McAllister, nine to two, and seven to one on the Reynolds twins, or ten to one if they shares you. Brother Seth is ten to one, and Saul McCoy is one hundred to eight, with twenty to one the field. But say, if you've made a deal you'd tell your uncle Roscoe, wouldn't you now? We'd split the winnings.'

Melody had been too appalled to speak as he calmly recited the odds on different men taking her virginity and could only manage a numb shake of her head in response to his question. He carried on.

'So you see how it is? You back out, and there's gonna be a riot, and hell, if you really don't want it, you know what you got to do.'

'What?'

'Just keep on running 'til sunset, that's what!'

'And then I'm free?'

'Sure honey child, same rules as usual.'

He laughed, and had turned on the microphone again before Melody could continue her objections, his voice once more booming out.

'She's feeling a bit shy, boys, an' wanted a word with her old uncle. Ain't that just the sweetest thing?'

The crowd responded with laughter and yells of approval. Most of them had beer bottles in their hands and many of their faces were already red with drink. It was all to easy to imagine their boozy cheerfulness giving way to anger if she refused to run, and the consequences. A lot of them were eating too; huge hamburgers dripping with mustard and ketchup, chilli dogs, wraps of bacon and beans, fried chicken. Most would be easy to outdistance, and none of them looked really fit. It was best to run.

'Okay, I'll do it.'

'That's my girl!'

As he spoke he gave her a resounding slap on her bottom, then went on.

'I always did love to smack that ass, and who wouldn't, huh boys? Okay, let's get serious. Now, as you all knows, this a handicap hunt, an' that means showing a bit of respect for the old folk by letting 'em go first. Then comes most of the rest of us, and last the whippersnappers. Judge Riley, over by the pen, he'll give you your numbers. That's about it, I reckon, so enjoy the jamboree, and remember, hunt starts at high noon.'

Melody had no watch, but glanced at the sun, which was already high up in the sky. She thought of running early, only for Boss Conklin's pudgy hand to close on her arm.

'Time we put you in the pig pen, I reckon.'

'The pig pen!?'

'Sure. Don't want any of the boys trying to get one in up that tight little girl hole early, do we?'

'No, definitely not, but … but I wanted to speak to my friend, Jane.'

'I'll send her over.'

He led her to the far side of the stage, where some steps led down to the grass. Nearby was a stall run by a man in a loud, yellow, check suit, a red bow tie and a bowler hat, obviously the bookie, as the sign said "Honest Ben Mahoney" and a large blackboard had names and odds chalked on it. Jed Nankins was still the favourite, and had gone down to two to one, while at the very bottom were the odds on her escape, at fifty to one. Her heart sank, but they had already reached a wooden stockade.

She was hustled inside and the door padlocked behind her, leaving her to look out through the chicken wire that stopped anybody from touching her but also prevented her escape. The door opened towards the narrow bridge she'd seen from the hill, with the big banner now close by, the words on it taunting her as she stood waiting, her senses flicking between numb shock and something close to panic.

The crowds had become a blur, the noise a throbbing ache in her head, while she had become acutely conscious of her sex and the tiny arc of skin that closed her off to men's cocks, which she couldn't normally feel except with an exploratory finger, but which now seemed both tight and swollen at the same time. It was hard to keep her hand from going between her legs in a pointless effort to shield herself, and to stop herself from running in circles around the pig pen, which was all too obviously what the little enclosure really was.

Jane appeared, to comfort Melody and to feed her water through the chicken wire, but her friend's words seemed distant and meaningless, while most of the water missed her mouth to run down her cleavage and over her breasts, leaving her shirt more revealing than ever. Yet it cleared her head enough to let her focus on her predicament and who she'd need to escape.

'Who's Jed Nankins?'

'Jed? Just over there, by the fried chicken stall.'

Melody followed Jane's gaze, to where a wiry youth with sandy yellow hair and huge, bony hands was laughing and joking with some friends. He wasn't eating or drinking, and looked as if he could run a marathon, but he was very definitely not the man she wanted to lose her virginity to. His face was long and horsey, and it was all too easy to imagine him grinning down at her with his body settled between her open thighs as his long, bony fingers fumbled at her shorts.

'Oh shit! How about Hank Sawyer, or Billy-Joe McAllister?'

'Hank's the guy drinking liquor at his grandpa's stall. Billy-Joe I don't see.'

Hank was better than Jed, a handsome young man with a look of arrogant self-confidence that immediately put Melody's back up, as if to him she would be just one more cut on a well notched bedpost. Her man had to be special, and once again she found herself considering the woodcutter's offer.

'Do you know a guy who lives in a cottage up on the ridge? He's a lumberjack or something.'

'Billy-Bob McCoy?'

Melody gave a violent shudder.

'No!'

'Then you must mean his cousin Saul McCoy. He's cute. Why, are you going to let him catch you?'

'Maybe, I'm not sure … I don't really want anyone to catch me.'

'Then you'd better run.'

Hunted

Melody ran.

Boss Conklin had opened the gate to the pig pen amid rolling drums and blaring car horns, leaving her a path between two rows of old men ready to give chase. Several of them managed to land smacks on her bottom before she reached the bridge, and their joyous whoops and calls to slow down followed her as she sped away up the path. They weren't going to be catching her in a hurry, but some of the younger ones would be hard to avoid, even if they were half drunk on beer and rough whiskey, while every single one of them presumably knew the woods. All she could hope to do was keep ahead of them long enough to elude pursuit, then hide.

She'd never run so fast in her life, her booted feet pushing the short turf back and the sound of the fair fading rapidly into the background. By the time the car horns sounded again she was halfway up the slope, but she knew it meant the old men were after her and forced herself forwards. They could still see her, and she knew it was pointless to enter the woods until she'd reached the ridge, but by then her legs were aching and her lungs felt as if they were about to burst.

Melody stopped, panting, to look back. The fair was far behind her, a cluster of toys on the broad green meadow. Men were coming up the path, but none at more than half the speed she'd run, yet as the car horns sounded yet again she had to force herself not to dash blindly into the woods.

Beyond the ridge she could see for miles, across a great forested bowl of land that led all the way to the distant mountains. One thing was obvious: however well the men knew the ground they might search all day and never find her, even if she wasn't very well hidden. She intended to be very well hidden indeed, and to have a back-up plan. Blue Ridge was obvious, a high col between two of the largest hills with a single pine tree growing from the exact middle. A tumble of huge, grey rocks to one side looked ideal for her hiding place, no doubt full of nooks and crannies but close enough to the pine for her to run for it and surrender herself to Saul McCoy if the worst came to the worst.

Below her the middle-aged men were starting up the slope, the fittest among them already ahead of the most decrepit or most drunken of the oldsters. She set off, their whoops of excitement quickly fading as she ran down the slope, determined to make the rocks before the first man reached the ridge. One glimpse of her red shirt and she'd be lost, tempting her to take it off, perhaps even use it to lay a false trail, but the idea of going topless as she was hunted made her feel so vulnerable that she changed her mind.

Getting to the rocks seemed to take for ever, and long before she'd reached them she realised that she'd badly misjudged the scale of the place. She reached the edge of the woods and looked back, to find men already on the ridge, and when the car horns sounded for thc fourth and final time panic began to bubble up in her throat. It took all her willpower not to run blindly into the open, and to focus on what seemed her only chance, to skirt the hill and come up again on the far side, even though it would mean running towards her pursuers.

Again she set off, stumbling over the grass, knowing they were getting nearer, which filled her head with awful images; of the bearded Pa Mulligan mounting her, his whiskey-sodden breath washing over her face as she wriggled beneath him, of the hatchet-faced Judge Riley forcing her to suck his cock hard before he put it up her, of her supposed uncle catching her and taking her from behind, using his hat to spank her bottom as he prepared to thrust himself up her virgin pussy.

At a yell from what seemed just metres behind her she tripped and went sprawling, face down on the turf, expecting rough hands to catch at her jeans at any instant. No man came, and she ran on, glancing over her shoulder again and again. Her resolve began to weaken as her strength went and the pain in her muscles grew, until she was telling herself how much easier it would be to give in, so simply strip off her own clothes and spread herself naked on the soft green grass, a prize for the first man who happened to stumble across her.

Only the screams and whoops of the pursuing rednecks kept her going, reminding her again and again of how they looked and what they were going to do to her. Soon she was praying, and babbling meaningless entreaties to the empty woods around her and the hillside above, her head full of images of erect cocks and her own burst hymen, with her on her back and her legs rolled high to show off the tuck of her bottom as her conqueror's balls slapped on her cheeks, spattering her skin with her virgin blood as it trickled down from her burst hole.

She screamed, the sound breaking from her throat unbidden, and dashed forward, running helter-skelter up the slope, no longer caring if she was seen or not, but unable to think of anything except flight. Only when utter exhaustion finally overcame her panic-stricken limbs did she realise she had gone far enough, and was sheltered from the woods. She could still hear her pursuers, and forced herself on as soon as she was able, sobbing and gasping in her desperation and yet with the need to give in growing stronger once more, until only by picturing the most vivid and humiliating pictures of her fate could she force herself to go on; being caught by several of them and made to choose, with the others using her mouth instead, or left tied on the ground like a spit-ready piglet while they played cards for who got to take her, or carried back to the fair over the shoulder of some hulking oaf, her hands tied behind her back and shorts pulled down to leave her virgin cunt on show, then fucked in public.

'No … they won't … not me, not Melody J!'

The rocks were all around her, triumph pushing aside her despair as she began to search for a crevice she could crawl into. The boulders were huge, far bigger than she'd realised, the smallest two to three times her height, and what had looked like inviting crevices were in fact gaping caves, open to view for anybody who walked past but barely deeper than they were wide. Again and again she thought she'd found somewhere suitable, only to be forced to admit it would never do, and all the while with their voices growing closer, loud with excitement and drink.

She began to panic again, wondering if they'd heard her scream or caught a glimpse of her red shirt as she fled through the woods. A lot of them seemed to be nearby, which might mean the faster, silent hunters were almost on her. The rattle of a stone dislodged by her own foot was too much. She scrambled down into a chink between the boulders, struggling to make herself as small as possible but knowing full well that anybody climbing the rocks above her could scarcely fail to see. A voice called out, just metres away.

'She's up here somewhere, bro. I can smell her cunt.'

Crude laughter answered the comment, from the same place, then another voice, identical to the first.

'Me too, bro. Time to get us some, I reckon, in right up to our balls.'

Melody immediately pictured the Reynolds twins, a pair of gangling young thugs who'd said they were going to share her. Another few paces and they'd have what they wanted, maybe making her adopt some unspeakably rude position so that they could penetrate her together, two cocks pushing in to tear her hymen and stretch her wide …

It would have to be Saul Mc Coy, if she could only get to him before the Reynolds twins caught her. She peered out from between the rocks, to where the lone pine rose not two hundred metres away. At first she could see nothing, before a movement caught her eye at the edge of the woods far below. A man emerged, bearded and heavy-set, a bottle of whiskey clutched in one big hand. Melody froze, not daring to move for fear of being seen. She could outrun him, but the

Reynolds boys would surely see her and they would be too fast. Yet the far slope of the hill beckoned, empty all the way down to where a tiny stream ran among dense ferns with woods beyond.

She almost ran, only for Jed Nankins to appear almost exactly where she'd been meaning to go. He was running, at a slow, easy lope, showing no signs of tiredness. Again one of the Reynolds boys called out, from beyond the very boulder she was hiding under, and at the same instant she realised that Saul McCoy was at the pine after all, leaning against the far side of the tree, one jean clad leg visible where he had raised it onto a boulder. Still she hesitated, but Jed Nankins had turned for her hiding place and the bearded man was coming up the slope. A moment more and she'd be cut off, but she was unable to make herself leave the sanctuary of the rocks. She wondered if she was under compulsion from her subconscious to give in to the Reynolds twins and a despairing sob broke from her lips, answered immediately.

'Hey, bro, did you hear that?'

'Yup, I heard. Cunt time!'

Melody burst from the rocks, finding her muscles at the shock of his crude words. She was in full view, both Jed Nankins and the bearded man immediately calling out and starting for her as fast as they could, while delighted cries from behind showed that the twins were on her tail. Yet the pine was close, surely close enough to reach before she was caught, and as she ran Saul McCoy seemed an angel of mercy for all that he would no doubt fuck her. As she neared the tree she screamed out his name.

'Saul, here! It's me!'

The booted leg moved as Melody hurled herself at the tree, with the thud of the Reynolds twins boots coming fast behind her. A body appeared, huge and male, and a face, not Saul McCoy, but his cousin Billy-Bob. Even as she realised her mistake she had slammed into the tree, and him, an instant before clutching fingers caught the back of her shirt.

‘I got her!’

She was jerked backwards, sprawling on the turf as the knot between her breasts gave way. Both fat globes spilt free and her hands went to cover them by instinct as the men surrounded her, the tall, lanky Reynolds boys and the vast bulk of Billy-Bob McCoy, quickly joined by Jed Nankins, who spoke first.

‘Hell, and I nearly had her!’

One of the Reynolds answered him.

‘Well, cousin Jed, you didn’t, but don’t you worry. You’ll get your turn.’

His brother was still holding Melody by her shirt, making it impossible for her to cover up, and her struggles and pleas were ignored as Billy-Bob McCoy spoke up.

‘You can all have your turn, when it comes, but first off, she’s mine.’

‘No she ain’t! I touched her first, didn’t I do so, Elvis.’

‘Sure did, Aaron.’

‘And you saw too, didn’t you, Jed?’

‘Well …’

Billy-Bob strode forward, planting one massive foot to either side of Melody’s prone body.

‘I touched her first. Leastways, she ran smack dab into me before you got her, and I say that counts for the same, but if you want to settle it the hard way, well …’

He trailed off, bunching one massive fist at the twins. Neither backed off, Aaron still keeping his grip on Melody’s shirt.

‘You’re a big man, Billy-Bob, but there’s two of us.’

‘I’d take you if you was four!’

Jed Nankins raised his hands in a calming gesture.

‘No call for fighting, boys. This is supposed to be a day for fun. What say we let her choose?’

There was an immediate babble of voices, Billy-Bob and both Reynolds boys asserting their rights, none of them taking any real notice of Melody. She jumped up, slipping her arms free of her shirt, to scamper away among the rocks bare breasted. All four gave chase, still yelling at each other as she sprinted for the woods, dodging to avoid the grip of the bearded man by an inch as he appeared as if from nowhere, slipping on a patch of mud and sprawling headlong among ferns and long grass. The men were on her in an instant, all five of them, standing above her in a ring as she lay with her chest heaving. Her thighs were pressed together and her hands over her nipples, but she was on the edge of giving in, her sex shamefully wet and ready for all her anguish. Jed Nankins was the first to recover his breath after the chase and drew in a deep sniff.

'Ain't she ripe, boys!? Just smell that cunt!'

The bearded man answered him.

'Yup, like happy hour in a Nawlins whorehouse. Who's first?'

The men began to argue again, but when the bearded man told them to shut up they went quiet.

'Rules is simple. First touch gets her cherry, an' seeing as how she ran plum into Billy-Bob, why, it's his cherry. Ain't that right?'

The Reynolds boys continued to grumble but went quiet when the older man spoke again.

'I'm right, an' y'all knows it, only Billy-Bob ain't never been the sort to do his friends out of a little fun, have you Billy-Bob?'

'That's right, Uncle Tom.'

'Sure is. There's plenty to go around, after all, ain't there, honey?'

Melody met his eyes and found she could barely manage a weary shake of her head. She was going to be fucked and there was nothing she could do, but even if it had to be Billy-Bob she wanted to make it as special as possible. She was ready anyway, wet and warm and easy, her resistance worn down, with no more than a lingering spark of defiance in her brain, more regret for her broken dreams than distaste for the actual act.

'Just one, please? And somewhere private.'

Billy-Bob clapped his hands together in glee.

'Looks like I've got me some virgin cunt, and it seems I'm special! Didn't I tell you so?'

Melody tried to rise, but one huge hand caught her by the seat of her jeans shorts. Thick, calloused fingers pushed in down the back, between the soft flesh of her bottom and the hem of her shorts, and deeper, spreading her cheeks to his knuckles and pulling the denim tight between her sex lips.

'Hey! Let go! What are you doing?'

She began to scrabble at the long grass as she was lifted by her shorts, but his grip was unbreakable. Her eyes popped and she blew out her breath, still struggling, but he carried her as easily as if she'd been a brace of rabbits instead of a full-grown woman. He started down the slope and the others fell into step, Melody still protesting as they entered the woods among tall pines.

'Let me up, you big pig! I said you could, didn't I? Come on, please, you're hurting!'

Her body had tipped forward, forcing her to fend off the ground with her hands to stop her breasts trailing in the carpet of pine needles while her legs were kicking wildly in the air, a sight that set the men laughing and once more filled her head with indignation.

'Where are we going!? Come on, this isn't fair! If you're going to have me, get it over with!'

Billy-Bob merely laughed and carried on, with Melody swinging in his grip like a sack of potatoes.

'Please! It's not fair!'

Finally he spoke to her.

'I ain't gonna fuck you here, sugar buns. I tell you what I'm gonna do. I'm gonna take you back to town and do you in your uncle Roscoe's bar, where everyone can see you get stripped down, an' see you get me nice an' hard in that little rosebud mouth, an' see you go down on your knees with your ass in the air, begging for Billy-Bob's cock, an' see you get it, an' see your cute little cherry go pop, that's what I'm going to do. Yes, sir, right in front of old Roscoe, and cousin Joe an' Aaron an' Elvis and Jed, and all my brothers, and Pa and Uncle Tom and all, so I can show 'em how you ought to take a virgin, good and hard, so she don't holler so much, and then when I'm done and I've shown 'em all the blood on my dick, why, I'll let you suck it off, and … and they can take turns with you from behind, and make you a spit roast … that's when one cock goes in that pretty little mouth of yours and one up your cunt, and … and …'

'No! You said in private! You did! Please, Billy-Bob, not in front of everybody, please? No, not that! Get me out of here!'

Arcadia

Melody squeaked in alarm as she was dumped face down on the forest floor, and again at the prickle of pine needles against her bare breasts. Her first thought was that he'd changed his mind and decided to have her then and there after all, but as she rolled over to defend her virginity she found herself looking up at towering pines and pale blue sky, but nothing else. Billy-Bob was gone.

She sat up, still cautious, her panic ebbing only slightly, but he had vanished completely, along with the others. Nor could she hear the drunken whoops of the remaining rednecks, nor the music of the fair. She was shaking badly, her heart hammering and her skin wet with sweat from her experience and her exertions, but very gradually she began to calm down. No human sound disturbed her, only the faint rustle of the breeze and the tinkle of water in the valley below.

At length she got up and brushed herself down. The button of her shorts had popped when Billy-Bob had lifted her by her waistband and it was nowhere to be found. Being topless made her feel exposed and reminded her of her still strong need for sex, so she turned up the slope in the hope of retrieving her shirt from where she had left it beside the pine on the ridge, only to discover that there was no pine and no ridge.

The woods ended more or less where they had before, but instead of coming out on to the rocky slope, she was in a meadow. Hills rose to either side, but they were not the hills of Redneck Creek, while the air was also different, fresher still and without the hint of wood smoke she'd barely realised was there. Obviously she was in some new environment.

It didn't seem threatening, but then nor had Redneck Creek or Metrocity, until she met the inhabitants, nearly all of who seemed determined to get her out of her knickers for one purpose or another. Wherever she now was, it seemed sensible to assume that the same would be true, a thought that filled her with apprehension but also anticipation. She shook her head, trying to rid herself of her sexual feelings, but they wouldn't go away, while there was no denying that while her relief was very real she also felt cheated.

Melody sat down on the trunk of a fallen pine, trying to make sense of what had happened. Even while she'd been fleeing in panic-stricken fear that her virginity would be taken there had been an underlying need for it to happen, not in the sense of wanting it to, but in that it was somehow necessary. Her pride rebelled at the thought, and yet she knew that all she had really needed was an excuse to surrender herself, while it was impossible to deny the responses of her body. She was still wet, her skin warm and sensitive, the urge to let her thighs come wide or to stick her bottom up still strong. There was also her sense of disappointment, and anger at Billy-Bob for pushing her too far by threatening to do her in public. That, she felt sure, was what had made the difference.

'Bastard! Oh well, his loss … he could have had me.'

She had spoken aloud, her voice breaking the silence to make the truth of what she'd said curiously potent. Her temper flared, her sense of regret welling up to become her dominant emotion and she was shouting at the empty forest.

'You could have had me, you stupid, redneck bastard, you could have fucked me! Do you hear that, you fucktard, you could have had me, Melody J!'

Her voice was swallowed by the vastness around her and she went quiet, her lower lip trembling as she struggled to hold back sudden, hot tears. They came anyway, rolling down her cheeks to splash on her naked breasts as she screamed out her frustration to the empty woods. She knew she was out of control, and expected her volition to switch off at any moment, but her emotions only grew hotter, until she had kicked her boots off and pushed down her shorts and the G-String beneath, stepping out of them to stand naked, her arms raised and her feet braced apart.

'Come and get me then! Come on, all you big, dirty men, here I am, naked and ready for you. This is what you want, isn't it? Come on!'

Not so much as a bird call answered her tirade. She sat down again, now bare bottom on the carpet of pine needles with her back to the tree trunk, her thighs open as she made one last effort to hold back from what she needed, only to give in.

'Oh, what the hell!'

She closed her eyes, her hands went to her breasts and sex, and she was masturbating. It was all too easy to let the dirty images rise up in her mind, first how it would have been if Saul McCoy had really caught her, taken on her back with the Reynolds twins and Jed Nankins as witnesses to her being deflowered. The idea was shocking, very far from her lifelong desire to be wanted while all the while keeping her most intimate moments for one man alone, but also compelling.

She pushed her shame away, telling herself that any chance of keeping herself mysterious had gone the first time she stripped on stage, and that she had been very rude indeed since. Yet she was still virgin, and as her fingers began to explore the tight arc of flesh at the mouth of her sex her fantasies were growing rapidly stronger.

It was still Saul on top of her, but with the others waiting their turns, big cocks sticking out of their jeans or dungarees as they got themselves erect. She'd have been rolled right up, the way she'd imagined herself as she fled the hunters, her legs trapped beneath Saul's body, her pussy spread for all to see, her hymen on plain show as Saul's fat cock prodded at her sex, found its target, and pushed.

Melody screamed as she imagined her hymen tearing to the head of the big redneck's cock, and the rhythm of her fingers on her clitoris had grown frantic as she began to come. She thought of how she'd look, with her bottom spread to the men's erections and her virgin blood trickling down to pool in her anus, her pussy a straining pink ring on the thick pole of male flesh inside, her skin pulling in and out as she was fucked.

Her orgasm held for an extraordinarily long time, allowing her to picture the moment again and again, and with ever more dirty details; the twins getting their cocks erect in her mouth and hands, Saul denying the others her pussy but letting them take turns up her bottom, sucking her virgin blood and his come off his cock afterwards, just as Billy-Bob had threatened to make her.

The last detail broke her orgasm and brought her shame rushing back. She stopped, allowing her body to slump slowly to one side, where she stayed, barely noticing the prickle of pine needles. Her thumb went to her mouth and she began to suck on it, wishing she was in Jane's arms with a nipple in her mouth, suckling for comfort after having her virginity taken, which was something she now felt she should not have escaped.

When she finally got up it was because the air had started to chill. She retrieved her G-String and shorts, pulling them on quickly, then her boots, and all the while wishing she was back in her house. Only when she was dressed did she realise that it was the first time she'd felt the cold since she had become virtual, and that just as Redneck Creek had seemed more real than Metrocity and Metrocity far more real than the first version of her house, so her current environment was more real still.

'Great, just when I'm half-naked. I don't suppose I can even play Dress Up?'

No text boxes appeared and there was little hope in her voice as she spoke again.

'Jeans: Black. Thick socks. Hiking boots.'

All three items appeared, although she had once again forgotten to strip first and so still had her shorts and the G-string on, although her cowboy boots had vanished to be replaced by stout, yellow leather hiking boots. She shook her head.

'Who knows … Jeans off. Shorts off. Knickers off. Plain white panties. A sensible bra. Baggy black jeans. Red jumper.'

She was dressed, her new clothes warm and comfortable, while the dress up session had also left her skin feeling fresh and clean. Her hair was also free of twigs and leaves, and brushed.

'That's good. I'm starving.'

The food at the fair had smelt good, for all that eating had been the last thing on her mind.

'Southern fried chicken? Jambalaya?'

Both appeared, served on plates with a knife and fork to either side and red paper napkins, all balanced on a flat section of the tree trunk. Melody sat down to eat, polishing off both dishes before she was full. Another request and there was a large, cool beer in her hand. The label showed the Weissinger Corporation logo, which was surprisingly reassuring. Full, and warm, seemingly able to get whatever she wanted just by asking, Melody began to feel moderately confident, but there was still the question of finding her house, or any house, and if the latter then what the inhabitants would be like.

'More perverts, I expect.'

She began to climb the nearest hill, hoping that the view from the top would include her house, or at very least a road. As she went, she talked to herself, now conscious of a creeping sense of loneliness. Halfway up she stopped.

'Some people maybe? Three girls. Friendly, with no nasty habits … well, not too nasty.'

Nothing happened.

'Bother. Um … Jane? Okay … my uncle Roscoe? Veldt Panther? Mr Hawker? Saul McCoy? Anybody!?'

There was only the silent hillside.

'Um … a fire extinguisher.'

A large, red canister appeared, marked with the same logo and instructions on use.

'Great! Okay, okay … a man? Some hulking pervert with a monster cock and a thing about virgins?'

A thrill of fear ran through her at her own words, but no man appeared. She carried on, climbing to the summit, which was bare and rocky, allowing her to look out in every direction. As she'd begun to fear, the entire, vast landscape was completely empty, beautiful but vacant. The sole evidence of human existence, of even of animal life, was herself and the red dot of the abandoned fire extinguisher.

She was safe; nobody to spank her, nobody to chase her and catch her and fuck her, but nobody to talk to either, to kiss or to hold. Her hands went to her hips as she looked out over the scenery.

'Now what? Can I speak to somebody please, anybody?'

Below her there was a man walking up the hill. He looked refreshingly normal if a little severe, in a black suit with a black tie, while he wore his hair in a conservative cut and carried a black clipboard. When he reached the fire extinguisher it vanished.

Melody had decided not to run, but grew increasingly nervous as he approached, even when he gave her a friendly, casual salute. As he drew close he took a pen from his top pocket, then spoke.

'Some view, huh?'

There was nothing remotely threatening in his voice and Melody relaxed a little.

'Yes. Um …'

'Are you Melody J, the pop star?'

'Yes, that's right.'

'Born April the twelfth, 2011, and now a BRAT?'

'That's me.'

'Pleased to meet you. I'm Joseph Rosenthal of the Weissinger Corporation.'

Rosenthal

It took a moment before Melody realised the full implications of what the man had said.

'You mean you're one of the guys who runs this place?'

'Yes, I am.'

He seemed to be enjoying himself, stretching and drawing in a deep breath of the fresh air as Melody tried to arrange the thousand and one questions she wanted to ask.

'So, er … where are we?'

'Arcadia. Didn't you know? You transferred out of Redneck Rampage. The good old boys got a bit much for you, I suppose?'

'Um … something like that.'

He gave a light chuckle and made a tick on his clipboard.

'Each BRAT has their own private Arcadia, as a place to rest. Now, you were in Metrocity before you decided to visit Redneck Creek, I believe. Was everything to your satisfaction?'

He sounded as if he were a waiter asking if her steak was properly cooked and the dam of Melody's words finally broke.

'To my satisfaction!? I got … I got molested, spanked … dressed up in every tarty outfit you can imagine, compelled to strip on stage, spanked … seduced by some weird teddy bear thing, made to toss a load of strange men off, spanked … made to parade myself with my bum on show, tricked into lesbian sex, caned in front of a load of perverts, spanked, and spanked and spanked and … mostly spanked, and you want to know if everything was to my satisfaction!?'

He seemed taken aback.

'Yes.'

'Well, I want you to know, Mr Rosenthal, that I am not used to being treated …'

'But you have an Orgasm Rating of nearly five.'

'A what?'

‘An Orgasm Rating, the average number of times you reached orgasm within each subjective period of twenty-four hours. We use it as a measure of contentment, and frankly, two to three is pretty high.’

Melody made a rapid shift of mental gear.

‘You know how many times I came!? You were watching me!?’

‘Not personally, no, but naturally these things are recorded. After all, we have to keep a close eye on our clients’ welfare.’

‘My welfare! I got molested, spanked … and as for Redneck Rampage, is that your idea of looking after my welfare, having me hunted down and fucked by a load of sex crazed hillbillies!?’

He shrugged, his voice defensive as he carried on.

‘You chose to transfer, Miss J, and you presumably read your manual first?’

‘Manual, what manual? One minute I was in Metrocity, the next I was here … or there … whatever.’

He gave a sigh and a shake of his head.

‘Your Games Manual, Miss J. Always read the manual.’

‘I don’t have one!’

‘No? Are you sure? It’s a big, yellow book with the company logo on the cover. You can’t miss it.’

‘I’ve never seen anything of the sort!’

‘Tut, tut, somebody’s going to be in trouble, but fortunately not me.’

He made another mark on his clipboard, turned the page and scribbled a few lines before speaking again.

‘Metrocity then. Would you say you were highly satisfied, satisfied, neutral, dissatisfied or highly dissatisfied?’

‘Highly dissatisfied!’

‘Despite your near record breaking Orgasm Rating?’

‘Yes! Nobody asked me if I wanted all those spankings, and I know about my subconscious desires and all that, but …’

'It is all in the Manual, Miss J, but then … no manual. That seems to be the root of the problem.'

'The root of the problem is the way I've been treated, as if … as if I was some sort of sex toy!'

'But you are.'

'What!? How dare …'

Only the discipline instilled into her by numerous trips across other people's knees prevented her from smacking him across the face, but she held herself back and went on.

'… I mean, yes, I suppose I am, but why? I mean, everybody seems to want a piece of me.'

'Well, yes. After all, that's what pays the bills.'

'What bills? I get money for my performances, don't I? And for my nursing work. There's plenty in my account.'

'Metrocity credits, yes. I mean the bill for your recording, and the trouble is, when people think of Melody J they think sex.'

'I'd hope they'd think music.'

'That too, I'm sure, but it's your sexy image that's endured.'

'I had five number ones!'

'Did you? I doubt one person in ten thousand could remember that now, but anybody who knows anything about late twenties pop remembers the way you used to dance, and those outfits!'

He blew his breath out and shook his head, leaving Melody feeling both flattered and embarrassed, but mostly annoyed.

'That was just Peter, my manager, the outfits anyway. He seemed to think I was just some talentless little tart he'd picked for her looks. I used to write my own songs, and not everybody can dance like that!'

'That's for sure.'

'Anyway, how do you mean the bill for my recording. That was settled.'

He turned up the pages on his clipboard, frowning as he

read before speaking again.

'Ah, no. I'm afraid not. This manager of yours, would that be Peter Lunt?'

'Yes. What's the bastard done?'

'Rather a lot, I'm afraid. You were one of the earliest recordings, I believe, when the technology was still new and expensive, very expensive.'

'I don't know. He handled that sort of thing.'

'Did he now? That might explain rather a lot. As far as I can see, he appears to have reneged on the payment, of … let me see … two million pounds sterling, and also taken out an insurance policy to the value of six million pounds sterling, all of which he kept, along with your earnings …'

'The utter bastard! I knew he was behind all this!'

'That's not entirely true. He simply absconded with your funds and went to live in Paraguay, where he married a Conchita Velasquez. She managed to divert most of the money to herself, then divorced him …'

'Good for her.'

'Not entirely, because the result was that your money became irretrievably lost, so that your recording was stored rather than re-embedded into a clone. The charges were also unpaid, until Simon Weissinger purchased your recording, for a very considerable sum. He was a fan of yours, apparently, and you were instrumental in the research that eventually led to the creation of his virtual worlds, including Metrocity.'

'Does he like pink?'

'Pink?'

'Yes, pink. My house was pink. Everything was pink pretty much, except all the kinky costumes he put me in, the little pervert!'

Joseph Rosenthal cleared his throat.

'I'm er … not privy to that information, but er … never mind, and frankly, as you owe him your continued existence I feel that you should do your best to overlook certain er …

personal peculiarities on his part.'

'Like being a dirty little smut merchant pervert?'

'He prefers to be called an eroticist.'

'He's a pervert, a sex freak.'

'Considering the enormous popularity of his games, I think that at the very least you should grant that he's normal. Either that or the majority of the population are perverts, but we can discuss erotic philosophy another time. Once the system was up and running you were introduced to Metrocity. Since then, you appear to have been thoroughly enjoying yourself, according to our records anyway. You feel otherwise?'

'Yes I do! It's … it's just that I … I masturbate a lot.'

She had gone red and her voice had sunk to a whisper as she made her admission, but he took no notice.

'So I see, but presumably if you didn't find Metrocity sexually stimulating you wouldn't have masturbated so often, while your fantasies were, it must be said, fully in keeping with what you'd been up to.'

'My fantasies? You mean you read my fantasies!?'

'Melody J fantasies are among our most popular, particularly when you masturbate anally …'

Melody's volition had gone off, the hit of shame at the thought of people sharing her rudest and most intimate moments too much for her to cope with. Rosenthal waited patiently until her full senses returned, switching off and on several times before she settled down to a state of red-faced embarrassment.

'I … I knew people were looking in, but …'

She gave a powerful shudder, thinking of all the times she'd played with herself in the warm darkness of her room, naked and open to her fingers, to the various implements she liked to slide up her bottom, to Teddy's cock. He carried on.

'Some are looking in, yes, but the majority simply buy a set of pre-made recordings and enjoy them in their own virtual space. I think "Melody Masturbates" is up to volume seventeen.'

'So … so that's why everybody in Metrocity treats me like a slut, or spanks me?'

'In part, yes. It's quite expensive to be a CAT, and a lot of people don't like to get that involved, because naturally their avatars are on display just as you are yourself. The great majority simply log on as ordinary members and watch or buy your recordings.'

'And when did I get asked if all these sickos could get off on me!?'

'We needed to pay off your debts.'

'Why couldn't I just perform, and I don't mean with a striptease thrown in?'

'Our analysis of your recording shows that you prefer sex, so I fear your concerns have very little to do with us, and are more a question of coming to terms with your submissive sexuality.'

'Submissive? I'm not submissive, not me, not Melody J!'

'Ah, now there you're making a classic error in confusing being submissive in general terms, which you're certainly not, and having a submissive sexuality, which you do. Remember, I've seen your recording. Nevertheless, you now have the manual, so you may do as you please. Here we are.'

He produced a large, yellow book from nowhere, passing it to Melody with a happy smile as he went on.

'Once your debts are cleared and you've built up sufficient credit you'll be able to have your recording transferred to a clone.'

'A new body?'

'Exactly.'

'And I'll be me again.'

'You are you. You were never anybody else. In fact, I would argue that you are more you than you were before. In any case, I strongly suggest that you enjoy yourself, and try your best to accept your sexuality. You could nip back to the Virgin Hunt, for instance, and let the Rednecks finish you off.'

A shudder passed through Melody's body and she shook her head.

'No? Well, there are plenty of other options, and you can stay here as long as you like. And that, I think, concludes our business, at least for the time being. Naturally you can consult me whenever you wish.'

'How do I get in touch?'

'It's all in the manual.'

'And how do I get out of here?'

'It's in the manual. Now I really must …'

'Hang on! You can't just go! I mean, I need to know …'

'I suspect that what you really need is a little time on your own, with the manual. Besides, I have other appointments.'

'Yes, but …'

He vanished, leaving Melody seated alone on the hill top. Her mind was full of questions, and of strong emotions, but before long she had opened the cover of the manual and begun to read. She stayed as she was for a long while, turning page after page as the sun sank slowly towards the distant mountains. When the light at last began to fade she turned to the index, and after a minute of intense study spoke a few quiet words. The sun shifted from west to east, not moving back across the sky, but instantaneously.

Melody stared in wonder for a moment, then went back to her reading. An hour later she closed the book and began to brood, her eyes filmed with tears as she stared out across the valley, her thoughts moving back and forth. At last she rose to her feet, to climb onto the highest rock of the summit, opening the book once more, as if about to deliver a sermon to the empty hills.

'Dress Up.'

She was nude.

'Red G-string.'

It appeared, a strange contrast to the sylvan beauty all around her. She immediately felt dirty, but bit back her shame.'

'White jeans shorts. Skin tight. Frayed.'

The new garment clung to her body like paint, following every contour of her bottom, her hips and the swell of her sex, the crotch tight between her lips, most of her cheeks showing behind. She undid the button and adjusted the zip, leaving a hint of her red panties on show.

'Red tartan shirt.'

It came done up, and she took a moment to adjust it, rolling up the sleeves and unbuttoning the front before tying a knot below her breasts, most of which were left showing, while her nipples stood out like small corks beneath the taut cotton.

'Socks. White leather cowgirl boots, knee-high.'

Both items appeared, encasing her lower legs and lifting her to tighten the muscles of her thighs and bottom.

'White cowgirl hat.'

She got it, a final touch to an outfit that made her look and feel exactly as she wanted to, sexually available. Her fingers were already trembling with nerves, but the thought of how her bottom would show as she bent to retrieve the manual sent a sharp, erotic thrill down her spine. Standing once more, she took a last look at the magnificent scenery and then spoke again, her voice defiant and loud.

'New Game. Redneck Rampage.'

Helter Skelter

Melody stood on top of the rock pile where she had tried to hide from the Reynolds twins, looking out across the slopes where she'd come so close to having her virginity taken. She felt more naked than before, and glanced down to find that her shorts and G-string were gone, leaving her bare behind so that if she bent even a little, anyone below her would get a full view of her sex lips peeping out from between her thighs. Her hands went to cover her sex and the tuck of her bottom by instinct, but there didn't seem to be anybody around to appreciate the view. Nor could she hear anybody, much less the raucous jabber of hunting rednecks. Puzzled, she consulted the manual, frowning over the pages until she found the right command.

'Identify Game.'

A text box appeared – Bare in the Woods.

'Oh … Jane mentioned that one, didn't she?'

She realised her mistake and was about to switch to Virgin Hunt, but hesitated. It felt rather nice to be bottomless; sexy, but also vulnerable in a way she was sure would make her surrender easier. An hour's walk would bring her to Saul McCoy's cottage, and he'd be sure to take her.

Her shaking was growing rapidly worse as she climbed down from the summit, every touch of the rock or so much as a blade of grass against her bare thighs or bottom cheeks forcing her to focus on her exposure, and her intentions. She still felt misgivings, and found herself secretly glad that something might happen before she got to Saul's cottage, because for all her need she felt unable to acknowledge him as the one. In ways, somebody she'd never met would be better, especially if he just took her, making her suck him hard and thrusting his cock into her virgin hole without even bothering to introduce himself.

The idea made her feel almost unbearably horny, making it easier to push down her apprehension as she started towards the woods at a fast walk, only to stop in her tracks, her mouth falling slowly open in horror. A bear had emerged from the trees below her, and it was not Teddy but a great, shaggy brown monster, at least half her height again and massive in proportion. It was wearing a collar and tie, also a hat, but what might have been comic details in a picture did nothing to reduce her fear as she began to back slowly away among the rocks and ferns.

It began to sniff the air and Melody had started to whimper as she realised it could smell her. Panic hit her and she turned to run, only to find another bear just a few metres along the slope. It was smaller, paler, wore a purple bow tie and an expression of amiable stupidity, but it was still a bear. Only one direction remained, back the way she had come, but even as she turned up slope two more beasts climbed onto the pile of rocks she had just vacated. They were also smaller, one dressed in a jumper, the other in a hat and coat, which was open at the front, displaying a large, pink erection.

'Oh no, not that! You are such a fucking pervert, Simon Weissinger, you really are.'

The bears had started to close in on her, all four standing on their hind legs and all four sporting erect cocks. Melody shook her head.

'Oh no you don't, not me, not Melody J, not like this!'

As she began to thumb through the manual the closest of the bears spoke up.

'Hey, pretty lady! How's about a nice fuck?'

Melody ignored him, at which the largest of the four spoke up.

'I don't like her manners. I really do not.'

Another answered him.

'Do you think she fucks for money?'

Melody's answer was instinctive.

'No I do not! Shit, why am I even talking to you!? Sorry, boys, got to go … What was the other one? What was the other one!? What was the … New Game: Helter Skelter.'

The bears vanished, leaving Melody standing alone on the slope. Her little white shorts were back, and the G-string beneath, exactly as she'd had them before. Otherwise, nothing seemed to have changed, but far off through the trees she could hear the sound of an axe. She set off, shaking badly but determined to go through with her plan. Her mouth was set in a nervous smile and her eyes were constantly flicking from side to side as she walked, alert for bears, the less appealing sort of redneck and anybody or anything else who might want to stick a cock up her but fall outside the scope of even her dirtiest fantasies.

She found it easy to follow the rhythmic thud of the axe, even when deep in the woods with huge trees rising on every side. It grew slowly louder, and worked on her imagination, so that every strike of metal into wood seemed to represent the thrust of a hard cock into her virgin sex. Several times she nearly lost her nerve, and by the time she drew close to the source of the noise she was moving forward with extreme caution.

It was just as well. Peering from behind a gigantic oak, she found herself looking across a clearing. On the far side a man was chopping wood, much as Saul McCoy had been, but there was no homely cottage and the man was very different in appearance. Well over six foot, he was heavily muscled and stripped to the waist, a sight that made Melody's sex tighten, but only briefly. A straggling beard of bright ginger hair framed his face and fringed a bald dome onto which he had pushed back a white plastic hockey mask to reveal a lumpy, irregular face and pale eyes that glittered and jumped, while the slit of his mouth worked in chronic and insane mirth as he smacked the axe down again and again with obvious glee. Beside the fallen tree from which he was cutting wood rested a chainsaw and a rifle, while a large hunting knife hung from his belt alongside two dead and bleeding rabbits.

Melody moved carefully back among the trees, retreating

until she was sure she could whisk herself away in time before opening the manual. A quick consultation of the index and she had found the game –

Redneck Rampage – Helter Skelter. One for the horror fans! Ever wondered how it would feel to be stalked through the woods by a psychopath? Ever wondered how it would feel to be caught? Now's your chance to find out! Deep in the woods around Redneck Creek live all sorts of crazies, and they like nothing better than a little fresh young ass. There's Sawblade Saggory, who'll chase you with his chainsaw; Vinton Vouls, who likes to keep his victims in an old cesspit; Pervis Peckerwood, who'll strip you and dress up in your clothes to fuck you; and last but not least, Cletus the Cuntboy, who'll gag you with your own panties and tie your arms around a tree to do you, or you might prefer a home grown maniac from your own subconscious, and who knows what he might get up to!

Options include …

Melody read on with increasing horror, through the introduction and on to the detailed commands, only to be drawn back to a sentence in the introduction -

… be rescued by the man of your dreams and let him take a hero's reward.

She nodded to herself as her finger moved down the page once more. As she had hoped, the "man of her dreams" would be a product of her own subconscious, something only available to BRATs. He would, by definition, be perfect; handsome, strong, a man among men, yet courteous and respectful to her. Admittedly all her subconscious had so far managed to produce so far was an array of sex maniacs, perverts and disciplinarians, but that had been in Metrocity and the manual was quite clear that he would be the man of her dreams, also that he would understand her need to surrender without having to be coaxed, which was exactly the way she wanted it. Again she nodded to herself, then spoke before she could have second thoughts.

'Option: Hero's Reward.'

Nothing happened, but she knew that somewhere in the woods around her was the man who would take her virginity, making her heart flutter as she moved on. It seemed to be tempting fate to head back towards the clearing where the man who was presumably Sawblade Saggory waited, so she struck off in another direction altogether. The sound of his axe had stopped anyway, which was not altogether reassuring. She found herself constantly glancing over her shoulder, only to have a man jumped out at her from behind a tree.

He was tall and unnaturally thin, his lanky body clad in badly sewn rags, his face long and cadaverous with two tiny, brilliant eyes staring out from deep pits. Melody screamed and tried to run, but a spidery hand had already closed on her wrist, pulling her in with a horrible strength. In just seconds her arms had been pulled either side of a young tree and her wrists lashed together, the man making weird bubbling noises and chortling to himself as he worked, but speaking only when he had Melody helpless.

'I'm Cletus. They call me the Cuntboy. Want to know why?'

Melody could guess, but she was too far gone in shock and fear to do more than babble for mercy. He grew more active still, prancing around her in a high-kneed, capering dance and filling the woods with wild laughter, then stopping, to stand stock still, his bony hips pushed out through the opening in his ragged long coat.

'Do you want to see what Cletus has got for the pretty lady?'

All Melody could manage was an urgent shake of her head and she moved to the far side of the tree, desperate to keep as far away from him as possible for all that she knew it was futile. He spoke again, now with his fingers on the tab of the huge zip that closed off his tattered, dirty trousers.

'Say you do, and maybe Cletus will let you go …'

'Oh shit … yes, okay … show me.'

'… after he's had your cunt.'

'Oh God, no … not like this …'

He was laughing as he drew down his zip, to let free a dirty brown cock, as long and thin and ugly as he was himself, and already full erect.

'Ain't he a beauty?'

'Oh God! No … New … New Game …'

There was a crash from one side. Cletus jumped high, let loose a torrent of obscenities and fled, his huge feet kicking up the leaf mould as he disappeared among the trees. Melody sank down, gasping, as a man stepped out in front of her. He was very different; tall, well formed, his skin the same golden brown as her own, his face calm and strong and noble. She looked up with something close to adoration as he bent to unfasten her wrists.

'You alright, Miss?'

'Now you're here, yes. Thank you.'

'My pleasure, Miss. You had a lucky escape there.'

'I know. Thank you … thank you … thank you …'

She knew she was babbling, but she couldn't stop herself, her reaction too strong to be held back. He seemed to know what to do by instinct, lifting her as she collapsed into his arms and carrying her as if she had no weight at all. Her top had become disarranged in her struggles to break free, leaving one stiff nipple peeping out, but she made no effort to cover herself up. It felt right to be exposed in front of him, and ungrateful to deny him anything, even her virginity.

His house proved to be only a little way off among the trees, a neat, wood-built cottage behind a white picket fence. The door was open and he carried her inside, to the single large room, plain and masculine, where he laid her down on the bed. Melody's heart was fluttering, but there was no resistance in her at all, her strongest need to let her thighs come apart and accept him between them. Again he seemed to know, gentle but firm as he spoke.

'I'm Mark Steel, Miss. Better get you out of those clothes and into bed.'

'Melody J, or Jay maybe. Yes, I suppose you're right.'

Melody began to undress. He watched, not indifferent, but more paternal than lustful as she undid her top and let her breasts free, kicked off her boots and pushed her shorts and socks off her legs. Only when she was down to her panties and had pulled the bed covers back did he speak again.

'Those too, Miss.'

It was a command, completely assured. Melody's hands went straight to her panties, pushing them down and off to go nude in front of him. It felt right, not just to be naked in his presence but to be naked while he was fully dressed. Before she could stop herself her thighs had come open, to show off her virgin sex in open surrender.

'I … I'd like to say thank you … properly.'

He nodded, cool and controlled, accepting her gift without needing to speak. His fingers went to his zip as he stepped forward, drawing it down to free a heavy, dark cock, thick and smooth and beautiful, also his balls. Melody took him in her mouth without hesitation, sucking eagerly for the thought that the perfect cock growing rapidly under her tongue would soon be in her pussy, her virginity surrendered.

Her hands went between her legs to get herself turned on, but it wasn't necessary. She was soaking, her sex wet and ready to accommodate him, her juice flowing so freely it had begun to run down between her cheeks and wet her anus. He was stiff too, his cock a rigid bar in her mouth as she stroked and squeezed at the heavy sack of his balls where they bulged from his open fly. She pulled back, looking up at the man who was about to receive her greatest gift with unashamed worship.

‘I’m yours.’

‘I know.’

As he climbed onto the bed Melody had spread her thighs as wide as they would go, deliberately making herself completely vulnerable. He took her by the hips, but instead of mounting her he turned her over into a kneeling position, her bottom high and her knees well parted. Melody sighed in pleasure as she was put into position, showing everything and glad she was, content to let him enjoy her in any way he pleased.

He was kneeling behind her, his magnificent cock rearing above her open, receptive sex. She felt him touch her as he took himself in hand, first his knuckles, then the round, firm cock head, rubbing in the wet of her pussy, and higher, pressing into the opening to her body, stretching out her hymen. Her mouth came wide in blissful expectation mingled with fear as she braced herself for penetration, only for his cock to slip higher still, rubbing in the shallow valley between her bottom cheeks and pushing at her anus.

‘Hey, no, not there! No, Mark! No, no … oh never mind …’

It was too late, the head of his cock was already in up her slippery bottom hole. The shaft quickly followed, pushed deep with a few firm thrusts that had Melody blowing out her cheeks and gasping for breath before his balls squashed to her empty sex. Her buggering began, the expression on her face flickering between resignation and ecstasy as the big cock worked in and out of her bottom hole.

With every push his balls slapped against her pussy, and as the breathless rhythm grew faster she realised she was going to come and that there was nothing she could do to stop it. Until then she’d been taking pleasure only in him and her own surrender, but as her excitement began to rise her control slipped. Soon she was wishing he’d spanked her first, a hard, bare bottom punishment for letting herself get caught by Cletus. Then it was worse, not merely across his knee with her bare bottom bouncing to the slaps, but done in the woods with the maniac peering out from behind a bush.

Mark had taken her by the hips, thrusting ever harder and deeper up her bottom as her orgasm rose and her fantasies grew dirtier still, imagining herself not merely spanked in front of the crazed pervert, but buggered, and as a final, self-inflicted humiliation made to take his hideous cock in her mouth, spit-roasted between the two men and left with come dribbling out at both ends. The awful image stayed in her mind as she rode her orgasm, panting out her ecstasy into the bedclothes with her still virgin hole in urgent contractions, also her anus, and as he grunted she realised that she was milking him up her bottom.

It was an exquisite thought, adding a final filthy touch to her ecstasy and bringing her to a second shuddering, screaming peak, but the moment he had stopped pumping inside her and the pleasure began to fade she was overwhelmed by shame and a sense of bitter frustration.

'Why … why didn't you take me … properly?'

'Oh, I wouldn't take your virginity, Miss. I've too much respect for you to do that.'

'But … but I thought … oh, never mind. You are such a pervert, Simon Weissinger, and so am I.'

'Beg pardon, Miss?'

'Never mind.'

Frustration

Melody stayed with Mark Steel for two days, hoping he would lose control and fuck her, but before long she was bored. For all his physical perfection and firm masculinity, he was simply too nice, too good. He did at least spank her, for going out into the woods on her own, and in a no-nonsense, paternal fashion with her shorts and panties pulled down across his lap in the woodshed at the back of his house. Unfortunately, while she was left with the juice running down the inside of her thighs and in urgent need of his cock he didn't seem to regard the punishment as erotic at all, but made her stand in the corner with her hands on her head and her red bottom on show for a full hour.

Twice more he buggered her, and once had her suck him off, but by the morning of the second day she had decided that the situation was hopeless. He might have been the man of her dreams, once, but her experiences had corrupted her, making her crave dirty, kinky sex, while the desire to have her virginity taken had grown to such an urgent need that she was having trouble holding herself back from running into the woods and hoping one of the psychopaths got her. Only two things held her back, worry for what else they might do to her and a nagging conviction that Mark would always turn up in the nick of time and spoil it.

At last she decided to switch game, feeling sorry for herself and her corrupted sexuality as she flicked through the pages of the manual. Mark had gone out to shoot their dinner, allowing her to concentrate. There was plenty of choice, with a huge range of games offering an astonishing selection of sexual scenarios, from simple, romantic liaisons to situations of extraordinary perversity. Most had options for conquest by some strong, authoritative man, and before long she had made her choice.

'Sorry, Mark. New Game: I Fought the Law. Option: Quick Capture.'

She was a on a moonlit rooftop, perhaps in Metrocity, perhaps elsewhere, but still in nothing but her plaid shirt and cowboy boots, the way she'd been wandering around Mark's house in the hope of enticing him to take her virginity.

'Shit! Um … Auto Dress Up On.'

Her dress changed, to a black cat suit that hugged her body like a second skin, with holes only for her eyes and mouth. She was nude underneath. Nearby was an attic window, temptingly open to the summer night. She eased it wide, thinking not of the loot the house might contain, but of the suave young detective who would be lying in wait for her, who would put her in cuffs and take advantage of her helplessness.

After the bright moonlight of the roof the inside of the house seemed absolutely black, and Melody eased herself down to the floor cautiously and in complete silence. As her feet touched floorboards the lights came on, startling her despite her knowledge of more or less what was going to happen. She froze, allowing the man who had been waiting to one side of the window to catch her easily, twisting her arms behind her back and quickly cuffing her as he spoke.

'What have we here then, a burglar, and a girl at that to judge by the feel of you.'

He had taken a grip on the back of her mask, which was pulled roughly down, and as Melody turned her head she found that she was looking up into the face of a tall, dark haired man in full police uniform with a sergeant's stripes on his sleeve. A badge gave his name – Stern – and she immediately thought of the brat spanker of Metrocity. Not that it mattered who he was, because she was helpless, while his voice had been cool and amused with not a hint of mercy. Already her choice seemed insane, and yet her body was responding for all the rapidly building emotions in her head.

'Let's have a look at you then.'

She was hustled into the middle of the room, an attic completely bare save for a plain wooden chair set close to one wall. Melody swallowed, already sure of its purpose and her bottom cheeks tightened in anticipation of a spanking. He had folded his arms across the breadth of his chest as he stood back, his mouth flickering into a cruel smile as he took her in.

'Well, well, very nice, and so young. This is your first offence, I suppose?'

Melody managed a weak nod and he went on.

'I guessed as much. No need to make this formal then, I don't think. In fact what a young girl like you really needs is a good old-fashioned spanking, which is exactly what I'm going to give you.'

She tried to answer, but all that escaped her lips was a whimper. He wasted no time, stepping forward to take a powerful grip on her elbow. Cuffed and helpless, Melody could do nothing to resist as she was frog-marched to the chair and placed across his lap in spanking position. She'd known it was going to happen, and she'd known she needed it before her fucking, but now that she was going to get it her stomach was fluttering and her muscles were twitching in apprehension as he laid one huge hand across the seat of her cat suit.

'Yes, a good old-fashioned spanking, and then …'

He didn't finish the sentence, but Melody knew what he meant and a sob escaped her lips at the thought, her bottom spanked pink before his cock was inserted between her rosy cheeks, only not up her bottom this time, but into her virgin sex. Not that he was in any hurry, fondling her cheeks through the taut material of her cat suit and applying only the occasional gentle slap to make her cheeks wobble. Suddenly her legs had been hauled wide, to show off the bulge of her pussy, every detail of her lips outlined in tight, wet, black cotton. A finger touched and he'd begun to trace the outline of her sex, setting her gasping and wriggling in helpless response. He gave a low chuckle.

'Horny little one, aren't you? But you needn't think

you're going to get away without a spanking.'

Melody shook her head, very sure she would be spanked, and hard. It said so in the manual. Again he began to caress her bottom, and to smack, only harder now, with firm, stinging slaps that made her yelp and kick her feet. She knew she'd soon be over the pain, her bottom hot and ready, but that did nothing to dilute it, nor her sense of humiliation as he spoke once more, his hand now resting across the meat of her cheeks.

'We'd better have this bare, I think, don't you?'

She gave a single, miserable nod, unable to deny the truth. He took a pinch of the seat of her cat suit, pulling it up and lifting her hips to make her bottom more prominent still. She felt him shift and twisted her head around to find that he had drawn a wicked looking knife from his belt. One cut and he had slit her cat suit, to leave her bottom bulging out through the ruined seat, a sight she knew would be as ridiculous as it was rude. He laughed to see and she felt a fresh flush of humiliation and arousal, knowing she was bare behind, and not just the flesh of her bottom, but her pussy too.

'And those great big titties too, don't you think? A shame not to have them out.'

Melody could only hang limp and helpless as the front of her cat suit was slit and her breasts were pulled out, groped, and then left dangling beneath her chest, plump and bare with her nipples as stiff and sensitive as ever. He went back to spanking her, now on the bare, and hard, to set her kicking and wriggling, her boobs jumping and her cheeks wobbling, her hair tossing and her feet drumming on the floor in her pain and embarrassment.

The state she was in set him laughing, a cruel sound that made her feelings stronger still, but her bottom had begun to warm and the sense of abject surrender she could only achieve after a good spanking was creeping up on her. When she began to stick her bottom up to the smacks he laughed all the louder, while his cock was now a hard lump, pressing to her flesh through what remained of her cat suit and his trousers.

When it stopped it was sudden, leaving Melody's bottom a blazing ball of heated flesh as he pulled her roughly to her feet and dropped her back over the chair. Melody gasped as the wind was knocked from her, but with her hands tight behind her back she had no choice but to give in to her fate, exactly the way she wanted it, to be taken helpless and bare by a man with the strength to give her what she needed.

She heard his zip rasp down, felt the hot rod of his cock against her equally hot bottom and braced herself, shaking but ready, her sex wet and juicy between her thighs, only to have it thrust at her mouth. He was already hard, but she took him in, eager both for the taste and feel of a cock in her mouth and the knowledge that she was being made to suck the man who was about to take her virginity. When he spoke his voice was as rough as gravel.

'Now I'm going to fuck you, you little tart.'

Melody stuck her bottom up and spread her thighs, in a state of utter surrender, as ready as she'd ever been, only for his cock to jerk, making her cheeks bulge as he came in her mouth. He cursed, but didn't stop, grabbing his shaft to toss himself off down her throat and pulling back only when he was finished, to leave Melody with a beard of sperm and saliva hanging from her chin and an agonising sense of frustration ringing in her head. Finally she found her voice.

'Not in my mouth, you idiot! You're supposed to fuck me!'

Sergeant Stern scratched his head.

'Sorry, love. That doesn't usually happen. I meant to fuck you.'

Melody made to answer him, but began to choke, coughing up spunk onto the floor until he helped her upright. With the cuffs unfastened she stretched her arms, furious, and also horny.

'You can lick me out then.'

'Hey, I'm the one who's in charge around here.'

'Oh yeah? Character: Sergeant Stern. Act: Oral Sex, Receptive.'

He got down without further complaint, cupping her hot bottom in his hands as he applied his tongue to her sex. At first Melody's anger was too strong to let her enjoy the sensation, but her natural responses quickly took over. She lay back, caressing her chest as she was licked and thinking of the way she'd been cut out of her clothes for her spanking, her pretty cat suit slit back and front to leave her with her bottom and tits out, humiliated and ready for punishment, and for fucking …

With the final thought she started to come, but there was as much regret as ecstasy in her sobs as she rode her orgasm with her nipples pinched tight in her fingers and her sex pushed into the face of the man who should have been pumping himself into her deflowered cunt at that very instant. Only at the very peak did her resolve to be taken break.

'Oh God! Yes … Act: Penetration. Now!'

Sergeant Stern continued to lick, and as Melody's need started to fade with her orgasm she glimpsed a text box from the corner of her eye, lit up with a single word – Override. She collapsed back, sobbing. The Sergeant got up, his tone of voice belying his words as he spoke again.

'I hope that will teach you a lesson.'

Melody blew out her breath.

'Not the lesson I wanted. Get me out of here.'

She was back in Arcadia, seated on a stump somewhere deep in the forest. The manual was by her side. Her bottom was still hot and she was still in the tattered remains of her cat suit, so she paused to make adjustments, going clean and fresh, then dressing herself in comfortable jeans and a baggy jumper. Consulting the index of commands, she read what she found out loud.

'Override – a command in hierarchy, allowing players to

negate the commands of lower level players. Hmm … that can't have been Sergeant Stern. He's a Giga. Maybe somebody was watching, Weissinger even? Fuck off, you pervert!'

Her last comment was screamed at the sky, but her words were lost among the trees and no response came. She sighed and began to turn the pages again.

'Okay, let's try again. Come on, somebody, I do so want a cock in my pussy … ho hum, let's see … oh yes, I'd love to get it from an army boy. Auto Dress Up On. New Game: Army Girls. Option: Punishment Parade.'

The forest vanished, replaced by a wide, perfectly flat expanse of grass with a group of single-story wooden huts some way in front of her. She was one of a line of girls, each stood rigid to attention and dressed in an identical uniform of polished black boots, knee-high khaki socks, shorts so tight they might have been painted onto her bottom and the bulge of her sex and so short that most of her cheeks were on show anyway, a tiny jacket, too small to cover her lower back or her tummy and held shut across her breasts by a single, straining button. A khaki forage cap sat on her head at a jaunty angle, while her hair was tied back in a luxurious pony-tail. Immediately in front of them was a man with sergeant's stripes on his sleeve, a man who might have been the older, rougher brother to Sergeant Stern. He was yelling at them.

'… and you know who I am, don't you? I'm Sergeant Rider. I'm the one who smacks your little tails when you've been naughty, aren't I? And what else do I do when you've been naughty, eh? Private Playgirl?'

A blonde girl two down from Melody stiffened in shock, making the button on her shirt pop and exposing two plump, pink breasts. She snatched for the sides of her shirt, only to snap back to attention at an inarticulate roar from the Sergeant, leaving her breasts bare as she answered him.

'You … you fuck us, Sergeant.'

He stepped close, admiring the girl's naked breasts for a moment before he replied, his voice now low and menacing.

'Yes, girls, that's what I do. I fuck you. I fuck whichever one I happen to fancy, sometimes two or three. Sometimes I put it up your bums, just for a little variety, but today I am going to fuck you. So who fancies eight inches of prime British beef in her cunt hole, eh?'

His voice had risen to a yell again as he finished, leaving Melody shaking as badly as any of her companions, while the pretty redhead standing next to her had wet herself, the pee spreading out in a dark stain over the seat of her shorts and making a harp shape over her sex, also trickling down the insides of her thighs to soil her socks and fill her boots. Sergeant Rider gave a snort of contempt at the sight and turned to bellow at the huts. A woman came running, her dress the same abbreviated uniform as the girls but with a single chevron on her arm. She was carrying two chairs. Sergeant Rider returned the newcomer's salute and once more spoke to the girls.

'Spankings first. Lance Corporal Hardyke here will take down your shorts and pants and you will come over my knee, then return to parade. Is that clear?'

Melody just managed to join in the immediate chorus, now shaking again and with her thighs pressed tight together for fear of disgracing herself in the same fashion as her neighbour, who was now standing in a pool of her own piddle, or worse. In front of her the Lance Corporal had set out the two chairs, well apart, before taking one while the Sergeant occupied the other.

The spankings were administered with military precision, each girl marching smartly forward to have her shorts and plain white panties pulled down by Lance Corporal Hardyke, to leave her bare-bottomed as she was placed across Sergeant Rider's knee. There were twelve girls to get through, but the Sergeant made a thorough job of the pretty black girl who'd been first in line, spanking her hard with her hair flying and her legs kicking in her panties as she had her bottom warmed. Her struggles made her button pop, leaving two fat black boobs jiggling under her chest as she was finished off and sent back into line to stand at attention once more. Her shorts had come off in her struggles, leaving her with her panties in a tangle around her knees and her bare chest heaving to her sobs.

By then most of the girls had were bare-bottomed and ready, with no choice but to stand in line and watch as their companions were turned over the Sergeant's knee and spanked. Melody was near the end, so that once her shorts and knickers had been pulled down she was forced to wait until only she and one other girl remained. The redhead was given extra for wetting herself, then sent back to Lance Corporal Hardyke to have her panties removed and pushed into her mouth before being put back on parade.

By then Melody was over the Sergeant's knee, fighting the pain and wishing that spanking didn't have to hurt so much before she got horny enough to enjoy it as her bottom was smacked with the full force of his brawny arm. He did a good job of it though, leaving her hot and ready for his cock as she scampered back into line to watch the last girl polished off. With all twelve girls back once more on parade Sergeant Rider stood up once more, grinning unpleasantly as he inspected them, walking slowly along the line and then coming around behind.

At least half the girls had their breasts out, while all twelve pairs of bottom cheeks were coloured up, from rich pink to a glossy purple. Melody found hers twitching under his gaze, but didn't dare turned around, standing stock still, only to jump as he bellowed out a fresh order.

'On your knees! Faces in the dirt, arses up, feet touching, knees apart!'

All twelve girls hastened to get into the lewd position, making a line of now open bottoms, their pussies and bumholes on show behind, each and all of them available to

Sergeant Rider should he choose to insert his cock into one or more warm, moist holes. He didn't, but left them in position as he walked back to where his assistant remained seated on her chair, motionless, her back straight, but with a worried look in her eyes as he unzipped and pulled out a large, heavily hooded penis.

'Lance Corporal Hardyke, suck me erect.'

The Lance Corporal didn't look too pleased at having to take a cock in her mouth, but she obeyed the order, even tickling his balls and tugging on his shaft as she worked her lips to push back his thick, leathery foreskin. Melody watched from the corner of her eye, scared, but deep in submission, at once hating the sadistic Sergeant and desperate to have him inside her. Yet he was plainly taking a lot of pleasure in his colleague's humiliation and took his time, only pulling out of her mouth when he was fully erect, his cock now a thick, vein-covered pole, rearing from his trousers above a pair of massive balls.

He took it in hand as he came behind the waiting girls, masturbating casually. Melody hung her head, knowing it would be her and yet still full of apprehension as he feasted his eyes on each upturned bottom in turn. When he finally stopped he was standing well to the side of her, behind the blonde girl who'd been the first to expose her breasts, his voice thick with lust and cruelty as she spoke.

'So who's it going to be then? There's no choice really, is there, because you're all sluts, except for one of you, and one of you is a virgin, isn't she? Well, Private Jay?'

Melody's answer was a mumble.

'Yes, Sergeant.'

'What was that? I did not hear you!'

The roar of his voice was so loud that she lost control, squirting out a little pee into her lowered knickers, but she forced herself to answer him.

'Yes, Sergeant.'

'Yes, Sergeant. That's right, you're a virgin, aren't you,

and a very silly little virgin too, to let herself end up on punishment parade, because you, Sergeant Jay, are about to have your cherry popped. How does that feel?'

Melody couldn't answer, unable to even begin to explain the tangle of desire and fear, need and horror in her mind, but she held her pose, her sex open to his cock as he came behind her, her hymen showing in the mouth of her hole, completely vulnerable. Again he spoke.

'That's right, my little virgin, you're about to have your cherry popped, and I'm going to get it on camera. Take a picture, Lance Corporal Hardyke, first of her cunt, then with my cock going in, and after, so we can all see she's lost it, and those pictures, Jay … those pictures are going up on the wall in the Sergeant's mess. How do you feel about …'

Lance Corporal Hardyke was still getting her camera ready, and Sergeant Rider had been masturbating as he spoke, only to break off with a grunt. Something hot and wet splashed over Melody's spanked skin, then again as he swore, and she realised he'd come all over her bottom.

'Not again!'

Melody ignored Sergeant Rider's furious commands as she produced her manual and opened it at random. Only when he began to belabour her with his swagger stick did she speak a single, irritable phrase, dismissing him from the game. She was so wet that she was dripping onto the ground as she knelt, frowning over the book until found what she wanted.

'New Game: Builder's Bum.'

She was on a wide, dusty road next to a construction site, dressed in a smart business suit over stockings and expensive silk panties, which, according to the manual, were due to be ripped off before half-a-dozen burly construction workers took turns with her, bending her across a section of concrete sewerage piping to be made into a spit-roast. Yet there was no sign of the men, who should have been working on the towering structure of iron girders and scaffolding that rose beyond a barrier of orangc painted wood.

Puzzled, Melody checked the manual, but it was quite definite. There were supposed to be workers, who would wolf-whistle her as she passed. If she responded they would move on to making remarks about the size of her breasts and the way her bottom wiggled under her skirt, then to inappropriate propositions. She could attempt to complain, at which she would be surrounded, taunted, her clothes ripped to get her bare and her mouth and pussy used over the section of sewerage pipe.

There wasn't so much as a tea boy visible, but she could hear noises from the far side of the wall and so pushed open the plywood door marked Site Access. Beyond was the building site, much as she had expected it to be, right down to the six sweaty, muscular workers. What she hadn't expected was for two of them to be bent over the sections of sewerage pipe meant for her, with the remaining four taking advantage, top and tail. All six paused as she spoke.

'Hey, you're not supposed to be gay! What about me?'

Only the largest of them, a huge black man with his cock up a younger blond's bottom, bothered to respond.

'You can watch, love. No, hang on, use this.'

He threw her a torch, which she caught by instinct. The handle was thick, ridged rubber, invitingly phallic and already well lubricated. Melody dropped it hurriedly, convinced it had been used to open the blond boy for his buggering. Annoyed, and more frustrated than ever, she consulted the manual once more, considering a command, then shook her head. The idea of being had by a group of gay man gave her a curious and very dirty thrill, but somehow she was sure it wouldn't work.

'One more try. What was it called … Redskin Raiders. New Game: Redskin Raiders. Option: Prairie Farm.'

She was in a farmhouse, the windows smashed, the door gone, with wide open sky and a burning barn visible beyond. Men were approaching, four hawk-nosed, red-skinned savages, naked but for breech clouts, beads and feathers, their faces full of lust and fury. All she wore was the tattered remains of her underwear, big, loose drawers torn at the back to leave her bottom showing, a ruined chemise with one plump boob half covered and the other sticking out. The room she was in had no other doors, and the windows were set with jagged glass, making escape impossible.

'Oh shit! Not like this … no … New … no, I've got to. Come on then, you bastards, take me, fuck me!'

The leading savage pulled his loincloth aside, exposing a huge, crooked penis. Melody squealed as she began to back away, bumping against a table. He was in the doorway, pushing through, his cock growing even as he ducked down to snatch at her ankles and tip her up onto the table, legs held open to spread her ready sex. Pushing close, he began to rub his cock and balls in the wet flesh of Melody's slit, growing quickly hard as he glared down at her, her face pure evil, then suddenly slack as a shot rang out.

He slumped to the floor, dead. Melody sat up, to find the

other redskins strewn across the ground outside like so many discarded dolls. A woman was walking towards the door, small, blonde and clad in buckskins, a smoking six gun in either hand. She had entered the farmhouse before Melody found her voice.

'You shot them!'

'Sure did, Miss. Catastrophe Kate's the name, shooting redskins is the game.'

'But … but you can't just go around killing people!'

The woman looked surprised and her Wild West accent vanished as she replied.

'Why not? They're only Semigigas, not even sentient.'

'But he … he was going to fuck me!'

She'd gone red as she said it, but the woman's look grew suddenly apologetic.

'Oh, sorry. I'd have let him have you, normally, but seeing as you're a virgin …'

'You know who I am?'

'Sure. You're Melody Jay. All the CATs know you.'

'You're a CAT then?'

'Sure. Look, if you want it that badly I could do you with a strap-on?'

It was said casually, as if suggesting that they have a cup of tea, and it took Melody a moment to answer.

'Er … no thanks. No offence, but it wouldn't be the same.'

'Sure, I understand, but still …'

The girl was looking at her in a familiar manner. Melody's mouth came open in outrage but shut again as quickly.

'Oh, alright, if you must.'

Melody lay back once more, to allow the girl to climb onto the table and push down her buckskins, showing off a pert pink bottom, the cheeks so slim that the pucker of her anus and a hint of cunt showed between. A moment later Kate had sat down on Melody's face, wriggling to make her cheeks spread. Melody began to lick, unable to stop herself enjoying being smothered in female bottom once more, so much so that her thighs had quickly come apart again.

Kate responded by pressing the still warm barrel of a gun to Melody's sex, rubbing firmly as she started to buck back and forth with a gentle rowing motion. Melody began to work faster, lapping at Kate's sex and between the neat little cheeks to taste her new friend's bumhole, then deeper, pushing her tongue in up each hole in turn. Kate gave a pleased moan and began to rub the gun barrel harder as she spoke.

'I heard you were dirty … go on, lick my bum … that's right, right in up my hole …'

Her voice broke off as Melody obeyed, pushing her tongue as deep as it would go up Kate's bottom, now snatching at her friend's cheeks and her own breasts as she started to come, lost in ecstasy for the girl sat on her face, what she was being made to do, and what was being done to her. Her climax lasted a long time, and was so good she even managed to push away her sense of regret, if only briefly.

It soon came back, along with the shame that always hit her after sex with another girl, but Kate had yet to come and Melody was left with no option but to keep on licking until it was done. Even then Kate stayed perched on Melody's face, squeezing her bottom and holding her cheeks wide until she had taken her full satisfaction, speaking again as she climbed off.

'That was great, thanks. Look, if you want to loose your virginity and you like it rough, you should try Leather Sluts.'

'Is that good?'

'Well, you'll get fucked. You'll be on a lead, with some guy as your master. They do as they like, and it's never long before you get a cock up you.'

'He'd probably just bugger me or something. Every time I try to give in it's the same. I think my desires are being over-ridden.'

'Not you. You're a BRAT. The problem must be in your subconscious.'

'No, I don't think so.'

'It must be. Nobody can override a BRAT, I'm pretty sure, not on a receptive command anyway. If you genuinely want to get fucked, you'll get fucked.'

'Right, thanks.'

'No problem. Anyway, got to go. I've got me some red injuns to shoot.'

She had pulled up her buckskins and was making for the door, only to turn at the last moment.

'See you again, sometime, I hope. I play Cheerleader Locker Room mostly, for the Warlords.'

'I'd like that. Thanks.'

Kate pretended to blow smoke from her guns and left. Melody stayed as she was, not even bothering to cover up as she pondered the situation. Of one thing she was certain: she wanted it.

'New Game: Leather Sluts.'

She was in a club, crawling on all fours across a floor wet with beer and littered with cigarette butts, dressed all in black leather, soft thigh boots, a corset and a little cap, her boobs and bottom bare to the crowd around her, her neck encircled by a collar. A dog lead led from the collar, up to the hand of the man who owned her, his powerful fingers gripping the loop. A strong need to rebel hit her instantly, but the feeling of being on all fours and ready for penetration was stronger still and she found herself looking up with more hope than resentment.

The man above her was huge, a true giant; his sculpted torso bare but for crossed leather straps, his ebony skin glistening with oil, his long, muscular legs clad in skin-tight black leather, while his crotch held an extremely promising bulge. Melody felt herself start to melt, her voice weak with need as she spoke.

'Use me as you please, Master.'

He looked down, his handsome face calm and confident but marred by a trace of irritation.

'Speak when you're spoken to, slut.'

'Sorry Master. Are you going to punish me, Master?'

Her voice was full of hope and fear, but his response was more angry still.

'I decide when you will be punished, and everything else. You're in chastity for a month. Now shut up.'

'What?'

He reached down, to smack her, only not on her bottom but across her face.

'Shut up, I said.'

'Fuck that, and fuck you, you great ape! Get me out of here!'

She was back in Arcadia, naked beside a woodland pool. Her Volition was off, but quickly came back.

'What a pig! Chastity! What bollocks. Give me a real man, please! Now what …'

The manual was by her side and as her voice trailed off she picked it up. A little voice in the back of her head was telling her to simply lie down on the warm grass and go to sleep, but she shook her head.

'No. I don't give up that easily. Not me, not Melody J.'

She opened the manual, flicking through with desperate haste before speaking once more.

'Um … New Game: Cowgirl Roundup. Option: Strip Poker.'

She was seated on a log in front of an open fire, the only girl in a ring of men. They were in jeans and leggings, plaid shirts and waistcoats, boots and wide brimmed leather hats. So was she, or at least, she had been. Her hat and waistcoat were off, also her boots and socks. Each of them had a pile of coins in front of him, but she didn't. On the ground in front of her lay five cards, three of them with four pips showing. One of the cowboys was grinning as he threw down his own hand.

‘Full house, jacks on nines. So what’s it gonna be, girl, your shirt, or your jeans?’

The question gave Melody a shock of mingled excitement and shame. There were five of them, all looking at her, and she knew she had to do it, either taking off her shirt to leave her breasts bare, or her jeans and she would have nothing but panties to cover her from the waist down. She also knew what they’d do once they’d got her in the nude, making her feel as vulnerable as she was excited, and keen for exposure. It would be her top.

All five men were watching as Melody stood up, their eyes fixed on her already straining cowboy shirt, their cocks bulging in their jeans. She began to undo her buttons, her fingers trembling as each one came wide. As usual, she had no bra and her nipples were stiff, so that even covered she was making a display of herself, and more so as her cleavage came on display, then her tummy as she untucked herself and moved to the lower button. At last only one remained, taking the strain imposed by her breasts.

‘Here we are, boys, is this what you want?’

She tweaked the button loose, the sides of her shirt pulled sharply back and her breasts were showing, full and round in the fire light, her nipples thrusting high. One of the men licked his lips, another gave a near animal grunt of appreciation, but only the one who had won the hand spoke up.

‘That and more, doll. Deal the cards, Larry.’

Melody shrugged her top off and sat down, bare-breasted and shaking, full of apprehension and yet wishing they’d just take her then and there, preferably with the dark man who’d won her top first. He was big and strong, his face bronzed by the sun and the wind, his hands powerful and seemingly capable, making her imagine his fingers on the softness of her hips as he prepared to penetrate her. Now was the time.

‘Um … what’s your name, please … sir?’

He looked up, surprised.

'You know my name, doll. John Cogburn. Now pick up your cards.'

'Of course. Sorry.'

Melody did as she was told, to find that she held three aces. It was a good hand, no doubt meant to delay her fate and make the tension worse. Each of the men threw a coin into a heap beside Larry the dealer and John spoke again, his blue-grey eyes looking straight into Melody's own.

'Jeans this time.'

'I … I'll raise you my panties, for two cards.'

There was a rustle of laughter and remarks at her comment, but John merely nodded. Larry passed Melody two new cards, a three and a seven. Only one of the other men threw out another coin for three cards, but John spoke up as he increased his own stake.

'A dollar, and I'll raise you a dollar. One card, Larry.'

Melody swallowed, knowing she'd be nude if she chose to throw in her cards, and her fate if she stayed in but then lost.

'Um … I can't … I haven't got anything left.'

There was an immediate burst of laughter, with Larry speaking.

'Oh yes you have, doll. You've got what every man wants, real bad, right there on that log. In fact, seems to me that that's one lucky log!'

There was more laughter as Melody went red, but John's voice cut through the other.

'Play the game. You in or not?'

The other man shook his head and turned over his cards, revealing a pair of nines and another of twos. Melody looked up, her pussy tightening at the thought of John's cock, which formed a long, thick ridge down one leg of his blue jeans. Her voice was thick with embarrassment as she spoke.

'Um … how about a … a spanking?'

A gust of raucous laughter greeted her suggestion and she went redder still, but John remained as calm as ever as he replied.

'Okay, a dime a smack. How many d'you want?'

'Two, please.'

Larry dealt out her cards, a king and the remaining ace. She felt her mouth flicker up into a smile at the sight of her now perfect hand, only to fade under a rush of disappointment.

'I'm suppose to lose!'

'Beg pardon, Miss?'

'Nothing. Are you in, John?'

He spent a moment watching her face, then tossed a further four coins onto the growing pile.

'I'm fine the way I am, Larry. What's it to be, Miss Jay, a smacked ass in front of the boys, or are you going to raise the stakes.'

'What if I raise the stakes?'

'Maybe you win. Maybe I get to take you out in the dark.'

Melody knew exactly what he meant, bringing her frustration to boiling point, but a spanking would only make it worse.

'I'll raise and see you.'

John gave a light chuckle and put down his cards, displaying fours queens and a joker.

'Five ladies, and it looks like I'll be getting me a sixth.'

Hope and fear surged up in Melody's chest as she realised she'd made a mistake. Jokers were obviously wild, which meant she'd lost. She put down her cards.

'Four aces.'

Larry clapped his hands together.

'Wee doggie! We get to see it all, and a leathering! Do her hard, John.'

John merely stood up, his hands going to the buckle of the thick belt of plain, dark leather at his waist.

'Strip. Then touch your toes, ass to the fire.'

'But, you said a spanking!'

'Yep, and that's what you're gonna get.'

'By hand, over your knee!'

'You're a bit big for that, doll. A girl like you, I reckon it's the belt. Now come on, or do I have to get the boys to hold you down?'

'No. But look …'

'It's only twenty strokes. Don't be a baby. Come on then boys …'

'No, that's okay. You can belt me, but why are you men always such pigs?'

He didn't bother to answer. As she stood up, Melody tried to console herself by recalling the state she'd been in after her caning. It did little good, and the tears were already rolling down her cheeks, yet she made a point of showing off, deliberately humiliating herself by sticking out her bottom and peeling her jeans slowly down as if she were a stripper or a prostitute. She even took them off before repeating the lewd display with the big white panties she had on underneath, only this time to expose herself fully, the wet, pouted lips of her sex showing as she bent and her cheeks parted to show off the little pinkish brown star between.

John was ready, the thick leather belt held back to strike, and as Melody stepped out of her panties he brought it down across her bare bottom, completely unexpectedly. Melody squealed in shock and pain as the belt cracked down onto her meat, stumbling forward to trip over her half removed panties and sprawl face first into Larry's arms. He had taken a grip before she could recover herself, holding her securely in place with her bottom stuck high in the air as John applied a second stroke.

Again she screamed, and began to struggle, wriggling in Larry's grip and kicking her feet up and down. The third stroke hit home with a ringing smack, and the fourth, and fifth, leaving Melody too far gone in her pain to care about the ludicrous display she was making, with her legs flying and her bumhole pulsing between her cheeks, juice squirting from her ready sex with every smack of the belt.

Larry began to fondle her breasts, but she barely noticed,

lost in the hurt of her bottom and the appalling helplessness and exposure of her situation. Smack after smack landed across her cheeks, until she had lost count of how many she'd taken, although her struggles grew more desperate and her yells louder, as did the cowboys' laughter as they watched her beaten. Only John stayed silent, bringing the belt down with hard, accurate strokes, until the whole of Melody's rear end was ablaze with heat and welted from the top of her crease to where her cheeks tucked under to meet her thighs.

She broke just before it finished, her screams changing to whimpers and her bottom lifting to the smacks, her pleas for mercy changing to pleas for more, and for John to fuck her as she was pushed into the same willing, grovelling state to which the cane had brought her. The cowboys thought her reaction was hilarious, smacking their thighs and urging John to make a good job of her as he brought down the twentieth and final cut, full across the back of Melody's thighs. Again she screamed, jumping up as Larry released her, to go into a frantic, uncontrolled dance of pain, with her breasts jiggling and her hair flying, her hands clutching convulsively at her beaten bottom.

John simply watched, waiting for her to calm down before taking her by the hand and leading her out of the circle of firelight, her head hung in submission and her spare hand rubbing at one smarting cheek. Behind her the cowboys were still whooping and laughing, calling advice out to John on how to handle her and speculating on whether they'd get a turn once he'd finished. Both John and Melody ignored them, and the fire was no more than a flicker in the distance before he laid her down on soft grass.

She had given in completely, spreading her thighs to him in abject surrender, her back arched and her sex pushed out to show off her virgin hole in light as red as the taut hymen blocking the entrance. John came to stand over her, looking down at her naked body for a long moment before he unzipped. This time there was to be no preamble, no cock sucking or getting ready in her hand or between her breasts. He was fully erect, his cock a magnificent tower of straining man-flesh, the head purple with blood and shiny with pressure.

Melody moaned as he knelt down between her thighs, pushing them up to make her as open as possible. He took a grip on his cock, his body settling onto hers, their mouths opening together in a passionate kiss as the bloated head moved to her hole. She felt her hymen push in, stretching, and she cried out against his mouth in overwhelming emotion as he took her under her shoulders and vanished.

'No! Not again! No, no, no, no! You bastards! You fucking pigs! Just take me will you, fuck me! Fuck me I said! Yes, that's right, fuck me!'

She was yelling at the men around the campfire, but they were gone and as she realised she was alone Melody was screaming her frustration at the stars, no longer articulate, the tears streaming down her face, until at last her words came back, weak with defeat.

'Why won't anybody fuck me!?'

Deflowered

When Melody had finally calmed down her overwhelming need was no longer for sex, but for a friend. She still felt open and badly in need of penetration, but confusion and self-pity had overcome even her lust. The fire had died to embers, leaving her in near blackness, but she knew the command she wanted.

'CAT: Jane. I want to be with Jane.'

She was in a vast stadium, as big as any she'd ever played in, but there was no stage, no band, just her. Her bottom still smarted from John's belt and she was still stark naked, standing in the exact centre of a pitch of some sort, with maybe a hundred thousand people looking at her, spectators, players and two groups of brightly clad girls, some in red, white and blue, the others in black and yellow. As always, her first instinct was to cover her sex and breasts, however futile the gesture, but she quickly recovered herself.

'Dress Up. A … a cheerleader's uniform. Um … black and yellow.'

It appeared instantly, complete with pom-poms, while her hair was now in bunches tied with ribbons in the same bright team colours. A happy voice called out to her.

'Melody, over here!'

Jane was among the cheerleaders for the same team, one of eleven, and immediately ran to meet Melody. They came together in a firm hug, Jane kissing Melody full on the lips, only to pull back a little almost immediately. Melody had burst into tears.

'What's the matter?'

'Everything. Can we talk?'

'Of course we can, but we're in the middle of a game …'

'That's not a problem. Hold onto me, really tight. Companion: CAT: Jane. New Location: Arcadia.'

'Wow! Where are we?'

'My own private world, Arcadia.'

'Okay … that's cool. So, what's the problem?'

As usual there was somewhere convenient to sit, in this case a tumble of water polished boulders beside a stream. Melody made herself comfortable, keeping a firm grip on Jane's hand as she began to talk. Their shadows had begun to lengthen before she finished with a shrug. Jane took a moment to reflect, then spoke.

'There's only one person who can override a BRAT, and that's Simon.'

'Simon Weissinger?'

'Who else?'

'But why? He seemed determined to make me be as dirty as possible. Apparently it's the best way to pay off the debts for my recording.'

'Maybe people buy more of your stuff because you're a virgin?'

'Maybe, yes.'

'In which case he's probably holding you back for something really special, so that he can make as much as possible.'

'That makes sense. Like giving an album a big build up before it's released. I'd kill the bastard if I could catch him! Then again, I suppose he's only trying to make money, and I do get a percentage. Joseph Rosenthal said I could apply for a cloned body when I'd earned enough.'

'Wow! We could meet …'

Jane trailed off, suddenly looking glum.

'What's wrong?'

'It's … I … I don't think it would work, being friends that is. You'd be a celebrity, and what am I, a legal secretary who spends most of her life in virtual worlds.'

'You can be my legal advisor.'

'You wouldn't like me. I don't even look the same. Okay, this is me when I was twenty, more or less, but I'm older and fatter …'

'I don't care!'

Melody hugged Jane to her, holding her friend as she had been held herself, but in silence, with no sound but the gentle murmur of the stream. At last Jane broke away with an embarrassed grin.

'I'm sorry.'

'Don't be. So what now?'

'Well, if Simon's saving you up for something special, why don't we try and give it to him?'

'How?'

'Go back to where we were. Weissinger's Warlords take no prisoners!'

'Were we playing Cheerleader Locker Room?'

'Yes.'

'And I'm not cheering for the Warlords, am I?'

'No, we're with the visiting team, the Wasps, and we've already lost.'

'We have?'

'Sure. The Warlords' girls were just giving us our forfeit, the first part anyway. Look.'

Jane stood up and turned to Melody, giggling as she flipped up the back of her skirt to show off not the big, colourful panties Melody was expecting, but her bare pink bottom, with a wisp of yellow material protruding from between her thighs. She had been spanked.

'What have they done to you?'

'Spanked us and stuck our panties up us, with the whole crowd looking on, over a hundred thousand people, and they were all cheering while we got it, even our own fans!'

'And they're going to do that to me!?'

'Don't worry, when they see you're still a virgin they stick them up your bum instead.'

'Thanks, that's a great consolation!'

'Come on, you'll love it!'

Melody hesitated, her emotions still raw.

'And what's the forfeit, aside from being spanked with our panties stuck up us?'

'We have to parade like that, and do our cheer routine, with our tits out too. After that we get sent back to the boys' locker room and they get to do what they like with us. You're bound to get it, because believe me a recording of Melody J being put through all that and then having her cherry popped will sell in the millions!'

Melody drew in a deep breath, but the idea was too horny to resist.

'Okay. New Game: Cheerleader Locker Room. Replay from break.'

They were back in the stadium, standing exactly as they had been before. Some of the Warlords' cheerleaders were coming towards them, led by Kate, no longer in her buckskins or armed, but with the same wicked smile on her pretty face.

'If it isn't little Miss Jay! Looks like we missed one, girls. Let's get her.'

Melody ran, although more from a desire not to make herself look a complete slut by surrendering without a fight than any real need for escape. She had no chance anyway, both the rival cheerleaders and the Warlords themselves fanning out to cut her off in what was obviously a well practised manoeuvre. They caught her before she'd made twenty metres, a ring of girls around her with the men further back, her colleagues further still and the crowd beyond, all watching. Kate stepped forward.

'Touch yours toes, loser.'

Melody hesitated only an instant.

'Make me!'

They grabbed her, twisting her arms behind her back and ignoring her squeals as her cheerleader skirt was turned up to show her knickers to the jeering, laughing crowd. She was still struggling and grimacing as she was bent over and quickly stripped below the waist, her pumps and socks pulled off, then her panties, to leaving everything showing behind. They held her, standing back to let the crowd get a good view of her bare bottom and the lips of her sex before the spanking began. Kate did it, holding Melody around the waist and slapping at her cheeks with an upward motion to make them bounce and wobble, also parting them to show off her bumhole.

Still Melody struggled, wriggling desperately in their grip even though she could feel herself coming on heat as her cheeks began to warm, and her overwhelming emotion when it suddenly stopped was disappointment. Kate obviously realised, because she laughed and gave Melody's bottom another slap.

'Don't worry, darling, we're not finished with you yet. Where are her panties? Who's got the lube?'

Melody began to struggle again, but five of the girls were holding her, making it impossible to escape or even make her position less blatantly rude. Two more grabbed her legs, spreading her open and it had got worse, then worse still as her bottom cheeks were hauled apart to stretch her anus wide for intimate inspection. Her top was pulled up, spilling out her breasts to dangle pink and plump in front of her face where she was looking back between her open legs. Kate was holding the bright yellow panties and a big jar marked with the Weissinger logo and a single word – Lube.

'She's still a virgin, look.'

At Kate's words, Melody's mouth came open in a gasp of unspeakable indignation. Her sex lips had been prized apart, to show off her virgin hole not just to the girls but to the entire stadium, including an improbably large number of photographers with lenses so huge that she was sure the pictures would show her hymen in the sort of detail that should only have belonged in a medical textbook.

'Hey, come on! That's not fair!'

Kate merely laughed and slapped Melody's bottom.

'Shut up, loser. It's not like I'm going to bust you. After all, we've all got two holes, haven't we?'

The girls began to chant, demanding Melody's panties go

up her bottom, a refrain quickly picked up by the players and then the crowd beyond. Melody began to sob, still wriggling feebly as one well lubricated finger was applied to her anus. It went in easily, the little tight hole opening to Kate's finger, then a second. The sensation was too much for Melody, who was quickly moaning as Kate's fingers worked in her hole. A third slipped in, a fourth, her thumb, and Melody's anus was stretched taut, making a tight pink ring around Kate's fist, which finally slipped in all the way.

Cameras were flashing on every side, and Melody was moaning and gasping as her bottom was fisted, with Kate's hand in up to the wrist, a sensation even more powerful than her buggerings. A mixture of juice from her sex and lubricant was running down her legs, but still she resisted, unable to cope with her overwhelming shame any more than she could with having her bumhole stretched wide on Kate's forearm. Kate was laughing as she spoke again.

'Hold this. I'm going to make her come.'

'No! Kate, please …'

Melody's begging broke off as Kate's other hand found her sex, one knuckle rubbing directly on the sensitive little bump between her lips. It was too much, too sudden to take, and Melody screamed as her muscles went into spasms, her thighs and bum cheeks clenching, her anal ring squeezing on Kate's wrist and juice squirting backwards from her pussy. She'd come, a sudden violent orgasm over which she'd had no control whatsoever, and which her audience seemed to think was hilarious.

The reaction to Melody's plight only encouraged Kate, who continued to rub, bringing Melody to peak after peak, until she'd been reduced to a sobbing, sweaty mess, hanging limp in her tormentors' grip with both cunt and anus in soft, rhythmic contractions, and as the fist was finally withdrawn from her rectum she was left gaping open to the entire crowd. Her voice came in a mumble.

'Put a cock in … bugger me.. please!'

Kate's hand came down hard across her cheeks.

'Slut! That comes later. For now, your panties go up.'

Melody stayed limp, utterly defeated as her big yellow panties were dipped in the jar of lubricant and pushed between her cheeks. Her hole had closed a little and she felt it spread once more as her knickers were jammed up her, Kate feeding in the bulk of the slippery cotton but leaving just a little hanging out from Melody's still distended bumhole to make it obvious what had been done to her.

With the panties up the spanking began again, each girl taking her turn to smack Melody's bottom, until her cheeks were hot and throbbing, while she'd come twice more as the more skilled and sadistic of them applied their swats across the rear of her sex lips. By the end she was too far gone even to care for the audience, begging to be spanked harder and to be given to the players for fucking.

The girls merely laughed at her as she was released, to stand, unsteady on her feet as she was given the final humiliation of having her little yellow and black skirt tucked up at the back to leave her smacked bottom on show with the scrap of yellow cotton hanging out from between her cheeks. Jane and the others were nearby, in the same sorry state, parading themselves for the crowd, all eleven with their skirts tucked high, their tops pulled up over their bare breasts and puffs of bright yellow material protruding from between their rear cheeks where their panties had been stuffed up their vaginas.

Melody was sent to join her team mates with a firm smack to her already glowing bottom. She joined the end of the line, next to Jane, and they were promptly marched off to make a slow circuit of the stadium, walking with their knees kicked high and well spaced out to make sure everybody got a good look and had plenty of opportunity to photograph them.

The parade ended back in the middle of the pitch, now completely clear. Melody had no idea what to expect as Kate called out for them to do their routine, but her dance training stood her in good stead. She followed the others as they did handstands and cartwheels, lifted each other into the air, jumped to make their boobs bounce and bent to show off their bare bottoms to the crowd. All of it kept her excited, especially when they finished by making a twelve girl pyramid, kneeling on each others backs, which they were made to hold while they were photographed with all twelve pairs of boobs dangling and all twelve bare bottoms well open with the mouths of their cunts stretched taut around the bright yellow panty material within, or in Melody's case, up her anus.

By then she was lost in a haze of desire, so far gone that had any man run out from the crowd and mounted her she would simply have given in, spreading her thighs to his cock and allowing him to take the prize of her virginity simply for his boldness. None did, and all twelve girls were marched from the pitch with their rivals running alongside to taunt them, telling them what they were going to get, slapping bottoms and tweaking nipples, also making very sure that nobody escaped.

They were taken to the locker room itself, Melody's nose wrinkling to the smell of male sweat as she entered and her sex tightening in anticipation of cock. The boys wasted no time, piling in with whoops of joy and grabbing whichever girl was nearest, even those from their own side. Jane had quickly been hustled down over a bench, her knickers removed from her hole and a cock substituted while another man filled her mouth. Kate fared no better, grabbed and put on her knees to suck a man's balls despite her protests, while she'd soon had her knickers pulled down to allow another man to rub his cock in her bottom crease in preparation for fucking her.

Only Melody was ignored, but not for long. One of the men took her hand, the running back, still in his helmet, who seemed to have the respect of the others for all that he was the smallest and obviously slimmer despite his padding.

Nobody contested his ownership of Melody as he led her through the locker room and into the showers, where a heavy wooden massage table stood at the centre of the room. Suddenly she was sure it was going to happen. He was too confident, too cool to be denied, his authority absolute as he lifted her by her bottom and sat her down on the table.

She put up no resistance at all, lying back with her thighs wide open and rolled up, showing off her virgin cunt in complete submission. He pushed down his trousers to expose lean, muscular legs and a long, pale cock, then climbed onto the table to feed himself into Melody's mouth. She took him in, sucking eagerly as she played with her breasts and making no complaint when he moved to dangle his balls into her mouth, nor even when he straddled her face to have his anus licked. Her tongue simply went in, licking the wrinkled little hole in an act as submissive as it was wanton, and all the while squeezing and stroking her naked breasts.

He was rock hard by the time he climbed off, and pushed his cock briefly back into Melody's mouth before coming round between her thighs to stand with it rearing up over her sex, long and pink and glistening with her saliva. Melody gave a deep sigh as she took hold of her legs, pulling them higher and wider still to make as blatant a display of her sex as she possibly could. He nodded, pleased by her acquiescence, and began to rub his cock in the wet mush of her open lips.

'In me … please, put it in me! Fuck me!'

'Do you want me?'

'Yes! Can't you see? Look at me!'

His cock moved lower, prodding at her hole and rubbing on her hymen, and Melody had begun to beg.

'Just do it, please! Put it up me, fuck me … fuck me, you bastard, please!'

'Do you really mean that!'

'Yes! Not this again, please no! Take me! I'll do anything for you, later, but take me! You can fuck my bottom … have me and Jane together … spank me … cane me … make me suck your dirty cock when it's been up my friend, anything, but just fuck me, now!'

He let go of his cock, keeping it pushed to her hole. She was still babbling entreaties, but watching too as his hands went to his helmet, pulling it off his head to reveal a strong, bony face. In a moment her mind had stripped away the years, his face no longer that of a grown man with all the strength and confidence of success, but of a boy, pale and uncertain yet full of mischief, the face of a clown or prankster, and one which Melody instantly recognised.

'I know who you are … you bastard, you're that little nerd who used to draw dirty pictures of me, aren't you? Aren't you!? You're Simon Weissinger!'

He nodded, his cock now tight to the mouth of her sex, pressed in hard enough to made her hymen bulge in up her hole. Melody gave a single, choking sob, and then she was screaming.

'Okay, do it then, you bastard! You pig! You've got me, okay … you can fuck me … fuck me, now … fuck me, you pervert, go on, right in … jam it up, deep … I'm yours you dirty little pig, you filthy, dirty, perverted little nerd, you …'

Her voice broke to a scream as he gave a single, firm thrust and her hymen tore, spattering his balls and the tuck of her bottom with her virgin blood.

Simon Weissinger

Melody sat on the massage table, still wet from the shower they'd taken together as she bound a towel around her hair, indifferent to being nude in front of him. He'd taken her, and somehow that made the idea of concealing herself from him in any way whatsoever not merely pointless but actually wrong. She felt she was his, in much the way she had expected to feel for the man who finally took her, despite the circumstances. After all, he had fought for her and won, although it was in a way she wouldn't even have understood before her transformation. Only a small cinder of resentment remained, smouldering in the back of her mind, along with the picture of him not as the handsome, confident young tycoon he had become, but as the smutty=-minded little nerd he had been before.

Watching him as he towelled himself down, it was easy to see both men, and impossible to shrug off a touch of disappointment at his lack of any real height or bulk.

'One thing, Simon. Why didn't you just make yourself like Mark Steel or somebody. I'd have given in, and I'd never have known.'

'That wouldn't have been the same. You had to give in to me, knowing who I was.'

'You're very good looking, and successful, an alpha male if ever there was one.'

'That's not what you used to think, is it?'

'No, but people change.'

'And it's not entirely what you think now, is it? I know you like a bigger man, Melody, and what was it you called me: a perverted little nerd?'

'I'm sorry.'

'That's quite alright. The description is accurate, after all, just as you are a brat.'

'I am n … okay, I suppose I am a bit of a brat, sometimes.'

'You always were, and I hope you always will be. Why do you think I invented the BRAT acronym? It was for you, because it suited you. You were the perfect self-obsessed pop star, and never in the entire history of the world has a girl needed spanking so badly.'

'Why did you like me so much then?'

'Because I fell in love with you, and I wanted to tame you, to have you for my own. We perverted little nerds aren't necessarily weak in our desires.'

'No, I can see that now, and you've won. I'm yours.'

He gave a pleased smile.

'I've waited more than twenty years to hear those words, Melody, but here, in my world, nobody belongs to another. We are free.'

'What if I want to belong to you?'

'Then I accept your gift, sincerely and in full appreciation of what it means, but I still don't expect you to be exclusive to me, except only for that one special thing, your virginity.'

Melody blushed despite herself.

'Thank you, but … but what if I need to be yours and yours alone?'

'Do you? What about Jane? What about Kate, or Ginger?'

'Um … girls are different, I suppose, and I don't mind if you watch, really.'

Her blush had grown rich and hot at the admission, making him smile once more before he went on.

'And what if I chose, shall we say, to have you spanked by Mark? He's a linebacker for the Warriors, by the way.'

'That … that would be your choice … okay, it would be nice, really nice actually, but half the pleasure would be because you'd given me to him.'

'And if I made you suck him off?'

The words sent a powerful thrill through Melody, whose face was now a burning crimson as she nodded.

'If I told you to let him bugger you?'

Again she nodded, no longer able to speak for her shame

and excitement.

'To fuck you?'

She shook her head and had to swallow twice before she could get out what she wanted to say.

'No. That's yours.'

'What is, exactly?'

'My sex … my pussy. She's yours.'

'Say it properly. I like the word cunt.'

Melody shivered.

'My … my cunt is yours, Simon, and only yours.'

'Good girl. So, what if you were playing Hero's Reward and Mark rescued you?'

'I … I'd let him have my bottom.'

'Good. That's just as well, as it goes, because I've promised the boys they could have a little fun with you.'

'What, here? Now?'

'Of course. We're still playing Cheerleader Locker Room, after all. Most get had by at least half the team.'

He had extended his hand, but she hesitated, unsure if she could face what was to happen to her and stalling for time.

'What about Teddy? He was going to fuck me.'

'Only up your bum.'

'Oh … but one other thing. Why … why was my house pink? Did you think it was my favourite colour?'

'No. I never really bothered with that sort of thing. That was just my little sister playing with your recording.'

'Your little sister!?'

'Yes. It was while I was developing my program, and letting her play with it was the best way of working out the bugs. Don't worry, you were quite safe.'

'Safe!? Well, maybe, but … so who used to dress me up in frilly panties, and school uniform, and little sailor suits, and who put me on stage?'

'That was me, of course. Well, mainly. I have no idea what Hannah dressed you in, but the concerts were my first venture into commerce.'

'Including having me strip?'

'That's what funded my first company. All this is built on those first recordings. You were still fresh in the public's memory when I released your first on stage striptease. It sold nearly eighty million copies.'

Melody flushed with pride, but quickly came back.

'How much of that went to paying off my debts?'

'At the time I only had a licence to use your recording. It cost me more than half my profits to renew that licence, and twice that to complete the purchase.'

'But you did it?'

'I'd have paid ten times as much.'

'Thank you, I suppose.'

'There was a long legal battle as well, during which your recording was dormant, although you wouldn't remember that. I only won because Hannah seduced the judge and took some interesting photos.'

'Your sister?'

'Yes, although she was grown up by then, obviously. You've met her. Remember Matron?'

'Matron? But she must be fifty if she's a day! Oh … no, I suppose not, but still …'

'She likes to be in charge, and she likes to spank naughty little brats. It was her who persuaded me to make you a nurse when we activated your recording the second time.'

'The second time?'

'Yes. That was after all the legal problems had been cleared up. By then Metrocity was fully functional, with over ten thousand CATs already signed up. Didn't you notice the improved technology?'

'Yes, I suppose so, but …'

'No more questions, Melody. Come on.'

His hand was still extended to her and she took it, allowing him to lead her from the shower block and back into the locker room. The game was going full swing, with bodies on every side, mostly near naked, so that the only way to tell one group of cheerleaders from the other was by the colour of their socks, although a few of the more dominant Warlords' girls still had their tops and skirts on, although tucked up to let them enjoy themselves. Their knickers were off, even Kate's, although only to let her mount Jane, bottom to face as the blonde girl was fucked by a massively built, black footballer who Melody immediately recognised.

'That's my friend Veldt Panther.'

'So it is. Why don't you suck his balls while he fucks your friend?'

'Um …'

'Do it.'

Simon's hand smacked against Melody's bottom, sending her forward. She managed an embarrassed smile for Veldt Panther, but he had heard Simon's order and returned a happy grin as he cocked one leg up on the bench on which Jane lay, showing off his balls. They looked huge, bulging in their dark, leathery sack and swinging back and forth to smack on the tuck of Jane's bottom with every thrust of his cock into her straining hole.

Melody got down, feeling shy for all her excitement, so that it took a little courage to poke out her tongue and start to dab at his scrotum as it swung back and forth against her face. The salty, male taste encouraged her, and she had quickly began to lick properly, and to nuzzle her face between his muscular, black buttocks. Simon came behind her, holding something which she saw was a thick plug with a flat, rounded base marked as a No Entry sign. A couple of gentle smacks and she had been made to lift her bottom, allowing him to slide the plug in up her vagina, barring access to any man but him.

With that her inhibitions gave way completely. Pushing her face hard between Veldt Panther's buttocks, she began to tongue his anus, and to squeeze on his balls as she licked him. It was too much for him. He grunted and thick, white come erupted from the mouth of Jane's sex, over his balls and into Melody's face. Jane twisted around, giggling, and she and Melody were sharing what he'd done, licking each others' faces and his cock and balls, then kissing open-mouthed to pass the ball of mess between them. Kate had seen, laughing at their filthy behaviour and taking them both by the hair to hold their heads firmly together until she was satisfied both had their fill.

'Now swallow, both of you.'

Melody obeyed, revelling in the dirty act, and all the more so because Simon was watching, his mouth curved up into a cool, knowing smile as she made a slut of herself. Kate was far from finished, straddling the two girls' heads to push her sex to Jane's face and her bottom to Melody's.

'Now me. On my clitty, Jane. Melody can do my bum.'

Melody obeyed without hesitation, pushing her tongue in up Kate's anus and licking eagerly. A man was approaching them, Mark Steel, clad in Warlords body armour from the waist up. Otherwise he was naked, his helmet off and his legs bare, also his cock, which was hard. Simon spoke up.

'Lift your bottom, Melody.'

It was easy to obey, even though she knew it would mean a cock in her anus in front of everybody else and for a potential audience of millions. Her knees came wide and her haunches up, never once removing her tongue from Kate's bottom hole as she offered her own. Mark gave a nodded thank you to Simon, dipped his erection into a pot of lube from a locker and squatted down behind Melody.

His cock touched between her cheeks, pushing to her anus. Melody relaxed, allowing her ring to spread to the pressure, so that he was quickly inside, pushing deep until his balls met her empty sex. She knew the sensation would make her come, even before his balls had begun to slap her cunt to the rhythm of her buggering. Her hands went to her breasts, feeling the heavy, sensitive globes of girlflesh, tugging at her nipples and struggling to stick her tongue yet further up Kate's bumhole as her pleasure rose.

Other men had began to gather around, each with at least one girl, but obviously wanting their turn with Melody, pushing her excitement higher still. She came on the thought, determined to cope however sore it made her, and whatever the consequences of the other girls' jealousy. As her bottom hole went into contraction Mark jammed himself deep one last time, holding Melody by the hips as the squeezing of her ring milked his cock into her rectum.

No sooner was he out than he'd been replaced, John Cogburn slipping his cock from another girl's mouth and easing himself in up Melody's still gaping hole. She was still coming, peak after peak tearing through her for the sensations of her body and the knowledge that there was a man's cock up her bottom while she was licking another girl's anus. Kate had already come under Jane's skilful licking, but kept Melody's head in place while she brought herself to a second climax under her fingers.

Only then did she step away, quickly beckoning a man in to take her place, Saul McCoy, who thrust his erection into Melody's mouth without preamble. Now penetrated at both ends, Melody gave no resistance as she was pushed down over the bench, her bottom lifted to John's thrusts at one side, her breasts dangling down at the other, her mouth full of Saul's meaty penis. Somebody called out.

'A spit roast, that's what I like to see! After you there, cousin Saul!'

Melody looked up from the corner of one eye. It was Billy-Bob, more massive than ever in his Warlords' gear, and with his monstrous cock and balls hanging out over the front, half erect and glistening with some other girl's saliva. Saul obliged, quickly taking hold of his cock to tug himself off into Melody's mouth and squeezing her throat to make her swallow before giving way to his cousin.

There was no resistance left in Melody. She was surrendered to any man so long as he left her pussy inviolate, happy to take their cocks up her bottom, to swallow come, to lick their balls and between their cheeks, anything to maintain the state of glorious ecstasy they had her in. Even when John Cogburn pulled out of her bottom to offer his cock to her mouth she only hesitated for an instant, before she had taken him in, sucking as willingly as ever as Billy-Bob eased himself in up her now vacant anus.

As they rocked her back and forth on their cocks she was squeezing her breasts and clutching at her sex to rub on her clitoris and push Simon's plug back and forth in the hole, although simply knowing it was in her gave enough pleasure to make her want to come again. When John spunked in her mouth she simply swallowed and opened up for the next man, one she hadn't even met, while Billy-Bob had soon finished himself off up her bottom and let Sergeant Rider take his place.

The coach had come in, standing just inside the open door with an indulgent smile spread across his weather-beaten features. Melody recognised him instantly, as her Uncle Roscoe from Redneck Rampage. As soon as the man in her mouth had finished himself off all over her face she beckoned to the older man, telling herself he wasn't really her uncle as she took his cock into her mouth but wishing he was.

He took his turn up her bottom too, while she sucked on Mr Hawker, and they were not the last, man after man taking advantage of the state she was in to push their cock into her mouth or anus, until she was slippery with come and dizzy with reaction, her jawing aching and her bumhole slack, her face and bottom smeared with spunk that even speckled her back and breasts. Even Teddy had made an appearance, as the club mascot in a miniature red, white and blue outfit, inserting himself in her mouth and bottom turn and turn about to the claps and encouraging yells of everybody else, until he finally came in Melody's hair.

It was far from over. With every last man satisfied at least once, the girls took over, not just the Warlords' cheerleaders, but the Wasps as well. Kate started it off by mounting Melody's back to keep her pinned down on the bench while another girl pushed a huge strap-on dildo in from behind. Ginger appeared, in nothing but a Warlords' top which she'd had pulled up under her armpits, first to rub her boobs in Melody's face and then to present herself kneeling to have her bumhole and cunt licked from behind.

The girls were crueller than the men, and less hurried, each taking her time and often two or three orgasms before she gave way. Kate rubbed herself off on Melody's back, riding her cowgirl style, then moved lower to pee all over her friend's already badly soiled bottom. Lance Corporal Hardyke was there too, using a strap to beat Melody before rubbing herself to orgasm on the hot, slippery flesh of one cheek. By then Jane was back, and had quickly turned Melody over and around, to lie her along the bench with her legs rolled up and her plugged vagina showing where her bottom stuck out over the end. With Melody in position, Jane mounted up, bum to face, wriggling down as she demanded her bottom and sex licked until she'd come. Simon stepped forward, to push his cock into Jane's mouth as a powerful hand took Melody by her ankles, rolling her high as if she were about to have a nappy changed, her bottom once more vulnerable. A familiar voice spoke up, Matron.

'I knew you'd end up like this, you dirty little slut, but that's not going to stop you getting your punishments!'

As she spoke something hard smacked down across Melody's cheeks, a leather strap. It stung crazily, but Melody was trapped, with Jane's bottom in her face and her ankles caught in a vicelike grip. Not that she wanted to escape, not any more, taking the pain of her beating as the strap came down across her bottom again and again, the meaty smacks booming out to draw laughter from the watching crowd.

Before long Melody was hot and needy, as she'd known she soon would be, her knees now cocked wide to spread herself to the blows, her tongue deep in up Jane's open bottom hole. The beating stopped and Simon had come between Melody's thighs, to ease the plug from her ready sex and substitute his cock, fucking her with slow, easy motions, even as his sister brought the strap down hard across Melody's heaving breasts.

Simon's thumb, or maybe Hannah's, found Melody's clitoris and she had utterly lost control, with the three people who had brought her more pleasure than any others working on her at the same time. Everything began to come together in her head; the way she'd been kept in a near constant state of arousal, being treated as a sex doll and made to display herself, being made to touch men's cocks, to suck and lick, being spanked and caned and strapped, always with her knickers down, having her enormous, sensitive boobs fucked and spunked on, playing with her anus and being buggered, licking girls and sticking her tongue up their bottoms, and as she started to come one more time, the final, perfect moment, as her hymen had burst to Simon Weissinger's cock.

Epiphany

Some months after losing her virginity Melody lay supine in the warm grass somewhere among the hills near Redneck Creek. Her thighs were open, her pussy in gentle contraction on the plug inside, her bottom hole dribbling sperm between her cheeks from the buggering she'd been given by Vinton Vouls and Pervis Peckerwood, who'd trapped her at the end of a long game of Helter Skelter and taken turns with her in the long grass where she'd finally been brought down. She was nude, because the white leather cowgirl outfit and tarty red underwear she'd created to play the game had been stolen by Pervis so that he could wear it while they used her. Both had now gone, chuckling together for what they'd done.

Idly wondering what had happened to Jane, Melody propped herself up on one elbow. A curious mixture of screams and delighted laughter from somewhere down in the valley suggested that her friend had been caught by either Sawblade Saggory or Cletus the Cuntboy, possibly both. Briefly Melody wondered if she should go down and join in, only to decide that it was hardly fair on Jane, who always seemed to get less than a fair share of attention when they were together.

Instead she increased the temperature a fraction, tidied herself up, created a pair of shades and a towel to lie on, then relaxed, intending to sunbathe, which in Helter Skelter came with the near certainty of being caught by one or another of the psychopaths, probably one conjured from the darker recesses of her own imagination. After all, sunbathing in the nude was definitely asking for it.

Just a few minutes later the snap of a twig gave her a now familiar twinge of fear and excitement, but as she sat up she discovered Simon himself walking towards her, casually dressed and not even armed. In one hand he held a sheath of papers. Melody lifted her shades.

'I didn't know you were playing. What's up?'

'I have some news. You now have enough in your account to afford a clone. All you need to do is sign and in a few days you'll be back in the real world.'

'Wow! And I'll finally get to meet you in the flesh, and Jane, and Hannah, and the other CATS. So sales have been good then?'

'Wonderful. Even the short spankings clips get several million downloads.'

He had come close and Melody took the papers, feeling excited and nervous as she scanned the lines of the contract that would bring her back to life. Yet she already felt alive, more so than ever before, while she had no worries either. The Weissinger Corporation computers, she had found, were embedded deep in the rock, cushioned against even the most violent earthquake or the worst possible war, and powered by a geothermal generator, while there were also extensive back-ups and fail-safes. She was safe from death, from disease, from growing old, and able to do exactly as she pleased, while even her willing surrender to Simon was ultimately her own free choice.

He had given her a pen, but she let it drop to the grass as she spoke.

'No. I'm happy as I am.'

When dark fantasy turns to darkest reality...

Self-bondage addict Paul is submissive to the core but craves constant hard discipline. A chance meeting with an old friend brings him within the thrilling orbit of top professional dominatrix Mistress Nikki and the ultra-sadistic Mistress Alicia.

An erotic novel with strong BDSM and Femdom content.

ISBN 9781906373825, price £7.99

A saucy romp set in a Victorian finishing school for young ladies...

Sweet English rose, Victoria, is packed off to the Venus School for Young Ladies to learn how to be a dutiful wife. But she discovers that she has a lot to learn in the arts of pleasure when she encounters the strictness of Principal Madame Thackeray and her assistant, the domineering Madame Hulot.
Returning home to England, she turns her newfound education to good use to save the family estate.

ISBN 9781906373696, price £7.99

More great books from Xcite...

Naughty Spanking One
Twenty bottom-tingling stories to make your buttocks blush!
9781906125837 £7.99

The True Confessions of a London Spank Daddy
Memoir by Peter Jones
9781906373320 £7.99

Girl Fun One
Lesbian anthology edited by Miranda Forbes
9781906373672 £7.99

Sex and Satisfaction Two
Erotic stories edited by Miranda Forbes
9781906373726 July 09 £7.99

Ultimate Curves
Erotic short stories edited by Miranda Forbes
9781906373788 Aug 09 £7.99

Naughty! The Xcite Guide to Sexy Fun
How To book exploring edgy, kinky sex
9781906373863 Oct 09 £9.99

For more information and great offers please visit
www.xcitebooks.com